PRAISE FOR MICHELLE DIENER'S VERDANT STRING SERIES

About **Breakaway**:

"This was a roller coaster plot filled with intrigue, resistance, and a side of romance." *Booknova*

About **High Flyer** (Winner of the RUBY Award for Best Speculative Fiction):

"Amazing science fiction romance!" *Amazon reviewer*

About **Wave Rider**:

"I love the worlds being built in the Verdant String novels, and that with each story you get a little piece more of the puzzle, but also a distinct story with its own characters, and well drawn world." *Karen G.*

1

The whistle of the wind rose and fell as it funneled through the rocks behind Anja and beat against her back.

The long, lonely note of it reminded her of the call to peace that happened every evening in the clifftop city of Nanganya on Aponi.

Evocative. Mournful, in a way.

But she was not in Nanganya anymore.

She was standing on a beach on Fynian, three days at least from Fynian's only city, Rinc, and she was alone.

And, she forced herself to admit, a little afraid.

It was the first time since she'd taken up residence in the research station four months ago that she'd felt this way.

She hunched her shoulders against the tug and cut of the icy air and shaded her eyes to look out over the sea one last time.

Nothing.

The pod was gone.

Not just foraging a little way off the coast, as they sometimes did; gone, gone.

She wanted to find out where and why.

But not today. Darkness was already pressing against the last light of the day and a storm was coming in. As she looked up, the dark purple clouds were building to the west.

She turned into the freezing blast and battled her way over the rocky beach and then up the hill to the cottage.

She reached the outer door with eyes that watered, her cheeks almost numb with the cold, and gasped with relief as the door closed behind her and she could finally hear herself think.

She stood in the small outer room for a moment, blinking her eyes clear, and then took off her jacket and boots.

When she was inside, she went straight to the comms unit.

The solar storms that raged continually over Fynian meant the only reliable communication method was fixed cable. The little unit was her lifeline, her only point of contact with Rinc and the scientific research headquarters.

She hesitated, her finger hovering over the button to dial in.

The rule was that she had to check in every day, talk to someone in real time.

It was a safety measure put in place because she was alone out here on the edge of the southern peninsula, with no easy means of getting out.

If no one heard from her by six in the evening, a runner would be sent to check on her.

But for the last three days she had not spoken to anyone. She'd gotten an automated voice telling her to leave a message, and no runner had come.

No one had called her back.

Hence the fear slowly blooming in her gut.

Something was wrong.

That it was happening at the same time the pod had disappeared did not seem to be a coincidence.

She blew out a breath, shook out the tension in her shoulders, and gently pressed down on the dial button.

Listened to the system trying to connect.

She hesitated again, and then moved her hand over to the visual comms control and cancelled it.

Over the last three days of trying to connect, the visual comms screen had been blank, but that didn't mean no one was there, looking back at her.

She shook her head at her paranoia, but didn't reactivate the visual comms.

"You have reached the Verdant String Scientific Exploration Office in Rinc. Please leave a message and we will respond as soon as possible."

Anja cleared her throat. "Dunc. This is day four of trying to reach you, and I'm worried. Get back to me, please. If I don't hear from you by tonight, I'm leaving tomorrow morning to come back to town on my hover." She hadn't realized she was going to suggest that, but now she had, she saw it was the only thing she could do in the circumstances.

Waiting on someone to come to her was not working out so well.

She thought about her route. "I'll go along the coast, rather than across the tundra. I know it'll take longer, but there are too many ways across the plains, and if you do manage to get off your ass and come looking for me, I'll be a lot harder to find." If she took the coastal route, it would also mean she could keep looking for the pod. At least she had a chance of spotting them from along the cliffs. She opened her mouth to say as much, and then closed it.

It hit hard that she didn't trust whoever was listening.

If anyone was.

She cleared her throat again. "I'm assuming something is wrong. And I hope you're okay, and that Jan and the kids are well, too. If I don't hear from you tonight, I'll see you in two or three days."

She cut off the connection in a quick, almost panicked movement and realized her hand was shaking.

The wind went suddenly still, and she walked over to the window and switched on the powerful telescope she'd set up. Bent a little to look through it.

The last pink of the sunset reflected off the small, choppy waves.

The clouds were darker now, and she guessed this was just the calm before the storm.

The pod was still nowhere to be seen. She searched the horizon for their long necks and arrow-shaped heads, but to no avail. Out of desperation, she switched the scope over to heat mode, even though the infrared function barely worked on Fynian.

Nothing.

Absolute silence pressed against her and she thought it might be the first time she'd experienced no sound at all since she'd gotten here.

She hadn't realized how noisy the leviathans were until they disappeared.

It felt lonely to her now, without the hoots and deep booming groans of the adults in the pod, and the higher-pitched yips of the babies.

She was the third scientist assigned to study this pod. There had been year-long gaps in the research, times when no one was here, but the other two researchers had both stayed at least 18 months at a time, and never had the pod strayed from the waters around the peninsula.

Never.

She thought of Devinia, the matriarch of the pod. What was the old girl thinking?

Anja had only been here four months, but in the last month, she had sensed a shift in Devinia's behavior. The leviathan had come closer, sliding on her back just under the small craft Anja had used to go out into the bay—before the ice made it too dangerous—looking up at Anja with her enormous eyes.

Anja had logged the new encounters, spending her evenings looking through Dr. Recknic and Dr. Carvello's notes to see if they'd experienced anything similar.

It didn't appear that they had.

She tilted the lens up to look at the gas giant Jero. The planet that Fynian orbited as a moon had two dark storm spots close together on its surface. They looked like eyes, changing daily. Sometimes round with surprise, sometimes thinning to angry slits.

This evening they looked sullen, the dull yellow of the surface muddier than usual. It was like living beneath an ever-changing, moody face.

Anja shut the telescope down and moved to the kitchen, putting together a quick meal and going through her supplies to choose what food she would take on her journey tomorrow while her dinner cooked.

When she slipped into bed, all packed for the next day and ready to go at dawn, she lay for a while, listening to the rattling of the roof and windows over the scream of the wind, as if some monster was trying to pry them off with icy, hard fingers.

She had put the comms unit right beside her so she wouldn't miss the chirp of an incoming call over what was now a raging storm.

It never came.

SOMETHING WAS DEFINITELY wrong at headquarters.

The fear that had blossomed the day before got a tighter hold on Anja as she listened to the same recorded message play one last time before she left the cottage and got on the tiny hover she had as her only way back to Rinc.

It was unthinkable there would be no one at the office for this many days in a row unless there was a serious problem.

She was about to cut the message off when a voice broke through.

"Hello?"

She could barely hear the greeting. It was a man, but the sound was distorted, the line full of static.

"Hello?" She couldn't help the eagerness in her voice. "Is that you, Duncan?"

"No—"

Something else was said, but she couldn't make it out.

"I can't hear you clearly." She shouted the words. "This is Anja Farucci, from the southern peninsula station, and I'm coming back to Rinc by way of the coast. If you can send me a runner, please do."

The comms unit speaker hissed and then died.

Anja hit the connect button again and was met with silence.

This shouldn't happen.

It was a fixed cable. Encased in protective piping to make it easy to access but safe from Fynian's extremely cold temperatures and wild weather.

And while the weather had certainly been wild last night, it had been like that more than a few times since she'd moved into the cottage.

She didn't even know if whoever had been on the other end of the comms unit had heard a word she'd said.

And so she would have to assume they hadn't.

She did a slow turn to make sure everything in her little house was locked down and put away to her satisfaction.

She had been comfortable here, but it somehow felt like a final goodbye.

She was done, she realized. No matter what happened, she wasn't coming back. Not for months on end on her own, anyway.

If she could get back to find Devinia, make sure she was all right, that would be the end of it for her.

She needed more company than this job provided. Needed people around her.

She just hadn't wanted to admit it. Admit defeat.

But enough was enough. Duncan's strange behavior was just the last straw.

She closed the door behind her, made sure it was locked.

She'd continue with the plan she'd already decided on, with the benefit—maybe—of someone knowing she was coming. Someone who could send a runner out to fetch her.

And if not . . . she would be uncomfortable and cold for the next three days. Two, if the weather and conditions cooperated.

She picked up the pack she'd stuffed with food to eat during the day, and a few extra layers of clothing, and slung it over her shoulder.

Time to go.

2

———————

Calder Mordova stood, dripping freezing sea water on the floor, and stared down at the comms unit that had just inexplicably died.

Then he looked around the small hut he'd taken shelter in. It was just as he remembered it. Basic but with everything needed to keep a wave rider alive should they wash up on the shore, until someone could send a hover from Rinc.

Certainly it was not a place Anja Farucci would call if she needed help.

The line was so bad, he'd only caught part of her name, but there was only one woman living out this way called Anja.

Only one woman living out this way, period.

He'd seen Anja around Rinc a few times, had even been introduced to her by Duncan Verne once in a cozy bar the wave riders liked to frequent.

Unlike the marine biologist who'd come before her, she'd been eager to talk to the wave riders about their relationships with the pods. She'd behaved as if she considered them experts on the magnificent beasts she had come to study, which had been a big point in her favor.

She was not an asshole like the others.

Maybe.

She was new, and attractive, and there had been a lot of competition for her time that night, but he hadn't forgotten her quick, easy laugh, or the gleam of light on her dark brown hair.

She hadn't sounded like laughing a few moments ago, though.

He thought he'd heard stress in her voice.

She thought she was calling Rinc. Her asking him if he was Duncan made that clear. But this was nothing but a wave rider hut, one of several dotted along the coast for emergency supplies and a place out of the cold.

He suddenly recalled that a message had been playing before he'd cut in to answer. He tapped the messages button on the unit and found it was only outgoing comms that weren't working. The message function worked fine.

He played the recording, listening in surprise.

It was as if the Scientific Exploration Office had somehow rerouted their calls to this hut.

With a faint beep, all the messages Anja had left over the last few days played back, starting four days before.

Anja had thought she was speaking to Duncan because that was who she'd been calling.

It didn't make any sense.

He was only here himself because Kada had dragged him here.

The adolescent male was in an awkward stage, no longer part of the matriarchal pod but unhappy being with the other males.

When Calder had approached Kada last night, instead of lowering his head as usual and letting Calder harvest his druk, the juvenile had grabbed the rope trailing from Calder's boat and swam away as only a leviathan could.

Cal thought he was playing at first, that he'd tire of the game, but as they moved further and further out, he realized this was either a fit of pique, or something had set Kada off.

It had been a long night, with Kada barely slowing down, and it was only when dawn broke and Cal had seen the beach, close enough that he could probably survive the short swim to shore through the icy water, that he'd dived off.

The hut, sitting up above the water line, had been a welcome sight. He could call for help from there.

Except, he couldn't. Not with the outgoing comms disabled.

A shiver shook his body, and he kicked off his boots, walked over to the tiny shower room and turned on the water, stepping into the hot stream, clothes and all.

When everything was soaked with hot water and his shivering had stopped, he stripped off his clothing and hung it on rails heated by the water as he showered.

By the time he stepped out, the room was steamy, but his smart fabric clothes were dry.

He dressed quickly, then rummaged through the cupboards, making himself a hot cup of jah and warming an instant meal.

Anja Farucci.

He'd been mulling over her message since they'd been cut off.

Something strange was going on.

He added Kada's behavior to the mix, as well.

The one snatch of conversation he'd heard from Anja was she was coming up the coast toward Rinc.

She would have to pass the hut on her way.

He could wait for her here.

Or he could go south and find her.

Her research station wasn't more than a two hour hike from here.

He opened the hut door and leaned in the doorway as he scooped up the last of his meal, looking out over the ocean.

Kada was in the distance, nosing Cal's boat and batting at it like it was a toy.

The young leviathan lifted his massive head and bellowed, then smacked his long neck down onto the surface of the water and disappeared completely beneath the waves.

"What are you up to?" Cal wondered.

Something was going on.

He turned back into the hut and cleaned away any trace of his presence, leaving it as he'd found it, as was the unwritten rule. He packed some food and water into a rucksack he'd found in the narrow cupboard next to the shower room, slung it over his shoulder, and closed the door behind him.

The cliffs ran along the length of the coast, looming above the hut, and he found a path up. When he reached the top, he looked over the sea for any sign of Kada, but the leviathan was gone.

His boat was just visible on the horizon.

He shrugged.

He'd get it back at some point.

No use getting annoyed about something he couldn't change.

He looked south down the beach, and wondered if Anja would come along the clifftop or the beach.

He decided he'd better stay on the cliffs, because that way he could see her, either way.

He caught a movement from the corner of his eye, and without understanding why, he crouched down, looking back toward the hut.

Two men walked in single file down a cliff path from the north, dressed in clothes so similar to his own, he wondered if he might know them.

Both of them had heavy packs on their backs.

He studied them a moment, but they were too far away.

There was a predatory air that seemed to settle over them as they approached the hut.

They entered it in a coordinated move, as if expecting trouble within, and then stepped out less than a minute later.

One of the men shielded his eyes and scanned the cliffs, looking for something.

For him, Cal admitted to himself.

They had heard him answer Anja Farucci's comm, maybe.

And had come to . . . ?

He didn't have an answer for what they may have had planned, but from the way they moved, he ruled out they were tourists on a trip to see the coast.

They were not here to see the leviathans and the majesty of Jero, with its two staring eyes.

Cal was a wave rider, fit enough, strong enough, to take on almost anyone he met, but he had no weapons, and the way these men moved, he had a feeling they did.

And Anja Farucci was coming this way.

The men walked back the way they'd come, one of them looking over his shoulder more than once until they disappeared between a crease in the sloping cliff face.

Cal rose up, looking in their direction for a moment longer, and then he turned south.

He'd take his small head start and run with it.

Whatever was going on, instinct told him those men were not here to play.

3

She was being followed.

Anja glanced to her left, across the beach, and fumbled her grip on the handlebars of the hover.

A boat was keeping pace with her along the shoreline. It was sleek, silver, and she recognized it as the type used by the wave riders in Rinc.

Except this one was empty.

She could just make out a shape below it in the water, and as she slowed more and more, a head slowly rose from the waves and a shockingly bright purple eye stared at her.

The leviathan rose to the surface, keeping his profile low in the water.

She came to a complete stop, and he nosed the boat, pushing it in her direction.

It hit the sand, ground to a stop, and she saw there was a rope attached to the front of it, which the leviathan must have been using to pull it along.

He wasn't part of Devinia's pod, although something in his striped markings made her wonder if he was related to the group.

If he was part of the group of males that she knew were associated with the three pods up around Rinc, he was either very brave coming into Devinia's territory, or her pod had really abandoned these waters, and the young males were moving into the vacuum.

She didn't want that to be true, but there were few other explanations.

He gave a huff, put half his head under the water then lifted it sharply, creating a wave that deposited the boat right in front of her.

It was almost as if he was asking her to get in.

That wasn't going to happen.

When she didn't react, the young male lifted his head and neck right out of the water and swung them in her direction.

He was young, but he was enormous, way bigger than most of the members in Devinia's pod, except Devinia herself, and he lowered his head very close to her without moving from his position in the water, resting his chin down on the sand.

He opened his mouth and lifted his lips, revealing his sharp teeth.

A round bead of druk was caught between two rows of teeth, and he angled his head for her to get it.

She swung off her hover but didn't go any closer.

"Sorry, I don't know how to do it. I'm not a wave rider." The druk was beautiful, though. Pearlescent, as all druk was, this one a pale green. And almost as big as two fists clenched together.

He inched his head a little closer, as if trying to tempt her, and she couldn't help the laugh that escaped her.

"You are quite the charmer, aren't you?"

A low buzz sounded, and the leviathan jerked back with a sharp growl. He turned his head to look at the base of the cliff, and she noticed a section of his cheek smoked a little. She spun in the direction he was looking and gaped.

Two men stood in the shadows thrown from the sheer rock face, one with a hand extended, holding what looked like a . . . laz.

She had only seen a laz occasionally when she'd been based in the military barracks on Aponi for a few months, but she was sure that's what it was.

They had shot the leviathan.

"What do you think you're doing?" She took a step toward them in outrage.

The man shot again, this time at her, and she stumbled back.

The shot sizzled into the sand, and she ducked behind her hover.

She was working out how quickly she could jump on the hover, start it up and escape when suddenly the boat sailed through the air and landed on the two men.

Anja turned to the leviathan, mute with shock. He had flipped the boat at their attackers.

But her rescuer was already ducking beneath the water, disappearing without so much as a ripple.

She forced herself to focus. The young leviathan had given her a chance to escape and she best not waste it.

She scrambled onto her hover while the two men heaved the boat off them. She turned back the way she'd come. As she raced away, she saw the flash of another laz strike, felt the hover jerk as she sped down the beach, looking for the best way up the cliffs.

She turned sharply at the first rough path she noticed, although the going was steep and the hover's engine was struggling. The whole vehicle was jerking by the time she reached the top, making a noise she knew meant some kind of death knell. As she accelerated through the bushes at the top and burst onto the clifftop, she managed to swallow a scream and to brake in time to not plough into the man standing in her way.

As the hover came to a stop, it died.

"Did they hurt you?" The man, dressed in the same dark clothing as her attackers, stepped in close.

"No. They hit the leviathan." She slid off the hover, heart sinking, but the man cursed at that news and ran to the cliff's edge to look down, leaving her alone beside the hover.

She wanted to see over the cliffs too, to find out what they were up to herself, but hesitated.

"Do I know you?"

He seemed familiar.

"Calder Mordova. We met in Rinc. I'm a wave rider." He glanced at her over his shoulder and as she caught his gaze, she remembered.

Duncan had introduced them.

She felt a sudden lurch in her chest. She had liked him, even though he was serious and quiet. Not as outgoing as the other wave riders she'd met that evening.

The relief at a familiar, friendly face made her a little weak as she moved to the cliff's edge.

"Do you know those men?" She joined him, looking down, but they were gone. The only thing left on the beach was the boat, wedged into the sand on its side.

Through the incredibly clear water in the shallows she saw the young leviathan, just visible under the surface, a little way off the beach. As she had noted before, he was enormous, almost as long as Devinia, although he still had the slenderness and striped coloring of a calf, faded though it was.

"How was he hurt?" Calder Mordova glanced at her, then back at the leviathan.

"The laz shot hit his cheek. It burned him."

Calder swore again.

"Where did they go?" She leaned out a little, and then saw a flash of movement through the bushes on the right side of the cliff.

There must be a narrow path there that she'd missed.

"They're coming up." She pointed.

"Time for us to be gone. Unless you have a laz on you to even the odds?" He turned toward her hover.

"No."

He moved to the back storage holder and lifted the lid, began hauling out her things. "What's most important? Because we'll have to carry them."

He was bossy.

And right.

Everything was important. But to stay alive . . . She pointed to her food, tent and clothing, grabbing some of it from him.

"Where to?"

He pointed east, toward the open escarpment. "We can hide in one of the fissures." He started moving right away.

Conscious her attackers were climbing up the path and could emerge at any moment, she jogged after him.

"Do you know if there are fissures close by?" She'd only gone down to look inside a few of the deep cracks in the ground, even though they were found all over the escarpment.

She guessed they would be good places to hide.

It would be impossible for their attackers to search them all.

Calder either didn't hear her question, or didn't consider it worth answering, because he simply kept going, looking back a few times to make sure she was keeping up.

She managed to stay close behind him, but she had a suspicion he was going slowly on her account.

She wouldn't have remembered his name, but his face was clear in her memory.

She had been overwhelmed by new faces the night Duncan had taken her to The Ice Breaker, the bar where the wave riders liked to socialize, but Calder had stood out.

Quiet. Handsome. Big.

A little gruff.

She'd been sorry they'd barely spoken.

Duncan had told her Calder was not only a wave rider, but also the government of Fynian's head of trade, which on Fynian meant negotiating the price of druk.

He had wanted to say more, she remembered him leaning in as if to tell her an even more interesting fact about him, when they'd been interrupted and the moment had passed.

She'd been overwhelmed by the noise and lights in the bar that night. It was too much after her first month alone at the station.

Calder Mordova had gone to sit in a chair by the fire, and she had longed to sit opposite him in silence and sip her drink.

She hoped that initial attraction meant she could trust him now. She was inclined to, but the situation was not clearcut.

She tripped over one of the limestone rocks hidden by the grass, and forced herself to concentrate. Calder was keeping the pace steady, but a sudden shout from behind them made him increase his stride.

In the distance, she heard the sound of a hover start up.

"They must have had a hover of their own and left it somewhere out of sight. They know they'll need one to hunt us." Calder edged around a fissure so narrow, even Anja didn't think she could fit into it.

She wanted to ask who 'they' were. And why they'd shot at her. But she needed her breath to keep up with the punishing pace he was setting.

They bypassed a few more fissures before he chose one. He looked back at her before he dropped down into it, as if to ask if she could keep up.

She nodded, jumping down after him. Strong arms came up to catch her, holding her against a wide chest and strong body before gently setting her down.

She went still with surprise, saw his quick frown, and then he turned, leaping from terrace to terrace, into the gloom.

It was so shadowed below, she couldn't see the floor.

She followed him without hesitation, and found the bottom wasn't that far down, but it formed a long, narrow passageway, and the ridges and terraces of natural stone hid them from above.

It was warmer in here. Or at least, it was out of the cutting wind, so perhaps it only felt warmer.

It was a relief, anyway.

"All right?" he asked as she made the last leap to land beside him.

She nodded again and he started moving, shifting the pack over his shoulder as it caught on the rocky protrusions that extended into the narrow passage.

The limestone was abrasive, razor sharp in places, and she grazed herself more than once before she stepped into a larger space.

Calder stood with the pack at his feet, gazing upward.

She did the same, and saw there was no direct view of the sky from here. The light was diffuse, filtering down from above through stepped terraces of stone.

They had been moving for more than half an hour and neither of them spoke, listening instead for the sounds of pursuit or the buzz of a hover.

"Do you know who they are?" she whispered at last, slowly sinking down to sit on a rock ledge that ran along one side of the space.

Her legs suddenly started shaking.

"I was hoping you did." He turned to face her, his gaze sharpening on her face. He bent, rummaging through her pack and pulling out a bottle of water, which he handed to her.

She took it gratefully, sipping carefully and slowly catching her breath.

"How are you mixed up in this, then?" She kept her voice to a low murmur.

He watched her with dark gray eyes. "I was in the wave rider safety hut just up from here this morning when the comm system there received a call. It was you, calling for the Rinc research headquarters, before you were cut off. It seemed as if research center comms had been diverted there. I listened to all your messages for Duncan."

"Diverted to a safety hut?" She leaned back, stunned. "So Duncan never got them?"

Calder lifted his shoulders. "Unless he was staying at the hut, but it looked unused to me."

"That still doesn't make any sense, because if he doesn't hear from me, if I miss even one check-in, protocol is that he comes out to find me."

Again, Calder lifted his shoulders.

"Well, have you seen him around Rinc?"

He frowned, suddenly thoughtful. "I haven't seen him recently. But sometimes I don't see him for days on end, so it isn't that unusual."

"I've trusted him since I arrived on Fynian. I wouldn't have thought he'd have abandoned me." Besides, part of his job was to see to her safety. He wasn't just her friend, he was her colleague, and had duties to fulfill.

If something had happened to him . . . She thought of how she had been shot at with a laz. A laz set to a strength that was enough to take out her hover engine. Strong enough to burn a leviathan's thick skin. "He could be dead."

"Or he could be one of them. Or he could have been tricked in some way." Calder crouched beside the pack and started pulling out food.

"What were you doing in the hut in the first place? It's a bit far from your pods, isn't it?"

He grunted in agreement. "I was harvesting druk last night, and one of the juveniles grabbed my boat and just took off with me. When dawn broke and I could finally see the coast, I dived off and swam for it. The hut was near where I came ashore."

Oh. It was his boat.

That made sense.

"Your boat saved my life."

For the first time since she'd met him, he gave a quick grin.

"Do they do that often? Grab a boat and tow you away?"

He shook his head. "First time it's ever happened, that I know of."

"I had the feeling the leviathan was trying to get me to climb into the boat."

Calder's head rose sharply. "How?"

"He nosed it toward the shore. That's why it was handy for him to flick at our attackers."

"Huh." He sat back on his haunches. "I wonder what's going on?"

"I'm surprised he's risked coming this far south. Devinia doesn't take kindly to strangers, especially males." Anja didn't want to think the pod was gone for good.

"In the messages I heard on the comms unit in the hut, you said she'd disappeared. Maybe he picked up on that."

Anja nodded reluctantly. "I wanted Duncan to come with the runner so we could look for her over the water. But it's possible the lack of sound from the pod has been noticed. I know they can hear for long distances underwater. If the other leviathans have stopped hearing the pod's interaction, maybe some of the northern pods are coming this way to see whether they can expand their territory."

"You sound unhappy about that."

She felt her cheeks heat. It was ridiculous of her, and she knew it. She was a scientist. This move by the pod should simply be an interesting new behavior to investigate, but instead, she was acting as if the pod had abandoned her.

She had obviously been at the station too long on her own, with only the pod for company.

It reinforced her decision this morning that this research project was over for her.

"I miss them." She lifted her shoulders and gave a slight smile at her own foolishness.

"You don't need to explain the connection you feel to them to me. I'm a wave rider. I'm almost part of the pods."

She nodded, took a last sip of water, and then they both went still at the sound of a hover above.

It sounded as if it were directly overhead when the engine cut out.

There was a low murmur of voices, but they were too distorted to hear.

Calder moved to the side and then, without warning, started climbing up the wall, silent and focused.

Anja watched him for a moment. She was fit. She spent a lot of her day outdoors, but she had nothing on a wave rider.

She knew they managed to jump from moving boats to the backs of the leviathan, then run up their long necks, balancing as the massive beasts moved around in the waves. They hung from the hard frills that ran down the leviathans' noses to harvest the druk from their teeth.

Looking at Calder climbing what seemed to be a sheer lime-stone wall, she had to admire his physicality.

He disappeared from view as he got higher, blocked by a protruding curve of rock, and then appeared again almost imme-diately, gesturing to her to join him.

She was already on her feet, and she moved over and began to climb, rubbing her fingers raw on the rough stone.

He extended a hand down to her and hauled her up easily onto the ledge he was crouched on.

"I'm too big to fit through the gap. But I think you could make it," he whispered into her ear, and she held herself very still at the feel of the hot air from his breath against her skin.

When he rose to his feet, he pulled her up with him, and then pointed to a small crack in the rock above them.

"How do I get there?" She couldn't see how.

"I'll lift you." He bent a knee, tapped his thigh, and feeling rushed, feeling anxious, she stepped onto it and found herself thrust upward.

There was a handhold right in front of her and she grabbed it, managed to pull herself up higher, and after a short scrabble, she found a small protrusion of rock to balance by one foot.

The wind was howling above, and she couldn't make out the voices at all anymore.

They could have moved on, although she hadn't heard the hover leave.

"They could be anywhere."

The voice shot a spike of ice through her. It sounded as if the man who was speaking was right beside her.

"It's impossible to search with only two of us. When's Sirco coming?" The second voice was a little more muffled and distorted, as if he was facing a different way. Anja wondered if they were sheltering under an overhang just above her.

"Don't know. But I'm not wasting my time looking for her in this weather, not with this many holes to search. She's going nowhere without her hover." The second voice was a little more audible than the first.

"And what about whoever answered her call this morning?" The first man asked.

"Maybe he's out here, maybe he isn't, but there was no sign anyone had been in that hut, so maybe it was a crossed signal or something. We cut her off really fast, so they might not have heard anything."

"Anything is possible on this fucked up moon planet with its solar storms and ice storms and wind storms. It can't even decide what it is. And those staring eyes looking down from Jero. This place gives me the creeps."

"Fucking right." There was the sound of a boot scraping on rock, and then she thought she heard the other man say something about heading back to the hut.

The engine started up and a moment later was gone.

She turned back to look for a way down, but Calder wrapped an arm around her shins, and she let him lower her to stand beside him.

She told him what she'd heard as they made their way back to the ground.

"They're right, we can't go far without your hover, but equally, this is a big place and there are only two of them. They won't find us."

"Three of them, if you count Sirco." Anja looked up at him. "You know Duncan. Do you know Sirco?"

"Sirco." Calder gave a nod. "Reg Sirco. He's friendly. I've spoken to him a few times. He socializes with the wave riders a lot."

"He arrived to work at headquarters a month after me. I met him the same weekend I met you in The Ice Breaker. I think he might even have been with Duncan and me that evening." Anja thought about the solar flare scientist. Fynian, with its constant solar storms, was considered a perfect research center to study solar activity. But Sirco hadn't had the enthusiasm of most of the scientists she'd met. He was new, should have been hyped up, but he'd come across as cynical and disinterested.

She'd wondered at the time why he'd put in for a transfer to Fynian if he seemed so unhappy about being here.

"He came to the research cottage. Three, maybe four weeks ago." Anja had almost forgotten about the visit. "It was strange . . ." She saw Calder was focused on her as she spoke.

"Strange?"

"He behaved strangely. Said he was taking some readings nearby and decided to stop by. He had a lot of equipment on the back of his hover. He was asking questions that made no sense."

"Like?"

"Like did I have any wireless comms equipment, just in case the solar flares died down." She lifted her hands. "I told him no, and it felt like when he came inside for a cup of jah that he was checking to make sure I was telling the truth."

"Needed to make sure when he cut you off from headquarters, you couldn't get in touch with someone some other way," Cal said.

He glanced over at her, and unspoken between them was if Sirco was involved, was Duncan, too?

"Do you know what this is about?" Anja lowered herself to the ground again.

"No." Calder found a wall to lean back against, and lowered himself down as well. "They were listening to your messages, and they made sure your office didn't get any of your comms, which means they wanted you isolated and out of touch."

"I hope Duncan is all right. He wouldn't leave me out here alone. It makes me worried about what's happened to him."

"Seems to me, the best thing we can do is get to Rinc."

Anja lifted her head, and their gazes clashed. She swallowed. Nodded. "I agree."

"I think we need to travel at night. You've got supplies, and so have I. We should be able to make it at least to the next hut up the coast. We can try the comms link to Rinc from there."

"Unless they've redirected that one, too."

Calder shrugged. "We'll find out soon enough, but we should still try."

She hugged her knees tighter. "I agree. Let's get some rest, then, and travel at dusk." The light from above was still bright, but she was suddenly exhausted.

She slid down, curling onto her side, and rested her head on her arm.

Calder leaned back against the stone wall and closed his eyes.

She was stuck with a stranger, but he seemed to be on her side.

She had little choice but to trust that he was.

4

Cal dozed rather than slept.

He was hyper aware of Anja, the way she sank into a deep sleep as if she had been living on the edge for too long, and he realized she probably had been.

Her sense of isolation had to have grown as days went by without any word from Duncan.

Cal hoped the scientist had a good excuse for leaving her out here on her own, because he'd have a few things to say to him, otherwise.

She was slightly wary of him, but the fact that she'd been able to sleep with him right there made him feel as if there was at least a thread of trust between them.

They would need to trust each other to survive.

Their attackers certainly didn't seem to have a problem with shooting to kill.

The casual violence of it, the fact that the attackers' laz settings had to have been set to kill for the shots to have disabled the hover, worried him.

These people were very far from harmless.

Not knowing what they wanted and why made his and Anja's survival even harder.

It was tempting to sneak out, let Anja sleep, and go back to the hut, see if he could overhear anything of use, but he didn't want to risk leaving her alone.

It was getting late, anyway, he realized. The sun set early on Fynian at this time of year, and it would be time to go soon.

He got up and took out the small flare heater he'd seen in Anja's pack, set it up to boil some water and make jah.

Anja stirred as the scent of the drink filled the small space, and when he looked up from the heater, he found her watching him.

"Did you sleep?" Her voice croaked a little.

"A bit." He poured the jah into the one cup they had between them and handed it to her. She drank half and handed it back.

As he drank his share, she slowly got to her feet and stretched, twisting her neck and shoulders to get out the kinks.

"You must have family that are worried about you."

"I live alone, but yes, by tonight, my sister or my mother will start to wonder where I am." His mother would then start lighting fires under everyone who she thought could help look for him. He was almost sorry for the chaos this would cause. Almost.

"Will they come looking?"

He nodded. "They'll come looking. And make a big noise about it while they do." He suppressed a smile. "That's one thing these people didn't anticipate. That there would be someone other than you out here. From what you told me last night, they're not even sure whether I'm out here with you or not."

"Will your family look for you by sea or land?"

"Both." He'd been part of many search and rescue missions himself. "My boat has a tracker, but they have to be close to pick it up over the solar flare interference. There'll be a runner that takes the cliff path, and then a lot of boats searching the water."

She gave a nod, her body relaxing a little, and he cursed Duncan Verne again for abandoning her.

"Do you think the southern pod disappearing has something to do with all this?" Anja secured her pack and straightened. "I can't think how, but it's just too coincidental that they vanished just as someone tries to isolate and then kill me."

"I don't know. But I agree it's strange. The same way Kada dragging me all the way from Rinc to here is strange. I've never heard of a leviathan doing something like that."

"I need to get hold of a runner, and go out looking for Devinia and her pod."

It was almost as if she'd forgotten they were being chased by murderous strangers. "We need to get these would-be killers into custody, first."

She blushed, a deep flush that heated her face and neck, and looked away.

"You're right. I've been accused of being a little too focused on my work more than once."

He gave a nod that she didn't see. Cleared his throat. "Let's go before the sun sets completely. It'll be good to start out with a little light to see by. It'll help orient us."

She stepped aside, tacitly ceding the lead to him, and he went back the way they'd come in. The climb up took much longer than the jump down, and the sun was almost completely set by the time he reached the top ledge, just below ground level. Still, he took the time to wait a few moments, listening for any sign of their attackers.

He couldn't sense anything and lifted himself up, crouching low on the lip of the deep incision into the earth and sweeping his gaze around the low scrub.

Nothing moved.

Anja scrambled up beside him. She was panting slightly, and he felt the warmth of her body as she pressed close to him.

"What is it?"

"Just checking it's clear." He forced himself to stand and start moving.

He'd been too distracted by her to realize that the wind had died down, making things easier to hear, but suddenly, out of the growing darkness, he heard the hoot of a leviathan, and then the boom as it leaped from the waves and smacked into the water.

Anja stopped at the same time he did, head turning toward the cliffs.

"I think it's Kada," he said.

"Can you tell from the call?" she asked.

"It's a little higher than some of the big males, so it's most likely him. I can tell a few of the older ones by ear."

"I can tell Devinia, but not the others," she said.

Night had almost completely fallen, although the creamy gold and lighter yellow bands in Jero's atmosphere made the gas giant just visible in the darkening sky.

He retraced their steps from earlier that day, heading for the top of the cliffs where Anja's hover had shorted out.

It was possible their attackers had left something useful behind.

The temperature had dropped, and while the wind was no longer howling, it would pick up again soon enough.

They would need every piece of equipment they could get.

It seemed to take longer to get back to where they'd started, but the lack of light had something to do with it. They had to pick their way through the rocks and stones hidden in the long grass.

He slowed when they approached the spot where she had come up from the beach, moving carefully through the gloom.

If their attackers were smart, they'd keep a watch on the hover, wait for Anja to return to it.

The hover was nowhere to be seen, though. Neither were their hunters.

He heard a strange sound as he reached the cliff's edge, and went completely still.

Anja came up close behind him, a hand on his shoulder.

"Air sailing," she whispered in his ear.

He frowned, and then her arm stretched out, finger pointed, and he finally saw the small, winged contraption, with its buzzing motor, black against an indigo sky.

A man hung from the frame by straps, and a second man stood silhouetted in the sunset, on the clifftop, at least half a thou to the north, close to the hut.

"It looks like the two who attacked me. What are they doing?" Anja sounded less bemused, more angry, than she had earlier. "Looking for my pod?"

"Why would they do that?" Cal didn't think it was likely. "There are at least twenty pods on Fynian for them to choose from."

"I don't know." Anja blew out a breath, then rubbed the back of her head in frustration. "Maybe I'm reading way too much into the southern pod's disappearance. Maybe I'm just too close to this and can't see clearly."

"Well, they're looking for something." Cal watched the man on the cliff help his friend land and unstrap from the glider, and then they bent over what looked like a screen before heading back in the direction of the hut.

As soon as they were swallowed by the darkness, Cal moved forward, was just able to make out the drag marks leading off the cliff.

Anja followed him, looking down to the beach below with him.

There, at the foot of the cliff, crumpled and almost half submerged by the tide, was her hover.

"They pushed it over." She spoke neutrally.

"It's clever. We definitely can't use it again, and if someone comes looking, they'll think you had an accident. At least at first."

He saw her throat work. At last she turned away from the sight. "At least we took quite a lot of my equipment out."

He had a feeling nothing he could say would dampen her anger. Nor did he think she'd appreciate it. "Ready to go?"

"I'm ready." She took the lead this time, walking at an angle from the direction taken by their two attackers, more inland, in case the two men were not finished flying their glider for the night.

Cal strode after her.

He had a feeling she was running on fury now.

If they came face to face with the men again, he might have to hold her back.

5

It was cold.

Anja hunched deeper into her jacket as she followed behind Cal, grateful for the smart fabric. She knew without it she would be in trouble right now. Even with the heat-trapping functions of her clothing, she was freezing, and . . . she looked up at the sky again. . . it was only going to get worse.

She was grateful that Cal had retaken the lead, steering them back to the quicker, smoother parts along the clifftop as soon as the hut was behind them.

They had passed it less than an hour after they'd watched the glider come in to land. The lights had been on inside, and Cal had studied it as they passed with something close to the anger she'd felt at the thought of these men hunting her pod.

She guessed he did not like that their attackers were making use of the wave riders' equipment and supplies. Especially as they'd shot Kada, a juvenile leviathan.

No wave rider that she'd ever heard of had ever done anything to hurt a leviathan.

Dr. Carvello, the scientist who'd lived in the research station before her, had left her a comm, warning her that the wave riders saw the pods differently, that they insisted they had relationships with members of the pods, and considered themselves almost part of the pods themselves. He told her to steer clear of the men and women who made their living plucking druk from between layers of razor sharp teeth, because they were not only a little bit mad, but their interactions with the leviathans threatened the scientific study of the beasts.

She had listened to Carvello's message, then gone out and asked Duncan to introduce her to the wave riders to make up her own mind.

She found he was right, in that the wave riders loved the pods.

They spoke of the matriarchs and their little clans, and the males in their looser groupings, with humor and affection.

They would no sooner hurt a leviathan than hurt a member of their own family.

The wave riders were wary of her initially, and she guessed neither Carvello, nor the scientist who'd come before him, Recknik, had made any effort to reach out to the people who were, by definition, the foremost authorities on the marine mammals they were studying.

She had tried to mend some bridges, but she also felt guilty over her close connection to the pod because of Carvello's warning.

She kept wondering if she had fallen into the trap of getting too personally attached to her study subjects.

Or, maybe, that connection should be part of the study. She had wondered for a while now how to examine the way the pod had changed her, just by her being in proximity to them. They had established a connection to her, and she wondered if that was intrinsically part of their nature.

They seemed to be capable of inter-species communication and . . . she didn't want to use the word, but friendship was the closest one she could land on to describe her feelings toward at least Devinia.

She would swear the matriarch felt the same way about her.

A piece of sleet hit her forehead, ran down her cheek, and under her shirt.

She grimaced, and then she was being pelted with ice, as the wind gushed around her.

Cal turned. "We need to put up the tent." He had to shout the words.

She nodded. She was extremely grateful they had managed to grab it from her hover. Now, they just had to find a good place to set it up. "Not near the cliff's edge," she called back.

His grim expression lightened for a moment. "No."

He veered right, away from the sea, and stopped at the top of a deep fissure. "There might be a space we could set up in down there."

"It would be out of the wind, and maybe give us some overhead protection from the sleet." And it was out of sight of their attackers, and whoever might be coming to join them. She clambered down the first terrace, and he jumped down beside her.

The crack in the ground wasn't as deep as the one they'd hidden in before, but it was still out of the wind.

The sleet managed to find its way down, making the going slippery. Cal was gone when she got to the bottom, and she followed the soft light he'd taken out as soon as they were inside the deep crack, until she found her way into a space that was a little wider than where they'd come down, but not by much.

"We could find another fissure, see if it's better," he said.

She shook her head. "This is big enough."

It was also protected from above. A ledge of rock protruded over the space, so they would be out of the wind and sleet.

It wasn't going to get any better than this.

Cal nodded and opened the slim pack containing her tent, let it inflate itself.

At least it had a built-in mattress, so they should be relatively comfortable on the hard, rocky ground.

Anja brought out the small heater, made some jah and opened a self-heating meal. They shared it, hunched down under the natural rocky awning, close together in the narrow space.

Cal's shoulder pressed against hers, and Anja turned her head to look at him.

"I'm glad you're here."

He lifted his brows in question.

She moistened her lips, suddenly feeling exposed by her openness. "If Kada hadn't dragged you out here, I'd be either dead or doing this on my own. I'm sorry you're caught up in whatever it is, but I'm glad to have your company."

He looked at her for a moment. "It's an isolated job out there, at the Southern Peninsula Station."

She nodded. "Too isolated. I didn't realize how much I disliked being on my own until I decided to make my way back to Rinc. The relief I felt was way too much. I should have come in for more weekends in the city."

"Duncan didn't want you to?" His face was neutral, but she had the sense he was angry.

"He didn't say as much, but that's not how things were done before. Carvello—"

"Carvello was an idiot." He bent his head over his meal.

She couldn't read his expression, had the sense he wasn't used to conversations like this.

She considered it. "Carvello was anti-social. I should have thought about that more when Dunc set up my schedule. He just assumed Carvello needed the time on the station to follow the pod, but it was probably more he was happy by himself. I should have pushed for more trips to Rinc."

"Duncan should have done a little thinking of his own." Cal's tone was short, and he turned away, disposing of his container.

She didn't want them to sink back into silence. She was so tired of it.

It had been her reality for a little too long.

"What's the biggest piece of druk you've ever found?" It wasn't the most subtle opening, but she was actually interested.

He turned back to her and to her delight, held out his hands to indicate a ball about as big as her head.

"What color?"

"The most common. Black. But it was the biggest ever recovered."

"Did they make something interesting out of it?"

He shook his head. "Because it was black, it was sent to be ground down for coating. It's somewhere out there," he looked skyward, "protecting a spaceship from being damaged by pieces of asteroid."

When Fynian had been discovered nearly a hundred years earlier, tiny pieces of druk—not big enough to be caught between massive leviathan teeth—had been found on the beaches. Scientists discovered when ground into a powder, it had a strange negative effect on most space debris, actively propelling it away.

Its properties made powdered druk the most prized coating for spaceship exteriors.

But even with druk being considered essential protection in space, that didn't stop most inhabitants of the Verdant String from prizing it just as much for jewelry. Particularly the rare pinks and lavenders. Silver was the most prized of all, but Anja seemed to recall only a few hundred tiny spheres of silver had ever been found.

"Looking at the beaches now, it's hard to imagine they were once covered in druk." She'd seen images since she'd moved to

Fynian. Beaches covered in tiny balls of pearlescent black and pink.

Those were all harvested and long gone. Scooped up and used as powder coating.

The wave riders were the main source of it now. Plucking it from between the leviathans' teeth.

The pieces the wave riders got were big, though. Much bigger than the pieces that had once covered the beaches.

Druk was created in the belly of the leviathans, a hard, glistening coating from their stomach that encased the poison darts from one of the leviathans' favorite fish. The wave riders now provided the only supply.

The pieces they pulled out from between the leviathans' teeth were balls that had been repeatedly swallowed, getting bigger each time, until they got caught fast between the teeth layers.

It seemed to be uncomfortable for the leviathans. Anja had seen Devinia's pod chewing on seaweed, in an attempt to get the balls out.

The pods in the north now sought the wave riders out, opening their mouth to have the druk removed.

A symbiosis that worked for everyone.

"I heard they're considering dragging the ocean bed, like they did the beaches, to get more druk. That there's a plan to make an exception to Fynian's sanctuary status." She'd heard the rumors since she'd arrived on Fynian.

"It'll never happen." Cal shrugged.

"Because the wave riders won't let it?"

He nodded. "Most of the people who live here are either wave riders, or have a wave rider in their family. We won't let the pods be disturbed by dredgers. There is no way it can be anything but invasive."

She agreed with that, wholeheartedly. "I'm glad."

He sent her a look. "Your predecessor, Carvello, put forward an opinion it could be done without causing the pods too much distress."

She blinked. "How did he figure that?"

"Something about doing it in stages, during the mating season."

"But . . ." She shook her head. The pods were so sensitive to sound, Carvello had to know doing anything in mating season might affect the pods' feeling of safety. It could be catastrophic.

"Duncan told me you're the trade emissary between Fynian and the rest of the VSC, negotiating the price of druk."

He glanced at her. "Yes."

"But you still work as a wave rider as well?"

"It's not something that's easy to give up. I wouldn't like to be inside all the time." He stretched out his legs. "I wouldn't have taken the trade emissary job but my mother persuaded me it would be a good thing to have someone who worked as a wave rider, who knew the true value of druk, doing the negotiating."

"At least you managed to keep the wave riding part of it." She agreed with his mother, though. It was good for Fynian, and for the leviathan, to have a wave rider managing the trade in druk. "I also prefer the outdoors. That's why I chose research in the field to a teaching position."

He nodded in agreement, looking at her strangely, but before she could ask him what it was, a sound suddenly crashed over them, making her flinch.

The sleet had turned into hail and small white stones of ice rattled down the side of the fissure.

"Maybe time to get under cover." Calder started to untie his shoes, and Anja shuffled closer to the entrance of the tent and did the same.

She elbowed him in the stomach at least once as they wriggled inside, but when they were finally in, pressed together, the warmth was worth the embarrassment and discomfort.

"I'm sorry. I hope I haven't seriously injured you."

He gave a grunt, and she couldn't tell if it was in amusement or not. He was hard to read. Taciturn and unsmiling most of the time, but he had stuck by her every step of the way.

The sound of hail had been a light clatter as they'd squeezed themselves into the tent, but as if a tap had been turned on, it was suddenly a raging downpour, like a giant shaking a bottle full of pebbles.

Safe under their little overhang, Anja was grateful they'd called it a night when they did.

"Thank you."

He hesitated, she could feel his body stiffen behind her. "For what?"

"Making the good call to find a place and set up the tent. For helping me."

"Huh." He paused. "I'm Fynian. There aren't a lot of us, and we help each other. This is a rough place. With the solar flares, we have no mobile comms and the weather is dangerous. I wouldn't leave anyone out here alone, but certainly not someone who's under attack by strangers and who's genuinely got the interests of the pods at heart."

It was the longest sentence she'd heard out of him. "You'd know if they were locals? They're definitely not from Fynian?"

"I haven't had a proper look at them yet, but no. They aren't ringing any bells. I think they've come down as tourists."

"They're only pretending to be tourists, if they're taking direction from Sirco. What I don't understand is what they're after."

"Whatever it is, they don't want witnesses." Cal shifted behind her. "Those two didn't want you coming across them doing reconnaissance off the cliffs in a glider, so they decided to intercept you when they heard your plan to come up the coast. To get rid of you."

Anja turned slightly to look at him, found his eyes were closed, and turned back.

"That would mean whatever they're doing is illegal."

"Not many things you can do out here that are legal. The whole of Fynian besides Rinc is a nature sanctuary. And whatever they're up to, they don't strike me as the type to care about the law."

No. Them trying to kill her clued her in on that.

That and shooting Kada.

Injuring a leviathan would carry as stiff a penalty as murder on Fynian, she would guess.

"I really wish I knew what they were doing with that glider." She mumbled the words, because the warmth had made her limbs heavy and having Cal pressed up against her back made her feel safe.

If he answered her, she didn't hear it.

6

—————

CAL WOKE WITH HIS CHIN ON TOP OF ANJA'S HEAD, HER HAIR tickling his nose.

She had slid down in the night and was tucked up tight against him.

He had somehow wrapped his arms around her as he'd slept, anchoring her to him. He should feel uncomfortable—he had never been a cuddler—but he didn't.

He didn't at all.

For a moment he lay still, listening for any sounds from outside their tent.

It was quiet, and the light seeping through the walls of the tent seemed strange, although he put that down to the overhang above them, and the fact that it must be close to midday.

Anja stirred in his arms, and turned slightly. "Hello."

Her voice was a little husky, a little rough.

It sent a shot of desire through him, so hot and strong he had to hold himself very still.

"Hello." He had to wait a moment to speak. Had to clear his throat.

"The light's weird." She was looking up at the roof of the tent.

"Yes." He rolled onto his back, although she was still tucked up against his side.

"Guess we'll know each other pretty well by the end of this journey." She shot him a quick look, a smile flashing and then gone.

He gave a grunt of acknowledgment and scooted carefully to the front of the tent, scooping up his boots as he unfastened the entrance flap.

He stuck his head out while he slid his feet into his shoes and paused.

"What is it?"

"A hail pile-up." He pushed out of the tent, having to bend a little because of the overhang, and stared at the pile of ice that filled the fissure.

The overhang had saved them from any of it landing on them, but there was a wall of it as high as he was in front of him.

He pushed at it, and it did not move. After the hail, he'd heard it rain, and that water must have frozen overnight, turning the pile of hailstones into a single piece of ice.

"Wow." Anja pressed up behind him, warm and smelling of something exotic and spicy, and then yawned near his ear.

He had to fight not to smile in amusement.

"Good thing we had the overhang." She turned and dealt with the tent, folding it away, while he looked for a way out.

There was one, fortunately. They would have to walk under the overhang for a short distance, but there was space enough for them to squeeze through and climb the wall of the fissure up to the top.

When he turned back, he found Anja crouched down, heating some water for jah.

"You sleep all right?" He joined her, and she nodded.

"Woke up a few times, because of the storm, but I feel rested."

He did, too. He wouldn't have thought it, but he felt full of energy.

They ate side by side, and her hair caught on his jacket, the long, gleaming strands of copper and brown spilling over his shoulder and upper arm.

He knew how it felt. Knew its scent.

He cleared his throat and gulped down the last of the jah.

"Your family might start looking for you today." She sounded hopeful.

"They will." It was standard procedure to check on everyone after a storm like last night's. If they hadn't started to miss him yesterday afternoon or evening, they would definitely be missing him now.

"That'll put a dent in those bastards' plans to fly around in that glider."

He inclined his head as he packed up the last of the gear but he needed to temper her expectations. "Search and rescue might not come south first. It's a big ocean, and there aren't enough people to cover every part of it. They'll get here, but it might not be right away."

She held his gaze. "What do you think they'll do?"

He thought about the other search and rescue missions he'd been on. "They'll have less to go on, because they won't know when I went missing, but most likely they'll send a runner along the south and north coast, looking for my boat's signal. The other runners will divide up the open ocean, and each take a sector."

"How many runners do they have?"

"Four, if all of them are in Rinc right now. Five if the Verdant String Research Center offers theirs."

They stared at each other for a moment.

"The runner that should have already come to fetch me."

He nodded. "Be interesting to see what happens with that."

"Interesting?" She gave a snort of half amusement, half disgust and he decided he would like to be there when she had words with Duncan Verne.

"If they're flying that glider near the wave rider hut again, we can keep going in the light. We're far enough past it we should be out of their line of sight." He hoped that was the case, because even though traveling at night had been his suggestion, it was hard going without a light, and the weather looked clear right now.

If they could safely travel in the daylight, they'd get to Rinc a lot faster. Especially if the weather held.

Anja looked relieved at the idea. She obviously hadn't liked tripping over rocks in the dark either. "Let's go up and see if we can tell where they are."

There wasn't enough width for them to climb up the side of the rock face with their bags, so he climbed up first and Anja handed the bags up to him one at a time.

When they were both standing on the lip of the fissure, the bags at their feet, a light sheen of sweat on both their faces despite the temperature, she turned south and then he heard it, too. The sound of the glider.

"Out late, up early." She made a face. "They're certainly keen."

"At least it means we can get going." He wondered what the men could possibly be looking for.

Cal had spent his life riding these seas, and he couldn't guess.

It was going to be his mission to find out.

THE GOING WAS slow and hard.

The weather was colder than it had been yesterday, the clouds that had trapped some of the sun's heat had blown away in the storm, leaving the sky a blue so pale, it was almost white.

And while walking along the clifftops meant they avoided the much rougher ground of the escarpment, the dark slabs of rock were slippery and the sea breeze came straight off the ocean and cut through even the smart fabric of Anja's clothing with icy precision.

She alternated between looking up at the skies, watching for the glider or a search and rescue runner, and at the ground, watching her footing.

The constant whistle of the wind made hearing difficult, and so it seemed to her the sound of the runner approaching them from the north suddenly engulfed them without warning.

"Here they come." Cal stopped, and she stepped up close beside him. He angled his body to shield her from the worst of the wind and she sent him a quick look of gratitude, but his full concentration was on the runner speeding toward them, hugging the coast just above the cliffs.

Cal lifted an arm, and after a moment the runner swung out over the sea, and sank out of sight.

Anja leaned over the cliff's edge and saw it had landed on the beach up ahead.

She turned to Cal, gave him a quick, hard hug. "We're rescued."

He glanced at her, but he didn't look as happy as she did.

"What is it?"

He surely had to be pleased about this.

"That's the research center's runner," he said.

The one that should have come for her days ago.

"Why did they land on the beach, not up on the escarpment?" She looked to the right, to what seemed like flat ground, but she knew all too well how many fissures dotted the landscape.

The pilot could probably see too many obstacles not obvious from this angle.

"It's possible there wasn't enough of a landing area. The beach would guarantee it." But Cal still didn't sound happy.

She gnawed on her lower lip, suddenly more cautious as they

walked north until they found a path to the beach and began the walk down.

If felt like they were descending into a trap, but she knew that was only because Cal had told her it was the research center's runner. She'd be racing down with nothing but relief otherwise.

Halfway down, Cal checked his step, looking back the way they'd come, and she thought she heard the sound of the glider, but when she looked back herself, there was nothing there.

She couldn't be sure she'd heard anything at all over the noise of the wind.

The path spat them out on the beach close to the runner, and as they started walking through the soft sand toward it, the door on the side of the runner opened and four people jumped out, two women and two men.

"Cal!" One of the women raced toward them, kicking up sand behind her as she ran, and Anja thought Cal lost some of his wariness.

"Your sister?" she asked, but it was obvious. The woman had the same dark hair and sharp features as the man beside her.

"My sister, Livia," he confirmed.

A fifth person stepped out from behind the four running toward them, holding back.

Sirco. Anja recognized him immediately, drew a breath to speak.

"I see him." Cal glanced at her and Anja moved closer to him, suddenly nervous, so they stood shoulder to shoulder.

But then they were surrounded by relieved wave riders, and her view of Sirco was obscured.

"What happened?" Livia grabbed both Cal's arms, pulled him close. "Mom's out of her mind with worry." She glanced at Anja, and there was interest and speculation in her gaze.

"Move a little to the side, Liv." Cal's voice was urgent, but soft. "I need to keep my eyes on Sirco."

"What?" Livia's mouth dropped open in surprise, but the woman with her gave a nod, as if something had been confirmed for her, and she angled her body back toward the runner and turned her head.

Sirco stood beside the runner, arm raised.

From behind them, Anja heard a buzzing sound and looked back.

The glider slid along the clifftops, faster than she expected, drifting out over the sea and then dipping low as it came in.

The burst of laz fire from the man hanging from the frame was sudden and shocking.

She turned, looking for a place to run, and remembered Sirco.

He started firing as well.

She should have trusted her feelings earlier. They were caught in a trap, Anja thought as Livia fell in front of her.

Nowhere to go.

Sea to one side, cliff to the other. Enemy before and behind.

A flash of purple blinded her and she felt the searing pain of a hit.

Cal grabbed her as she went down, and they fell together.

The sand made for a soft landing, but she was half-blind, half-deaf, immobile.

The buzzing sound seemed to be everywhere and sand swirled around her before the world went dark.

WHEN SHE STRUGGLED BACK to consciousness, she didn't know how much time had passed.

She was in the back of the runner and roughly piled together with Cal and the four wave riders.

It was a struggle to keep her eyes open, and she could feel the tingle in her arms and legs, as if her system was fighting to work again, but she couldn't move yet.

The engine tone changed and someone came toward them from the front.

"Any trouble?" Sirco asked, and she realized with a fearful leap of her heart that the glider pilot was standing behind her. Had been there the whole time.

"Nah. They're out."

She let her eyelids flutter shut. Sirco bent over her, and she felt her chest tighten in panic as the two men picked her up, each taking an end.

She opened her eyes again, blinking hard. Better to see what was happening than play dead.

"You're already coming round." Sirco sounded surprised. "That won't help you."

The men stood at the now open side door of the runner, and swung her, out into the air, back in the hold, and then a final heave as they let her go.

There was a sudden cold rush of air around her as she fell.

She hit the water hard enough that even with her system being numb, she felt it jar all the way through her bones.

As she sank under the waves, she tried to scream with rage and frustration, but no sound escaped.

7

———

Cal felt Anja being dragged off him. It was hard to concentrate, but he was aware of Livia, Demi, Ritt and Walef piled up against him.

They were alive, he assured himself. For now, they were all alive.

The door of the runner opened, and the rush of cold air helped to clear his head.

As his eyes began to focus, he saw what they were doing with Anja, and the panic and rage cleared his head even more.

He fought against the fog in his head, the tight constriction of his chest. He struggled for breath, and his arms and legs felt like they were on fire.

"This one'll be a bit heavier than her." Sirco was suddenly looming over him, getting his hands under Calder's armpits.

"You sure you want to get rid of this one? The heat will go up. Especially if we kill him and his sister." The glider pilot grabbed his feet, and he was hoisted up.

Both men hesitated, holding him aloft.

"We've gone too far now. There's no turning back, and keeping him, any of them, will just slow us down. We don't have enough crew to watch them. Better if they just disappear." Sirco started to move.

So Sirco was aware of who he and Livia were. Who they were related to. He would understand the implications of harming them.

Not that it was going to stop him, obviously.

Cal could just feel his fingers start to work again, but that wasn't going to cut it.

He could feel the buffeting wind, and then he was dropped onto the floor.

"If I swing him, I might go out with him. He's a big bastard." The glider pilot grunted with effort as he grabbed Calder's arm.

Sirco must have done the same, because he was suddenly shoved, head first, out the door. He was in free fall.

He already knew what was coming, but there was no bracing for impact in his current state.

He hit the water hard and blacked out for a moment, coming to just under the surface.

The shock of the cold seemed to shake up his system, because he was able to move his arms and legs a little, get his head above water.

Anja.

Cal gulped in a deep breath of air and then sank back under the water, eyes wide open, looking for any sign of her.

Nothing.

And then a splash and bubbles obscured his view, and Livia was suddenly beside him in the water.

He grabbed her, forcing his arms to move, and as they broke the surface, Demi landed feet first.

She wasn't as affected, he noticed. She managed to fight her way up on her own, and then dived after Walef as he plummeted past them.

The runner was hovering above them, and by the time Ritt was thrown into the sea, Livia was more herself.

"Look for Anja," he shouted to them all, giving one last look at the runner as it started to move away, before he went under again, sinking deeper than he had before, slowly turning in the clear water, looking for her.

He saw a shadow, just out of the corner of his eye, and tried to track it, but to no avail before he was forced to make for the surface, gasping for breath. He looked for any sign of her among the waves.

The water was freezing.

"Anja!" He shouted loudly, his voice cracking in panic.

"I don't see her." Walef rose up, light hair sleek against his head, his breath puffing out in a plume of icy condensation.

"What does it matter?" Ritt coughed, trying to stay afloat. "We're going to die of exposure in a few minutes anyway."

Cal didn't like that he was right.

They were all as good as dead out here in the freezing water.

He was shivering already, even with his smart fabric clothing, and knew they didn't have long.

Anja would have even less.

He tipped back his head and saw the runner disappear beyond the horizon, felt a rage so hot, he was surprised it didn't warm the water around him.

His muscles began to cramp, making every movement to keep afloat a painful ordeal, and he was struggling to get his chest to expand enough to draw breath.

Ritt went under, and as he lunged to grab the back of his jacket, something bumped into his side.

He barely had the energy to glance over, but Demi shouted something, and so he forced himself to turn.

It was his boat.

It took him three tries before he managed to hook his arm over the side, but he couldn't pull himself up.

He felt his arm begin to slip, and then suddenly, both he and the boat rose up, out of the water.

Ritt lay, coughing up water, beside him.

He crouched beside the vessel, looking down to work out what was going on, his frozen brain slow to register what was happening.

He was on Kada's back.

He extended a hand, still hunched over like an old man, and hauled Livia, Demi, and Walef up.

They clambered over the leviathan's back, helped Ritt over the side, and fell into the boat in shocked silence.

Walef was the last to get in, and as he lifted his foot off Kada's back, the leviathan sank back down, leaving the boat to float on the water.

For a moment, Cal just lay still, exhausted and grateful as the small vessel rocked and shuddered under the onslaught of the choppy waves.

Suddenly, with a jerk, the boat began to move, racing across the water just like it had two nights ago when Kada had grabbed the rope the first time.

Walef swore as he fell back and hit his head on the side of the boat, and the others struggled up on hands and knees to work out what was going on.

Cal had played this game before.

"It's Kada."

"This is what happened the other night?" Livia looked over the side, eyes wide. "I've never heard of anything like this. Do you think he's just playing?"

"I've heard the stories about them saving wave riders. We all have. This is something else." Demi moved to the front of the boat and looked down into the water. "This is one to be added to the legends."

"And the woman with you? Anja?" Ritt shivered, hunched over on a bench, seeming beyond caring about Kada, or why they were moving.

"She's the scientist at the southern peninsula, isn't she?" Walef asked. "Studying the southern pod?"

Cal nodded. "Except the pod has disappeared. She was headed for Rinc when we bumped into each other. No one was answering her calls for help from research headquarters."

"That's why you were suspicious of Sirco," Demi nodded. "I thought he was too jumpy."

"You should have said." Livia turned to her. "I didn't pick it up."

"You were worried about Cal." Demi shrugged. "And . . ." Her voice trailed off, and she shook her head and turned away.

Livia stared at her back, as if she knew what Demi had been going to say, and Cal saw her mouth form an unhappy line.

"There's more to this?" he asked her. "You and Sirco—"

"There is no me and Sirco." Liv's eyes blazed. "But he was very friendly. Always at the same places I was. I thought he was nice."

Cal left it. He'd been scanning the water for any sign of Anja while they spoke, but he realized he'd stopped shivering, which was dangerous. The important thing was to get warm and functioning again so he could look for her. If it wasn't too late.

He unclipped a storage box lid and pulled out what he needed, throwing spare towels to the others. He dried himself down, stripping his wet clothes off, and then dressed in one of the sets of clothing he kept stored in case of accidents.

Demi did the same, sorting through clothes that might fit, and he was glad he had a lot of blankets, because he didn't have spare clothes for everyone, but at least they could strip the wet gear off and warm up while their clothes dried.

By the time they all had a hot cup of jah in their hands, he was able to breathe a full breath again.

Except, they could have passed Anja a hundred times over.

And even if he'd been looking at the water every moment, if she was under the surface, it still wouldn't have made any difference.

The boat hit a big wave, and Cal adjusted to keep his balance.

"Where's he taking us?" Ritt asked. He finally looked a little better, even if he was in nothing but a blanket, clutching a cup of jah in his hands.

Kada had turned, heading out into open water, toward the archipelago of islands that curved like the wing of a bird away from the coast.

"Looks like to the islands." Cal didn't know what was out there. Maybe nothing. Maybe Kada really was just playing a game.

Beside the boat he saw a ripple in the water, and the dark shadow of a massive body just below the surface.

As he turned for a better look, a head rose up, and there was a loud huff of exhalation. Spray drifted over to them on the cutting breeze.

Cal kept his balance as Devinia rose up enough out of the water for her eyes to be visible. She seemed to be watching him.

He recognized her from the breeding season, where the pods all congregated at the tip of the archipelago every year.

She was mature. Nearly at the end of her hundred year life cycle, the ridges on her nose prominent, her eyes the dark purple they seemed to get with age.

Except his grandfather had sworn Devinia was already mature when he was a young wave rider, which would mean the old girl was pushing a hundred and fifty, at least.

Which didn't seem likely.

She seemed to focus on him before she lifted her whole head

out of the water, keeping pace easily with the boat, and opened her mouth slightly.

"Is that . . .?" Livia had come up to stand beside him, and she leaned against him as she peered forward, holding onto the side of the boat with white knuckled hands. "Is that Anja in her mouth?"

Just past the leviathan's massive teeth, Cal could see the dark orange of Anja's coat, the black of a glove.

Devinia closed her mouth again and slid silently back under the water.

"Is she still alive?" Demi's whisper was shocked.

Cal couldn't respond.

Devinia must have scooped her up when she'd hit the water. That would have kept her warm as well as stopped her from drowning.

He had to believe Devinia had saved her.

And it looked as if Devinia and Kada were working together. Heading for the same destination. It was a level of cooperation he'd never seen before in leviathans who were not in the same pod.

They seemed to be headed for a small island with steep cliffs, one of thousands in the vast archipelago.

The journey might just be coming to an end.

8

————

WHATEVER SHE WAS LYING ON WAS ALIVE.

Anja lay still, in complete darkness, and felt the pulse of life in the surface beneath her. As soon as she moved, light leaked in from all around her, illuminating her surroundings.

Teeth. She was surrounded by sharp layers—four or maybe five—of teeth.

As the light increased, she looked down and found herself lying on what she slowly worked out was a tongue.

Suddenly, there was a sound like an explosion going off above her head.

It was only her months of studying the leviathans that she worked out it was an exhalation of breath.

She was in a leviathan's mouth.

She lay, still and shocked, coming to terms with it.

A leviathan had snatched her unconscious body out of the freezing water and was carrying her in its mouth.

She felt a surge of gratitude so strong, it was hard to contain, and the scientist in her was fascinated in equal measure.

This was incredible.

A level of inter-species cooperation she had never heard of before. Not even from the wave riders.

At the thought of wave riders, she made a sound of distress.

Cal and his friends.

She had a sense they had been piled around her in the runner. Had they been thrown in after her, or taken elsewhere?

She felt the hot prickle of tears at the thought that Cal was somewhere in the freezing water and blinked them away, suddenly refusing to accept it.

She didn't understand enough about the situation to know what was going on, what had really happened to him.

She chose to believe he was all right, and so were his friends.

This whole situation was unbelievable, and yet, she needed to adapt to it. To survive so she could find Cal and the others as fast as possible.

A metallic gleam caught her eye, resting near her hand, and she reached out to pick it up.

It was similar to a small piece of druk, round and smooth, but it wasn't like any druk she'd seen before. It looked like a silver bead.

As she lifted it closer to her face, it seemed to melt into her palm and she blinked, bringing her hand right up in front of her eyes.

Suddenly, the light disappeared as the leviathan's mouth snapped shut, and they sank down. The tongue lifted, pressing her gently into the roof of the mouth, and she forced herself not to panic.

Could this be an instinctive reaction? Something that happened every time a leviathan dived?

Before she could start to feel claustrophobic, the mouth opened again, wide this time, in a space that was gloomy although not completely dark.

The leviathan rested its chin onto a solid surface and opened its mouth even wider.

Trying to move carefully, Anja crawled forward and edged her way between the rows of teeth, half-falling, half-jumping onto the slick metal floor the leviathan's head was resting on.

She looked behind her.

"Devinia." She had guessed who her rescuer had been, but now she knew. "Thank you."

She reached forward to touch the matriarch's ridged nose, but with a huff, Devinia slid back into the dark water and disappeared.

She stared after her rescuer for a moment, while the water left in her wake slapped at the sides of the room she was in. She turned slowly on her knees, to find the light faintly illuminating the space was coming from an open door behind her.

She was in a place that had once been a chamber or room, but something had smashed into the side of it, and let the sea water in.

The rip must be enormous, and the original structure huge, to allow a leviathan access.

She slowly rose to her feet, careful how she moved because the floor was slick beneath her boots and angled downward. She shuffled in small, incremental steps in the direction of the source of light.

She finally relaxed a little when she reached the doorway, and a more even surface.

A light was affixed to a wall in a narrow corridor, and she studied it, reaching out to touch the round, smooth fixture. It was framed in some kind of metal, but that was deeply corroded. Whatever the light itself was made from seemed unaffected by the ocean, though.

She stepped back and looked both right and left, before choosing to go left.

The air was icy, and the passage had obviously been filled with water at one point. There were tiny barnacles attached to the walls and floor, and places where the metal was discolored and rusted.

It smelled briny and the floor of the passage was just as slick as it had been in the room where Devinia had let her out.

She was just thinking that she felt far better than she should, almost stronger with every step she took, when her leg seized and she went down on one knee.

She put out both hands and cried out as she just avoided cutting herself on a sharp, corroded metal pipe sticking up from a jagged hole in the floor.

She stood slowly, rubbing her knee, but the pain was already gone as she edged around the dangerous rip. The floor groaned as she moved and she guessed the whole thing was close to giving way.

She hugged the wall carefully after that, moving slowly.

As she moved deeper into the structure, doors began to appear, all of them open. She peered inside each of them as she passed.

Some seemed to be bedrooms, others lounges or dining halls, but all were lit only from the weak light in the passageway, and she didn't want to step into their enclosing darkness.

This had been some kind of installation.

The whole place looked like a military barracks to her. She'd been stationed at an Aponi military base for a few months at the start of her career, and this looked very similar.

Up ahead, the passageway took a sharp right turn, but there was a spiral staircase set in the corner that wound upward.

Beside it was what looked like a captain's suite; a larger room with a bed and a small lounge area. The light from the passage illuminated bedding lying on the floor, and she stepped inside.

As she did, a single light flickered to life, low down to the ground.

Emergency lighting, perhaps, and motion activated.

She prodded the bedding with a boot. It must have been underwater for a long time, and then left to dry in this cold, dank environment.

It stank.

The fabric that had once covered the chairs had rotted away, leaving a strange skeleton of rusted springs and wood.

Another open door tempted her deeper into the space, and she stepped up to it cautiously and peered beyond.

A shower.

This room, like everywhere else, had clearly been underwater, but there was a drain in the floor, and she guessed when the ship had been lifted off the bottom of the ocean, the water in this room had been sucked out.

It made it the least dank, slimy place she'd seen so far.

More out of optimistic wish fulfillment than any real expectation, she turned the tap and made a sound of surprise when water began to fall from the wide shower head.

When it began to steam, she gave in to temptation, bent, took off her boots, and stepped beneath it.

A container attached to the wall dispensed some liquid soap into her hand. It smelled strange—some unknown fragrance—or more likely it had gone off in the many years since this place had been submerged and abandoned.

She let the water run over her clothes and stepped out of them one by one, rubbing the soap over each salt-water and saliva-coated item.

Even though Devinia's body heat had kept her warm, the hot water felt like the most wonderful gift she had ever been given.

She stood under the spray until her skin began to wrinkle and then she stepped out and hung her clothes over hooks to dry.

They would dry quickly, but she felt suddenly exposed and unsafe in the dimly lit space.

From somewhere above her, she heard a crash, and then what sounded very much like footsteps.

She scrambled into her wet underwear and stood, looking up at the ceiling, listening.

Her mind went straight to Sirco. Had he followed her here?

She moved out into the bedroom, then looked back into the bathroom at her dripping clothes. She wanted them on, but wearing them would only create a wet, dripping trail for whoever was above to follow.

Decision made, she moved in silence on bare feet, slipping back into the passageway and listening again.

Someone gave a shout that seemed to come from the floor above and she flinched.

It would be good to find a weapon.

She began to move again, careful on the slick floor. She edged past the staircase and turned into the passageway leading away from it, glancing into rooms as she went for anything that she could use for protection.

The ring of boots on the metal stairs panicked her into darting into the next room she came to, but the emergency lighting flickered on the moment she did.

It would be a beacon for whoever was walking around. A sign pointing to her hiding place.

A sense of calm came over her.

She had the strangest sensation of an out-of-body experience, as if she was observing herself.

She crouched beside the low light fixture, aware that something other than herself was directing her movement, and then twisted off the rusted bolts in deft movements, ripping the corroded metal frame off the wall, and pulling out the twisted guts of its wiring.

The light flickered out and died.

She was now in darkness, the only light coming from the passageway.

Although, she could deal with that, too, the new voice inside her said with confidence.

She could deal with it from right here. Because the wiring was connected.

She looked down at her hands, and extended a finger, touching one of the wires, and suddenly the light in the passage died.

She was plunged into absolute darkness.

She turned, pressing her back up against the wall, and slid down to the floor, ignoring the cold as her bare skin came into contact with it.

What was going on?

She flexed her hand, curled her fingers into a fist, and remembered the small metal ball.

She heard a bang, and then voices; footsteps ringing.

"Not surprising the lights shorted." The man who spoke sounded Fynian. He had the strong accent that defined the locals.

Whoever he and his companion were, they had a light of their own. It flickered, as if they were playing it from side to side as they made their way down the passage.

"What is this place, though? Did the Arkhorans have a military base here when they first discovered Fynian and the VSC forgot to mention it?"

It was a woman who spoke this time, and she sounded Fynian as well.

Maybe this wasn't Sirco and his crew.

She heard another pair of boots, a straggler catching up.

"Any sign of her?"

The question sent a chill through her.

Whoever these people were, they weren't here by happenstance. They were looking for her.

She had a sudden vision of the room she was hiding in, before it had been plunged into darkness. It lit up inside her brain.

She knew what objects were in here. And exactly where they were.

She shouldn't know. She didn't think she'd been paying that much attention.

As she darted forward, she also knew she had never moved so fast before. Or so quietly.

Her hand closed over a black box that had been lying on the floor in the middle of the room, and then she was back by the door, standing pressed against the wall, box gripped in her hand as a weapon.

It should worry her, whatever was happening inside her. It would, when she had time to think about it, rather than keeping quiet as the ring of boots on metal came closer.

The lights they were holding swept dizzily up and down in the absolute blackness.

"We'll never find her in this place with no lights."

The whispered words startled her.

They sounded so near. And yet, she had a feeling her hearing was just better—they were not right beside the door, as it sounded.

She held her breath.

"Do you think the others are having more luck?"

She felt herself go very still as the woman spoke. There were more of them. Hunting her.

Anja stood, gripped by indecision, as they passed her by. The Fynian accents made it a possibility these people might be friends. Searching for her.

She considered taking the chance of stepping out and revealing herself.

There was a strange sensation within her, a push-pull that was both worried and protective, yet also a sense of urgency—that she was up against a deadline which these people could help to meet.

She didn't understand it, and the moment passed, with the voices of the searchers fading away into the distance.

She rubbed her arms as she realized she was still in her underwear and it was cold.

She should be shivering, but she wasn't.

Whatever was doing the weird stuff inside her was working hard to keep her from feeling the cold too much.

But it wasn't sustainable.

She needed to get back to her clothes.

To eat something.

To work out what to do next.

She had a sudden flash of thought, of swimming through the water, strong and powerful, but not fully reaching her potential. Not doing what she had been created to do.

It felt like . . . the memories of a leviathan.

She flexed her hand again. The silver ball had been inside Devinia's mouth. And she didn't know why, but she had a strong feeling there was a connection to that ball and what was happening to her now.

She forced herself to let it go.

One problem at a time.

She stepped out of the room cautiously, picking her bare feet over the rusted, mollusk-covered floor, and then realized the darkness would make things very difficult in finding the room where her clothes were.

There was a sense of sudden contrition from the new part of her that was separate, a flash of realization that it had been too quick to act, and could not undo what it had done.

Not from here, anyway.

She would have to make her way in the darkness.

She started back the way she'd come, moving carefully along the wall toward the staircase.

As soon as she turned the corner, she saw a movement of light inside the room where she'd showered, heard footsteps.

Someone had found her clothes.

She turned, looking back the way she'd come, but there were others looking for her that way.

The light moved again, coming closer, and she darted to the stairs, running up it as quietly as she could.

It spiraled upward to a small landing. In the pitch darkness, she had no idea of the layout but the movement of air made her think there was another passageway stretching right and left.

There was something directly in front of her, and when she stepped up to it and reached her hands out to feel, she encountered what seemed to be a reinforced door.

It was then that she heard the footsteps running on the stairs behind her.

Get inside.

It was like a shout inside her head.

She felt her hand being moved, slapped down on what seemed like a smooth surface beside the door, and then the slow, creaking groan as the door slid open.

She squeezed through as soon as it was wide enough, and then paused in astonishment at the sight that met her.

Light flooded the room, streaming in. There was a concentrated beam in the middle of the space from above, and then more diffuse light entered from a transparent wall to the front.

She momentarily forgot about the footsteps on the stairs behind her, and walked into the beam of light, looking up to find its source.

It was sunlight, streaming down through a rip in the ceiling. After the dark and the cold below, she could not make herself leave its warm, golden embrace as she studied the light coming from in front of her. She was looking down into an area which was lower than the platform where she stood, accessed by five shallow steps.

There was a transparent wall, like the window in the front of a hover, and it was underwater. Sunlight from above filtered through dancing, swaying waves to throw bright spots of light all around the room.

She was in a command center, she realized. Standing on the bridge, looking down at what was once control stations.

No sign of life remained, but then, the rip above her head would have seen to that, even if there were people who had been in this place when it plunged into the ocean.

From behind her she heard the door grind and creak again, and she suddenly remembered she hadn't heard it close after she'd entered.

Someone was forcing their way through the narrow opening she had used.

Someone bigger than her.

9

———

For a moment, Cal felt as if the world shifted, and reality went with it.

Anja stood in a beam of light in front of him; barefoot, in nothing but underwear.

She didn't move, her gaze forward.

The door seemed to be rusted in place or blocked by debris, and he shoved it hard to get in.

She made a gasping sound and spun, but something about the way she moved made his hind brain take notice.

This was a threat, not to be taken lightly.

She stared at him for a moment, her stance defensive.

"Cal?"

Her voice was rough.

They had slept locked tight around each other, faced death together, but they hardly knew anything about each other.

Even so, he didn't think twice before stepping toward her, arms out, and she flew at him, leaping the last few steps.

He caught her easily, his hands on her bare back, as she gripped his hips with her knees.

For a moment they simply stared at each other, gazes locked.

He bent his head, just a little, as she lifted her face to his, and they kissed, lips brushing lightly.

She shivered in his arms, and he suddenly deepened the kiss, his arm snaking up to hold her even closer, cupping the back of her head with one hand.

He had thought of this too many times since last night not to take the chance when offered.

Her hair was damp, but she smelled of perfume, not the sea, as if she'd showered and washed her hair.

He couldn't stop the sound of need that escaped his throat, and the raw emotion of it sounded a warning in his head.

This was not the place, and not the time.

He forced himself to lift his head, and Anja leaned back reluctantly, angling her head up to watch him, her dark eyes framed with thick lashes.

He cleared his throat, aware of her still in his arms, pressed against him. "I hoped Devinia had brought you here. I guessed those were your clothes in the bathroom downstairs."

"It was you looking around in there?" She sighed in relief, dropped her head onto his shoulder. "I heard someone and ran up the stairs."

"How did you get in here?" He reluctantly set her back on her feet and lifted his gaze to the light-flooded room. "We tried to get in earlier, but it wouldn't open."

"We?" She tilted her head.

"My sister and my friends. My fellow wave riders, who came with Sirco to find us. Kada rescued us with the boat and brought us here."

"I was so worried about you. I should have remembered Kada and your boat." Her voice cracked and she drew in a deep breath. She lifted her gaze to his. "I am very happy to see you."

She didn't step away from him, and he didn't drop his arms, so they stood loosely in each other's embrace, unwilling to lose their physical connection to each other.

"Didn't you hear the others? They went down the other corridor."

"I heard people looking for me, but I wasn't sure who they were so I hid." She lifted her shoulders. "I heard you coming up the stairs and panicked, so I can't remember exactly how I got in here, but I think there was a scan plate by the door."

"Where did Devinia spit you out?" He spoke into her hair.

She gave a low chuckle at that. "Some strange room. It's really big, farther down the passage where I took my shower."

"I saw it. I left Livia there to wait in case Devinia brought you in while I went to fetch the others."

"What do you think this place is?"

At last he forced himself to drop his arms. To step back. "I think it's a spaceship, wedged under the island. A lot of the archipelago consists of islands where the rock at the base of the cliffs has been eaten into over the years by the waves, creating an arch below the island surface. On some of them, the water has reached all the way through to the other side."

She turned her head as he stepped up beside her. "Why do you think it's a spaceship? I thought it might be a military installation. How could a spaceship crash on Fynian and we don't know about it?"

"If it crashed thousands of years ago we wouldn't. I also thought it might be an old Arkhoran military station, until I saw the atrium where Devinia brought you in. And now this . . ." Calder gestured to the bridge. "How much information have you gotten out on the peninsula these last few months?"

"Not a lot. It takes too long to come through the fixed cable so I stopped bothering."

He wondered what she did, out there on her own. Probably

worked most of the time. Duncan should have never left her out there on her own so long.

"A couple of months ago, the Faldine head-of-planet and one of his pilots discovered what seems to be an original ancestral spaceship in the Faldine mountains."

She lifted her brows. "Similar to the one they found floating in space about six months ago?"

He nodded. "Both ships had a massive atrium which scientists think was used to grow food. I saw some footage, and looking around the place where Devinia brought you in, I think it's the same."

"You think this is an ancestral spaceship?" Her eyes lit up in excitement. "If that's true, it would be amazing."

"It would." Even more amazing, he had a strong suspicion the spaceship hadn't ended up under this island by accident. It had been on the bottom of the ocean for a long time, that was clear. Something had moved it.

And there was only one creature he could think of with the strength to tow it any distance at all.

Although why the leviathans would do something like that, he had no idea.

If they had done it, their strange behavior had been going on for a long time, because while the spaceship had probably spent centuries under the ocean, it had been hauled into the shallows of the island some time ago, too.

Long enough for it to be covered in mollusks and barnacles on the outside, enough so that it was impossible to distinguish it from the island rock.

Anja's eyes narrowed, and she stepped back into the beam of light coming in from the hole in the ceiling. "It didn't crash here, though, did it? It's been moved. Lifted off the ocean floor."

She was working it out, too.

Cal nodded.

"The leviathans." Her whisper was full of wonder. "They dragged it here. Hid it."

"I don't see how else it could have been so cleverly tucked away."

When she turned to him, her eyes were alight with excitement. "This shows a level of intelligence far beyond—" She stopped talking and stared, looking into a dark corner of the bridge.

Just as he was about to ask her what it was, he saw it, too. A blinking light coming from one of the comms units.

It had probably been blinking the whole time they'd been in here.

Anja walked toward it and scratched at the sludge that had hardened around it. "The writing's not Aponi or Arkhoran, but it looks similar. It sort of looks like the Aponi word for disaster."

"Emergency," Cal said, leaning over her shoulder to look. "It's the Arkhoran word for emergency."

"Crashing into an ocean would be an emergency." Anja slowly lifted her head. "When did the first signal coming from Fynian get picked up?" She turned to look at him.

"About ninety-five years ago. That's what led the Arkhoran to the Jero system and to Fynian. It disappeared after a few days, but it was enough to lead them here. They set up an outpost but couldn't trace where the signal had come from." Cal walked slowly toward the unit. "The Mysterious Signal we call it, more as a joke than anything else. It's been detected again over the years, three more times, and the theory is that it's always transmitting, but it's usually masked by the solar storm activity. Every twenty years or so the solar flare abates for a few days and the signal is detectable once again."

"And Sirco by coincidence works in the solar flare office." Anja put her hands on her hips, and Cal was reminded again that she was in nothing but her underwear, although she seemed to have forgotten. She gave a dry laugh. "They weren't out on that glider looking for my missing pod; they knew the solar storm was about to die down for a few days, and they were trying to find the signal. They were looking for this spaceship."

Something landed hard on the roof above them, and then a sound like boots drumming over metal.

Calder looked toward the hole in the ceiling. "It seems as if they've found it."

10

She was underdressed for a fight.

Anja looked up at the hole in the ceiling and regretted she was in her underwear.

But the stomp of boots began moving away, and Cal turned to her, face calm.

"He's probably seen out how we came inside." He kept his voice low. "There's a hatch farther down, and we left it open."

She gave a tight nod. "I need to get my clothes."

He sent her a sudden, quick grin, full of mischief, despite the circumstances—a change from the silent, gruff man she'd come to know over the last few days. "A pity, but yes, that would be best." He started toward the door, his face morphing to worry. "I need to get to Livia. She's waiting alone in the atrium."

The sound of footsteps on the stairs had him going still, and Anja slid to the side, out of sight of anyone looking in, adrenalin flooding her system as she settled into a stance she didn't think she'd ever used before.

Cal glanced at her. "Don't move," he mouthed. He took a silent step closer.

A man peered around the door, and Cal's body language changed. "Walef." He glanced at Anja, and she thought she saw something flash in his eyes. A sudden protectiveness.

One of the men she recognized from the beach earlier, before they'd all been shot, stepped into the room. His hair was blond, a sharp contrast to his dark features, and stood in spikes. His startled gaze landed on her, took in her lack of clothing, and his eyes widened.

Then his attention was captured by the dancing of sunlight through water and the pillar of light pouring in from the hole in the ceiling.

She noticed Cal shrug out of his jacket and blinked in surprise as he held it out to her.

"I should have offered this earlier," he whispered.

She shook her head. "I'll just get my own," she mouthed back. Aponi was warm, and her people's love of communal bathing in the many warm water springs and bath houses meant she was very decently covered, even in her underwear, by Aponi standards.

She didn't know enough Fynians to know how they did things, but the cold weather probably meant she was wearing a lot less than they were used to.

"Cal?" A tall woman stepped in behind Walef, and then a second man crowded in on her heels.

Cal put his finger to his lips, and the woman went still.

"Wow." The man behind her, also tall, and as broad in the shoulders as Cal, didn't see the warning, and didn't lower his voice. He also didn't notice Anja at all, his gaze going to the big transparent window and the room itself.

The woman had noticed her straight away. "What is it?" she asked Cal softly, her hand grabbing the arm of the man behind her so she had his attention, and then raising her finger to her lips.

"Sirco or one of his men just landed on the roof." Cal's whisper had them all turning to him, suddenly very focused. "Whoever it is is heading for the open hatch."

"Shit." Walef glanced upward, then toward Anja and Cal. "Where's Livia?"

"We were on our way to get her. She's downstairs." Cal began moving to the door again, keeping his voice whisper soft. "Let's go."

Cal led the way, with Anja right behind him.

She could feel the eyes of the others on her as she ran lightly down the stairs.

Cal stopped at the room where her clothes were and handed her his light. "We'll wait here."

"I'll be quick." She took the light gratefully and disappeared into the bathroom.

She could hear the low sound of a conversation as she hurriedly pulled on clothes that were fortunately very close to being dry.

When she stepped back out into the passage and handed Cal back his light, the talking stopped abruptly.

No one had introduced themselves to her, but she was aware of the shared urgency they felt.

She thought she heard a clang from above and raised her head, but no one else seemed to hear it so she didn't say anything.

They jogged in silence along the passage, keeping close to the wall as they avoided the hole in the floor that had nearly tripped her up earlier, and then stepped into the space where Devinia had deposited her.

A woman stood near the door. She must have heard them coming toward her and seen the light, because she was obviously waiting for them.

"You found her," she said to Cal, her gaze on Anja. "I'm Cal's sister, Livia."

Anja smiled at her. "I'm Anja. Pleased to meet you."

The other woman in the group cleared her throat. "I'm Demi, this is Ritt and Walef."

She turned to nod to them, and noticed varying degrees of curiosity in their eyes as they nodded back.

"What's wrong?" Livia must have picked up the tension they were all feeling.

"Someone landed on the roof, and they'll be coming through the hatch." Cal stepped past her and crouched on the sloping metal floor, to look into the water.

Demi and Ritt had lights, as well as Livia and Cal, and Anja at last saw the place properly.

It could easily have once been an atrium, as Cal thought. They were standing on an old platform or bridge that would have spanned the space before the crash. Cal said it was stories deep, and that made sense, too. Devinia would not have been able to fit in to anything less.

"How do you think they found us?" Walef asked softly. "We hid your boat pretty well, Cal."

"You might not have noticed it, but there was evidence of a signal flashing in that control room."

"The Mysterious Signal?" Demi asked, voice hushed.

Cal gave a nod. "Maybe."

"That's what this is about? They're looking for the source of the signal?" Ritt sounded winded, and for the first time, Anja saw he didn't look well. He moved carefully, as if he was injured.

His dark curly hair framed a handsome face that looked pinched with pain.

"And they didn't want any witnesses while they searched." Walef didn't make it a question.

"They still don't." Cal looked toward the door, but Anja hadn't heard anyone coming down the passage.

With a sudden exhale of air and water, Kada's head rose from the water, and Anja jumped in reaction.

Demi slid a quick look at her, eyes wide.

She looked down at herself, realized that she had taken up that same, strange stance again, and forced herself to straighten.

Cal let out a low laugh as he came closer, and Anja saw the leviathan was towing the boat again.

"I tied that boat to the outside of this structure." Cal spoke in a half-exasperated, half-amused way, and Anja felt a strange tumble inside her chest at his tone.

Kada nudged the boat up onto the floor with a screech of metal on metal.

It sounded too loud in the quiet, and everyone seemed to glance toward the passage and wince.

Livia moved around the front of the boat and rubbed a hand on Kada's nose. "Come to rescue us, have you?"

There was a beat of silence, and Kada banged the boat onto the floor impatiently.

"He wants us to get in." Ritt shuffled back a bit, his hand going to his side.

"I think he does." Demi's tone was dry, but she watched her friend with worried eyes.

"How many of them are there?" Ritt asked. "Can't we take them?"

"There's possibly only one but as many as three." Anja glanced at Cal and he nodded.

"Chances are they're all here. This is their end destination, after all. I'd say we could take them as the odds are in our favor two to one, but we aren't armed. They haven't hesitated to use their weapons and I'm guessing the only reason they didn't kill us when they attacked us earlier is they didn't want to leave dead bodies on the beach. It would have drawn attention."

"What was dropping us in the ocean about then?" Ritt asked, and there was a wheeze to his voice.

"If anyone found our bodies, the evidence would be we died of hypothermia and drowning. Not because we were hit with laz fire. They kept it on a low setting that would be difficult to detect, is my guess." Cal turned away from him, putting out a hand to help Livia into the boat, but Anja kept her gaze on Ritt.

"You don't want to get in the boat because you have broken ribs," she said, holding his eye. "Do you want to stay here and hide and we'll get help?"

Livia turned, her hand still in Cal's, mouth open. "Ritt, you've got broken ribs? And you said nothing?"

"You asshole." Walef stared at him, too. "When you hit the water?"

Ritt gave a brief nod. "I was so cold, I didn't realize until we were in Cal's boat."

Cal's gaze flicked to Anja, an unreadable expression on his face, before he turned to Ritt. "There's a med kit in the boat."

Kada thumped his chin against the metal floor and the whole thing creaked alarmingly, and moved a little.

Everyone went still.

"He really wants us to go." Walef looked down the passage again. "I'm going to say I think he's a better bet than whoever is stomping around on the roof with a laz."

Everyone looked at Ritt for acceptance, and he gave a reluctant nod.

Walef and Cal flanked him, and lifted him into the boat in an easy move that spoke of shared tasks in the past.

Anja could see they moved as a team, even though she knew the work of a wave rider was usually a solo effort.

Still, they went out together to the pods, and they obviously trusted one another.

Cal turned to her. "You up for this?"

She nodded, and when she stepped closer he boosted her over the side of the boat, then did the same for his sister and Demi.

Walef hauled out the medkit for Ritt.

As soon as they were all onboard, Kada sank down into the water with a huff and the boat jerked back and then swung around as he towed it away.

"You would think there would be some light from outside seeping in if he was able to tow the boat in here," Walef commented.

That was true, now that Anja thought about it, but when Kada had pulled them the length of the space, she saw why it was so dark.

The opening, which turned out to be a massive gash in the side of the spaceship, was deep inside a cave.

"This spaceship looks relatively small from the ocean side, but it's been wedged deep into a cave that must almost stretch the whole width of the island." Cal was looking up at the cave's roof as he spoke.

"Like Archway," Demi said.

"Exactly like Archway." Cal turned to Anja. "Have you seen it?"

She shook her head. "I've heard about it, though. Dunc told me."

She'd hoped she'd have a chance to visit the island with the tunnel that ran its full width, open on both ends like a long, low archway.

"It's unlikely the spaceship just happened to end up hidden beneath one of these archways." Livia's words were hushed, but still echoed around them.

"You're right." Demi reached out a hand and touched the outside of the spaceship, her short brown hair stirring in the wind. "It was wedged in here."

"Could the pods have really managed this?" Walef sounded incredulous.

"Who else?" Cal asked.

Who else, indeed.

Anja felt the breeze pick up as Kada pulled them down a

narrow channel between the bulky spaceship and the wall of the cave.

If Cal was right, this channel might open on both ends, so Kada could take them left or right and they would come out on either side of the island.

He pulled them right, into the cold breeze which lifted her damp hair off her face and tugged at her clothes.

As they got closer to the opening, Anja could hear the groaning of a leviathan in distress.

"That's Devinia." She felt her heart leap in her chest. "Something's wrong."

The others didn't say anything, but she could see their faces were hard and their eyes narrow. They would know the sound of a leviathan in trouble better than she would.

"Maybe that's why Kada wanted us to come with him. Devinia needs help." Livia was crouched at the prow, and she leaned forward, as if it would make them go faster.

Anja looked around at the others. Walef was watching Ritt, who was pulling down his shirt over newly taped ribs.

Demi stood just behind Livia, gaze fixed ahead.

Cal stood near her, in the middle of the boat, and her gaze met his.

She thought for a brief moment of the kiss they'd shared in the control room, and something fluttered in her stomach.

He stared back until a sudden lurch of the boat forced them both to adjust their stances.

Light was visible up ahead, dull, as though it was fading, and she realized the sun would be setting soon.

It had been a long, hard day, and it wasn't over yet.

11

They were all tense as Kada towed them out into the open, looking around for any sign of Sirco, his runner, and his crew.

A buzz behind her had Anja turning around.

The cliffs towered above them from behind, cutting off the sky, but as they moved away, out into the open water, the glider became visible, a black slash against the gray of a clouded, late afternoon sky.

Kada was moving fast and as the angle changed with distance, Anja could see the top of the cliffs. Sirco had set his runner down a little way from the edge. Other than the glider, there was no sign of their attackers, but she guessed they would be inside the spaceship.

A long cry rose up again, and something in the sound set every one of Anja's senses on edge. Like a screaming baby, it hit her at a visceral level.

"She's in pain." Cal's words were grim, his forehead creased with worry.

"Look." Demi pointed up ahead and Anja stepped up onto the bench that ran along the side of the boat to get a better view.

82

The water seemed to boil in the distance, and she tried to make sense of what she was seeing.

"The pod." The joy she would have felt if she'd found them before now was tempered with worry for Devinia. They were circling their matriarch, churning the water.

It wasn't the whole pod, she saw, just the three most senior females after Devinia.

They turned toward the boat as it drew closer and bellowed to Kada.

She hadn't heard that sound before, but she had never seen a leviathan approach the pod who was not part of it.

"They're warning him?" she asked.

"I don't know." Livia glanced back at her. "It's clear Kada is related to Devinia. You can see it in the eye color and striping. I'd guess he's her grandson. One of the males in the bachelor pod up by Rinc must be one of Devinia's sons."

Livia's throwaway comment left her speechless. She hadn't considered it, even though she remembered thinking Kada's markings were similar to Devinia's when he'd originally tried to get her into the boat on the beach, before she'd even met up with Cal.

It would explain a lot if there was a familial link between the two leviathans.

It would certainly explain their cooperation—to an extent—although up until now, Anja hadn't observed, or read any notes from the scientists who'd come before her, of this level of complex coordination.

At least she knew why Devinia tolerated Kada in her waters.

The bellows of the leviathans swelled as they got closer, enough that Anja worried the usually calm, gentle giants might attack.

Instead of any aggressive displays, though, like smacking their necks onto the sea's surface, they moved aside.

They had been clustered around Devinia, who lay on her side in the water, her back to them, an injury clear along her spine.

"A laz burn?" Ritt had managed to struggle to his feet, and his voice was hushed. "They used their runner's laz cannon on a leviathan?"

Silence fell, the shock so evident, Anja could taste it in the air. It had the flavor of ashes and bitter salt.

Kada towed the boat around to Devinia's front, and she huffed out what seemed to be a greeting at the sight of him.

He gave a tug on the rope, and the boat glided forward and bumped gently against Devinia's side.

Her eyes were a little cloudy, and Anja's heart gave a frightened leap in her chest.

That was not good.

She leaned forward, gently running a hand down the leviathan's cheek, her touch so light she doubted Devinia would even be able to feel it.

The matriarch fixed her eye on Anja, and then opened her mouth and tilted her head, and all the wave riders seemed to come to attention.

"She wants us to harvest her druk." Cal spoke slowly.

"But she's not part of the Rinc pods. She wouldn't have had druk harvested before." That was why Anja was working so far from the city and the slightly warmer waters where most of the pods lived.

"I know. She has the action down perfectly, as if she's done this before, although I know she hasn't." Cal glanced at Anja, then back at Devinia's open mouth. "There's the druk."

Glistening among her layers of teeth lay silver balls, exactly five. They were too spherical to be druk, which was usually round, but not perfectly so.

She thought of the silver ball she had picked up inside Devinia's mouth, and something inside her shivered and then stretched, holding her in place for a moment, before she panicked, flailing in her head against the control. It let her go so fast, she stumbled, although nothing had been physically holding her down.

"Wait."

Everyone turned to her, and the sound of the glider following them became suddenly louder in the silence.

"He's coming closer," Walef said, shielding his eyes against the glare off the sea.

"What is it?" Cal had turned to face her.

"I don't think that's druk in her mouth."

Everyone turned back to look at the silver balls caught between Devinia's teeth.

"No, it's just that silver's rare. Really rare." Demi leaned closer to Devinia's massive, gaping jaw. "Although quite small to be caught in her teeth. And look how round!"

"I think they're . . ." She couldn't say any more, her mind seemed to be frozen, her throat closed, as Demi took one of the balls.

She tried to shout, but nothing came out, not even the air in her lungs.

Cal leaned over and took a ball as well. They both stepped back, lifting the balls to get a good look at them, and Livia plucked the remaining three out.

"Let's have a look, I've never even seen a silver one," Walef said, and she handed one to him and one to Ritt.

At last, whatever held Anja in place released her, and she fell to her knees, gasping.

"Anja?" Cal took a step toward her, and then frowned down at his hand.

"It's disappeared, hasn't it?" she wheezed.

He crouched beside her, frowning. "It doesn't matter about that. What's wrong?"

"It does matter." She coughed, and then finally got her full breath back.

"Where'd it go?" Walef held out his hand, and the others all looked down and then across at her.

"I tried to tell you, before it stopped me. That wasn't druk. It's . . . something else. I picked one up in Devinia's mouth, when she was carrying me to the spaceship."

They waited for her to finish, only there wasn't any more to say.

She cleared her throat. "It melted into my hand. It's . . . whatever it is . . . is inside me now." She looked at Cal, searching his face for the disbelief he was sure to be feeling. "Inside you, too."

"What are you saying?" Walef crouched on the other side of her, his eyes slightly panicked.

She hesitated, then shrugged. "It's made me . . . different."

"You'd only have picked it up four hours ago at most," Walef said.

She nodded. "In that time, it's saved me from hurting myself in the dark, used my finger to short out the power in the entire spaceship to keep you from spotting me in a bedroom, helped me open the door to the control room, and made me feel stronger than I have before."

Devinia gave a sudden groan, and the wave riders turned away from Anja toward her.

"She's dying." Cal ran a hand down her neck. "I think she was dying before, but this laz strike has tipped the balance."

"And the balls aren't in her anymore. Helping her." Anja spoke the words without thinking, but as they came out of her mouth, she knew they were true. "They withdrew from her to come to us, and she's finally feeling her age."

Everyone stared at her, as if she had lost her grip.

Suddenly an image bloomed in Anja's mind. It was basic, not the images she'd seen before in the spaceship, which felt more complex, like a person explaining how it felt to be a leviathan. This felt like it was from a more primitive mind, from a leviathan itself.

It was of Devinia, finding the spaceship on the ocean floor, swimming into the atrium. And the silver balls rolling off the upper level, falling through the water to disappear into her broad back.

But they were never meant for her.

And they wanted to fulfill their destiny.

"They were made for us." The words escaped before she could stop them. "Beings like us."

"The balls?" Cal asked, his gaze never leaving her face.

"I think Kada just told me something." She glanced at the young leviathan, sure the strong images had been from him. "The balls were designed to work inside people, and while they've helped Devinia live a long life, they felt the call of the signal as the solar storm has begun to die down the last few weeks, and she wants to pass on now, her time is done. She called us to her so she could give them to us."

"Called us to her?" Ritt coughed and then hunched over in pain.

"They'll heal you, I think." Anja recalled how good she felt even though by rights she should be in a med facility. "Of everyone, you should feel the effects first."

She didn't like how blue Ritt's skin was around his mouth, how sunken his eyes.

Help was so far away, it might as well not exist.

At least the ball that had sunk into his hand would hopefully help him.

"Are you saying we've just absorbed some nanotech, or something like that?" Demi widened her stance, but her question was almost drowned out by the sound of the glider, and they all turned to look up at it.

It had been coming steadily closer, but what was happening with Devinia had commanded all their attention until now.

The man hanging from the straps beneath the wings was holding a laz in his hand, although it wasn't pointed at them.

Yet.

Suddenly, the boat jerked beneath them, sending them tumbling, as Kada hauled them away.

The three leviathans around Devinia began to circle her protectively, and seemed to be urging her to move.

Anja felt like a wave of fire burned through her blood as she looked up at the man who'd shot her earlier; who was menacing them now.

He had been part of hurting Devinia. Hurting her and Cal and the others.

He needed to pay.

She'd fallen onto the bottom of the boat as Kada pulled them away from Devinia, and as she turned, hand out to push herself up, she saw a box of flares tucked beneath the bench.

She'd pulled it out, flipped open the lid and had the flare gun in her hand before she could even formulate a plan. Before she had even consciously made the decision to act.

The flares were ancient tech, but necessary on Fynian, where the solar storms interfered with more modern methods of communication in a crisis. And they would do fine for the purpose she had in mind.

She stepped up onto the bench, legs bent a little to keep her balance as the boat hit the choppy waves around the island, flare gun lifted up to the sky.

"Anja?"

She ignored Cal's questioning shout and fired at the glider's wing.

The flare left the gun with a whoosh of sound, arcing up in an almost blinding pink light.

"A hit!" Livia's shout was full of glee.

She felt a sudden resonance with Livia, and turned to grin at her.

The flare had struck the glider's wing and done some damage. She could see a rip on the left side.

The man shouted in rage and she thought she saw the laz in his hand fall into the water, but couldn't be sure.

He turned the glider back toward the island, the whole thing listing to the left. Anja could hear him screaming abuse at her as the glider shuddered away.

"Do you think he'll make it?" Livia asked.

"Do we care?" Demi shaded her eyes as she tracked his progress.

"That was a good idea." Cal picked up the flare box and Anja leapt lightly down from the bench and set the gun back in the custom holder.

Kada had slowed their pace now that the glider had turned away, and circled the boat back to follow Devinia.

She and the other three leviathans were moving in that particular way they had—seemingly slow, but actually anything but. Even ill as she was, Devinia was still the matriarch of a leviathan pod. She could move fast if she needed to.

The small pod had almost reached the next island along from the one where the spaceship was stashed, and were disappearing behind it.

The glider had made the safety of the cliffs, Anja saw, and while the landing looked awkward, the pilot was probably fine.

One of the leviathans in the pod with Devinia bellowed out across the water to Kada, and he answered in a low, booming response.

She had missed the sounds of the pod's communication when they had disappeared, but this seemed so much more specific than the back and forth she'd recorded in the months she'd watched them.

Like they were having a high level conversation with each other.

Her biologist's heart sped up at the thought.

She glanced over at Cal, wanting to share the moment of excitement with someone, and found him looking at her.

Something passed between them, a flash of heat and desire, that made her already speeding heart skip a beat.

She had to suck in a breath of cold, moisture-laden air, and look away.

She felt Cal move beside her, and with a quick glance up at him, she slid her hand along his back, around his waist, as his own arm came around her shoulders.

She leaned into him as he leaned into her, and where their bodies touched, she felt the bloom of a warmth that was more than just the result of body heat.

Livia glanced back at them, and she saw Cal's sister's eyes widen at the sight of them locked together, then turn back, as if to process what she'd seen.

Anja tilted her head to look up at Cal, and the eyes that met hers were amused.

As long as he wasn't concerned about it, she wouldn't be, either.

Satisfied, Anja went back to resting her head on his shoulder.

Devinia and her protectors had disappeared when they rounded the island, but Kada's speed meant they were soon rounding the rocks themselves, and had the leviathans back in sight.

Devinia was moving into a small bay, and with a feeling of delight, despite the circumstances, Anja saw the rest of the pod was waiting for her there.

The babies, their mothers, and the older males that were no longer looking for mates and deemed acceptable to Devinia again.

The roar of a runner engine behind them cut off any feeling of joy at seeing the leviathans again, though.

She and Cal turned to look back together. With a sinking sensation in her stomach, she saw the runner that had been parked on the clifftop of the adjacent island lifting off.

"Maybe it's going back to Rinc," Walef said.

"Or maybe it's coming straight for us." Demi had both hands on her hips, her long, slim body quivering in readiness.

The runner went straight up, then turned slowly to face them.

Kada was still towing them at speed toward the pod, but Anja realized that was dangerous. If they started shooting, the leviathans would be in danger.

Before she could say anything, though, the runner's nose tipped down and laz fire blossomed from its sides, the bright purple light strafing the water as the runner flew toward them.

"Out of the boat." Cal's shout jolted them all out of their shock. "Now!"

The wave riders obeyed without question, diving straight into the water.

Anja hesitated a moment, thinking through his order, but followed directly behind him.

He was right.

If they weren't in the boat, Sirco, or whoever was in the runner, wouldn't chase after Kada, they would fire at where everyone had gone into the sea.

The icy water was a shock to her system, enveloping her in a numbing hug, but she didn't feel any fear at all.

She let herself sink deep underwater and began to swim for the island, and while she had been a relatively good swimmer before, now she was powering through the water faster than she ever had.

Was that the result of the optimization of whatever nanotech had entered her body, or the fact that it had previously inhabited the body of a leviathan, one of the strongest swimmers Anja had ever studied?

Maybe it was a bit of both.

The water was clear, it always was on Fynian, and she found the others easily.

No one had gone to the surface, and above their heads she could hear the strange slapping explosion of laz fire hitting the water.

They fell into a clear formation, one she recognized all too well from her drone footage of the pod.

A tingle ran down her spine at the implications, but now was not the time to process the information. She needed to move to safety, to conserve her air.

The laz fire stopped abruptly, and Anja guessed the hover had passed overhead.

It was probably swinging around to do another run, but now was the time to get a fix on their location and a lungful of air.

She headed up, and the others did the same a moment later, in a synchronized movement that started the tingle up again.

She broke the surface, taking a deep, measured breath, her gaze going skyward.

"See it?" Cal asked, coming up right beside her.

"No." She could hear it, though.

"It's probably over the island." Ritt sounded short of breath, but when Anja looked over at him, she thought even in these dire circumstances, he looked better than he had on the spaceship.

The silver ball was helping him recover from his injuries, just as she suspected.

There was a change in the runner's engine tone, and then they all heard the sound of its engine getting louder.

From up ahead, a leviathan bellowed, and then slapped its neck on the water.

"Back under we go," Walef shouted, and they sank down beneath the short, choppy waves and dived deeper, out of laz fire range.

The cold was no longer affecting her that much, Anja realized.

She should be hyperthermic by now, but she was managing the low temperatures.

Not for long, the biologist in her knew. Even if the nanotech was helping keep her from going into shock, there was only so much leeway her body had.

They needed to get out of the water and to safety as fast as possible.

And then suddenly, they were surrounded by leviathans.

The massive bodies bracketed their little pod formation, shielding them.

Feeling weakened, knowing she was nearing the end of her tether, Anja fought her way to the surface just in time to see the runner hover over them for a moment, searching, and then turn back toward the island hiding the spaceship.

She gulped in air and then pulled herself onto the back of the leviathan she had called Helga during the months she'd watched the young female.

She looked down into the water, stretching her hand out to Livia to help her up.

As she hauled Cal's sister up beside her, she looked around to see where everyone else was. Cal had climbed up onto Kada's back, and was helping Ritt. Demi and Walef had found their own rides.

With another bellow, this time in victory, the leviathans turned and moved back to the small cove where they huddled with Devinia.

By the time they reached the calm bay, the cold had won out over whatever magic the silver balls had managed to work so far.

Anja's head pounded, and her movements were clumsy as she slid from Helga's back into the shallows and stumbled toward the shore.

They needed to get a fire going.

"Look for driftwood," Anja said to Livia, through chattering teeth.

Cal was already walking toward them with an armful of it, and soon they had a big pile on the sand.

Everyone had waterproof lighters except Anja. It seemed to be standard wave rider equipment, for which she was extremely grateful.

The moment the flames began to lick up the wood, they all stepped closer, hands out, in a move that looked a little choreographed.

Everyone noticed it, not just Anja, and they all glanced at each other, afraid.

"This isn't going to turn us into some kind of hive mind, is it?" Walef asked.

"A bit of warning would have been nice." Ritt flicked a look at Anja, and she felt a sudden fizz in her blood at his attack, a strange confusion that Ritt would blame her.

She didn't know Ritt, had no idea if he was the type to look for someone to blame, so this sense of shock had to be from the silver ball.

"I wasn't able to say anything. My throat closed up."

"You expect us to believe—" His derisive words were cut off and Anja tilted her head in interest as he clearly tried to speak but couldn't.

After a moment, he fell to his knees, coughing.

"Like that," Anja said to him.

"Did you do this to me?" Ritt gasped as he looked up at her.

"No." She didn't think she had.

"I saw Anja struggling to speak on the boat. She even managed to tell us to wait, not that we listened, but she was obviously trying to say more." Demi moved to stand beside her.

Ritt glared up at her with suspicious eyes, and she held his gaze, staring back until at last he looked away with a nod of acceptance.

Cal was suddenly standing beside him. He put out a hand to help Ritt back to his feet, but something in his grip told Anja it wasn't as friendly as it looked.

Ritt made a sound of protest, and then met Cal's gaze. Gave another nod.

"Okay. I was wrong." He held his hand to his chest as he stepped back.

"We need to exert more control over whatever it is inside us than it does over us." Cal's voice was calm. "It's used to Devinia. I'm not sure if she had the capacity to direct it the way we can. It may be used to being in charge."

Anja cleared her throat. "I agree. A few times it's sensed my panic and released me. But I think when we all do something the same, it's because it's trying to help. It thinks that's the best action we can take. Like warming ourselves at the fire. And maybe some of it is because all the balls were in Devinia together. They're used to being part of a single organism, working as one."

"So we'll lose the spooky clone moves over time?" Demi shuffled even closer to the fire. "As we push back and assert ourselves?"

"I hope so." Anja stepped a little closer to the heat of the fire and closed her eyes.

"I can breathe better now." Ritt's voice was quiet. Slightly apologetic. "I could almost feel my ribs knitting back together."

"It's taken something out of you, though." Livia studied him. "You're much thinner."

"We all are. It's diverted resources to keep us warm." Cal threw another piece of wood onto the fire. "We need food and water, or we're all going to hit a wall soon."

"Is there food and water on your boat?" Anja asked him.

Cal gave a nod. "But it's still out in the ocean."

She turned to look out over the bay, and saw Kada was floating close to Devinia, not very far away. She remembered the message she was sure he'd sent her before, of how Devinia had come into possession of the silver balls.

If he could send to her, surely she could send to him?

She kept her thoughts simple. She focused on Kada and then thought of the boat. And then thought of the boat resting on the shore by the fire.

Kada slowly, almost reluctantly, slipped under the water and disappeared, and Anja watched the water's surface intently.

Cal came up beside her, and she flashed him a smile as he bumped shoulders with her.

"You've sent Kada off to fetch the boat, have you?" Cal's tone was half-joking, but he was looking out intently into the growing dusk.

Anja could just make out the shape of Kada coming back. "I think he projected what Devinia had shared with him about her first encounter with the silver balls to me earlier. I assumed it was a two-way comm."

Cal went still, turned to look at her with eyebrows raised.

"Kada's bringing us the boat?" Walef came to stand on her other side, mouth slightly agape at the sight of Kada towing the boat into the bay.

"Thanks to Anja." Cal began moving to the shoreline.

"How did you do that?" Walef hurried after her as she joined Cal.

"I sent an image of the boat to him, then another of it resting on the shore."

Walef glanced at her, and then back out as Kada pushed the

boat up the sand with a grumpy grunt and then went back to lie close to his grandmother.

The others noticed when the boat was pushed up, and they all moved toward it.

"This isn't coincidence, is it?" Livia asked.

"Anja asked Kada to fetch it for us and he did." Walef tapped the side of his head as he spoke.

"Asked as in telepathy?" Demi stopped dead and turned to look at her.

"Asked as in used the communication ability the little silver balls have between each other." She reached the boat and jumped in, looking for supplies.

"But Kada doesn't have little silver balls, Devinia had them and then they came to us." Livia crouched beside her, and they pulled out a container from under a seat together.

"Maybe he has a more organic version of the balls naturally in his system. Maybe all Devinia's children and grandchildren do." Cal had a water container in each hand.

"They mutated in her system but the original ones remained apart?" Ritt stood outside the boat, grabbing what the others were passing over to him.

When the boat was stripped bare, they all jumped back onto the sand and crouched in front of the fire, looking through their haul.

It was enough to last one, maybe two, meals if they were careful.

They ate and drank with almost no conversation and Anja finally began to feel the hollow, shivery feeling subside within her.

"Calling Kada was clever." Demi's eyes gleamed in the light.

Anja lifted her shoulders. "He tried to explain why the silver balls needed us. I decided to see if the channel ran both ways."

They were all silent again, until Ritt shuffled forward.

"Did you see how we formed a pod formation when we were in the water?" he asked. "And the way we all swam?"

"It freaked me out a bit," Demi said. "Except that it felt as if we were moving through the water faster than I ever have before, on my own or with a group. The leviathans must have worked out the perfect formation for efficiency of movement through the ocean."

"Either they have, or the silver balls did, and Devinia has been teaching the others." Cal's words silenced everyone again, as they contemplated the information.

"Devinia has to be, what, a hundred years old?" Walef asked. He had found a piece of driftwood to sit on, and he stared contemplatively into the fire.

"More," Cal said. "My mother said she was the matriarch of the Southern Peninsula pod back when my grandparents were wave riders."

"The silver balls may have kept her younger and more active than she normally would be." Anja looked out over the bay again. "Now the silver balls have taken their leave, she's back to her old self."

"She was dying before they left her, though," Livia reminded them. "Maybe she was tired of living, and she and the balls came to an amicable parting of ways."

"I hope so." Ritt rubbed his side. "Given how well I'm feeling since one of them dissolved into me, I can imagine her life was a lot longer than an average leviathan."

"Whatever that amicable parting of ways involved, it included Kada luring Cal out of Rinc harbor." Demi looked thoughtful.

"Kada tried to get me to get into that boat when Cal jumped out." Anja remembered how insistent he'd been on the beach before Sirco's two thugs had tried to shoot her. "But I don't understand why she and the pod disappeared from the peninsula."

"They wanted more than one person or they'd all have gone into you when you were in Devinia's mouth. They were waiting for

Kada to bring them more people." Cal was crouched near her, and his gaze met hers. "Maybe they thought you'd call in others to help you look for the pod if they vanished."

"Except Duncan didn't come. Could that be why Kada grabbed Cal instead?" That seemed like complicated, sophisticated reasoning. It also reminded her that Duncan was nowhere to be seen in this. She hoped he wasn't in trouble.

"Either that, or Devinia needed to come to calm waters to die, that's why they disappeared from the peninsula." Walef tipped his head in the direction of the pod. "We know they always do that when it's time for one of them to pass on."

Anja nodded. The notes she'd read had all said the pod would surround a dying leviathan in calm waters, and because of the recent storms, the rough waters around the peninsula certainly wouldn't have been ideal.

Maybe it was as simple as that. No matter what agenda the silver balls had, they couldn't override the leviathans' fundamental nature.

It was comforting, in a way.

She felt a flash of hopefulness inside her. A feeling of unity.

It calmed her even more.

I want to trust you, she thought to whatever was inside her now. *Don't make me regret it.*

12

———————

Cal wanted this moment to last a little longer.

The crackle of fire, the warmth and sense of well-being now they'd had something to eat and drink.

Anja sat beside him and he liked the way their legs touched, a casual intimacy that he wished for the time and privacy to pursue.

But they had none.

He was about to break up the happy home.

"We have to go back to the spaceship."

Everyone lifted their heads to look at him.

"Sirco hasn't taken the runner back to Rinc. Which means as far as the search and rescue teams are concerned, he and the rest of you have gone missing, too."

"Oh." Livia looked up from the flames. "Mom will be going nuts."

"Two of her babies missing from the pod?" Demi said, her voice dry. "She'll be going more than nuts if I know your mother."

"We all know your mother will be gathering an army to look for you, but why does that mean we have to go back to the space-ship?" Walef asked.

"Because when she realizes Sirco isn't coming back, she'll take the route he did to come looking for us." Cal could just imagine it. And he shuddered at the thought of his mother and whatever crew she put together being caught in laz fire as they approached Sirco's runner.

"You think Sirco will shoot at them?" Livia half-stood, then sat down with a thump. "Isn't he trying to keep this discreet?"

"That must have been the original plan, but he's obviously been caught by circumstances. The signal has been found, so he hasn't gone back to Rinc. Discretion has been superseded by other considerations."

"So you want to sneak in and destroy his ability to shoot at Mom?" Livia asked.

"At the very least." Cal met her gaze.

She gave a nod. "Count me in on that."

"If we go nosing around, we might also get some insight into why Sirco and his friends are doing this. I mean, they wanted to find the spaceship, but what for?" Anja leaned forward.

"Weren't there some people trying to steal tech from the ancestral spaceship they found on Faldine?" Ritt asked.

"That part of the story was a little murky. I don't think the VSC said who was behind the attack on the Faldine head of planet, but someone definitely tried to steal something." Demi threw a stick onto the fire. "You think these are the same people? Some of them got away, the way I heard it."

Everyone was silent for a moment.

"It makes sense, because they planned ahead." Cal leaned forward. "They didn't just stumble upon this spaceship. They put Sirco in place at the solar flare department months ago. They've been monitoring Anja's comms, so they must have narrowed down the source of the signal to the southern peninsula. They tried to prevent anyone going down that way while they were waiting for the signal to reemerge. That sounds like people who thought it was a spaceship emitting that signal and were waiting for the right time to find it." Cal looked up at the sky. "It makes me wonder if someone's up there, waiting for Sirco to signal them. They can't expect to strip the spaceship of tech with nothing but that scientific runner."

"Except Sirco can't signal them. Even if the solar flare has died down for a few days, the wireless comms are disabled on all the Fynian runners, because even though they're standard VSC models, the wireless function drains the power by constantly looking for a signal it can't find," Walef said. "My brother's the engineer who maintains it, and it was decided years ago that the random few days of signal capability weren't worth the power loss."

"So how will he let them know?" Cal wondered.

As if in answer, the sound of a runner engine made them all look up. Cal could just make out the runner's burners as it screamed upward.

"Guess he's going in person." Demi's voice had a smile in it.

Cal thought of Sirco assuming he could signal up to nearspace because of the lack of solar storms, and then finding out he couldn't. Smiled himself.

"That's our cue. Let's go have a look around while Sirco's off-planet." He stood, and Anja pushed gracefully to her feet beside him. "And when he comes back, we'll be waiting for him."

"Do you think the other two will have gone with him?" Walef asked.

Cal shook his head. "Assume they're both still there."

"Doing what?" Demi wondered.

"Poking around? Marking things that look interesting so they know what to strip out?" Anja had both feet planted, hands on hips, as she tipped her head back, watching the runner wink out into nearspace.

"Sounds about right," Livia said. "I assume you don't want us to be seen by them?"

Cal shook his head. "Not if we can help it. Let them keep thinking we're either dead or stranded in the archipelago."

Since this thing had started, they'd been reacting to whatever Sirco and his crew had thrown at them, and that was understandable. They hadn't known what was going on.

But now they did, it was time to switch gears.

They would be the ones taking the initiative from now, if Cal had his way.

13

———————

Anja looked over at Devinia and the pod as Cal steered his boat, with its quiet motor, out of the bay.

Kada watched them pass, but made no move to abandon his grandmother to tow them again.

"I feel like I should stay with her." She glanced at Cal. "We're leaving her alone here."

"We're leaving her to die in peace. We aren't part of the pod, no matter how much we feel like we are. It's a lesson all wave riders have to learn." He put a hand on her shoulder.

The water around Devinia churned a little as more and more of the pod lifted their heads above the surface and watched them leave in silence.

"It's when they're quiet that they're the most scary," Ritt said, voice low.

"That and the way their eyes are tracking us." Anja had never seen anything like it. The sea was lit with the iridescent gleam of various shades of purple, as more of the pod emerged from below the surface, the gleam of their eyes as intimidating as it was beautiful.

Anja had the sense of tension. Of anything being possible.

Then one of the older males blew out a breath, and the spell was broken.

Anja felt everyone in the boat relax along with her.

She kept her gaze on Devinia, but the old matriarch had her own eyes closed, and her pod was crowding around her, making it difficult to distinguish who was who.

Cal steered the boat out of the bay, toward what Anja was beginning to think of as spaceship island, and the leviathans were suddenly out of sight.

"Why do you think Sirco shot Devinia?" For that alone, she wanted to bring him down.

"Maybe she tried to stop them getting to the spaceship while we were on it?" Demi said. "That would make sense. She wanted us to be safe, so she could give the balls to us."

Anja thought about that in silence as they hit the rougher sea between the islands, and everyone concentrated on holding on.

The sky was dark except for Jero, gleaming gold, yellow and mustard in the sky, so it wasn't difficult to spot the sudden flare of engine fire above.

"Looks like we have company." She pointed.

"That was quick." Livia came to stand beside her.

"Looks like Sirco has some friends coming to join him." Cal sounded calm, but when Anja followed his pointed finger, she saw what looked like a cloud of individual black canopies, and beneath them, the occasional flare of a booster.

"Droppers?" She whispered the word.

It had a similar effect on the others. Everyone went quiet, looking up.

"How many of them?" Livia whispered over the slap and crash of the choppy water against the side of the boat.

"Twenty?" Walef was studying the sky intently. He turned to Cal. "What do we do?"

"We keep going. We'll get there after them, given how close they are already, but not by much." He glanced at her. "They're probably here to help strip the spaceship bare."

Even though he spoke neutrally, she had the sense he was worried.

"And it means there'll be more resistance to your mother if she comes looking for you."

"It's not a case of if," Cal said, and increased the boat's speed. "It's a case of when."

***

SHE WAS with people who knew how to navigate the tiny inlets and sharp outcrops of the archipelago.

Anja admired the skill Cal showed in getting them to a tiny beach at the back of the small island, and how the others moved together to pull the boat up and hide it.

She helped, and as they stepped back, dusting their hands of sand, she realized she had been a productive member of the team, although she had never done this before.

"It's like you've worked a wave rider team before." Demi tilted her head to look at her.

She gave a nod. It did seem like it. And the silver balls had made that possible, she was sure.

She wanted to rage against it—it felt like a loss of autonomy— but she couldn't argue with the results.

Cal put a hand on her shoulder, pointed up to the cliff face. "The waterfall that's usually here isn't flowing at the moment. We can climb up it."

She turned so they were face to face, and looked up at him.

Their eyes met, and she tried to see into their depths.

He bent his head, so his lips were close to her ear. He hesitated, as if thinking what to say.

"Time for that after we've taken down a tech-stealing consortium who are trying to kill us all." Walef's words were accompanied by a slap on Cal's back.

Cal looked over at him for a beat, then turned to her and kissed her temple. "There's never a bad time for this," Cal answered him back. "And that's especially true when you're about to take down a murderous, tech-stealing consortium."

Anja knew her mouth had fallen open at his words, and he brushed a second kiss along her lips, then flashed her a grin.

When he strode away, she stood for a moment, watching him go.

"He's always been deep and quiet. Certainly never this openly affectionate."

Anja turned to find Livia beside her.

"You knew him before all this? In Rinc?" Cal's sister asked.

Before she could respond, Livia sent her a grin exactly like her brother's and then followed him across the sand to the cliff face.

Anja shook off her surprise and jogged after them.

It took half an hour for all of them to reach the top, and Anja had the sense it would have taken longer if they hadn't all had a silver ball inside them.

She assumed she was moving like the others, with maximum efficiency and a gracefulness and competence that was a thing of beauty to watch.

They moved over the rocky ground in the darkness much more easily than she and Cal had before, and when Cal lifted a clenched fist, they all came to a stop.

"How do I know that means stop?" Demi whispered. "I've never seen that before."

Everyone turned to look at her, suddenly realising they didn't know how they knew, either.

Anja shook her head. "The people who had the balls in them before must have known."

There was a beat of silence.

"You think we aren't the first people the balls have lived inside?" Walef asked. He sounded slightly horrified.

She shrugged. "Do you think they were just rolling around in the spaceship unused, or do you think they were inside people who were killed in the crash and when they died the balls went looking for other . . . hosts?" She didn't want to say host, but it was the most accurate description she could think of for what they were in this relationship.

She got pushback immediately in her head.

"Something in my brain is saying not host, protected beloved." Demi clutched her head and looked up, frowning.

"Protected beloved." Livia nodded. "My ball agrees."

"We can argue what our part in this relationship is later." Cal's voice was low but sharp. "And Demi's right about the signal, I don't know why I made it, I meant to say stop and be quiet, not that anyone *has* been quiet."

They all went silent, and Anja saw why Cal had stopped them.

The last of the droppers were landing up ahead, the blue green flare of their boosters as they touched down giving away their position.

"Who do you reckon they are?" Ritt asked.

Cal shrugged. "Not VSC military, obviously, so either the final dregs of the pirate crews from the Halatian disaster, insurgents that escaped the Faldine war, or enforcers who worked in the former breakaway planets."

"Criminals and mercenaries." Demi spoke softly.

"Let's just say, don't get caught by one." Cal turned to look at them. "Don't take chances. Not just for us, but for whoever on the search team comes riding to the rescue."

They all gave a nod, and Anja thought the motion held more meaning than it should. Like a vow of some kind.

She felt connected to the others by her agreement.

Stop it, she said firmly in her head. *This is an agreement on tactics. Nothing more.*

There was a sudden feeling of stillness inside her, as if the ball was considering what she'd said, and then the feeling of being caught in a binding oath lessened.

The others drew in deep breaths all around her, as if they too had been released from something.

Livia shook out her shoulders. "So what now?"

"We follow them in." Cal was watching the droppers gather their equipment and store it against one of the rocks near the landing spot. Then they moved toward a light that flashed a signal to them, talking softly among themselves.

Cal led the way, almost disappearing into the darkness, but Anja knew exactly where he was. Where everyone on the team was.

It was a good sense to have, as long as they were all working together.

The thought that it might one day be otherwise caused the ball to recoil. It couldn't imagine them ever being at odds.

Don't worry, right now, neither can I.

Her response seemed to settle it down again, and she moved forward, falling into a formation she could see *was* a formation, but one they had created instinctively.

Just like when they'd swum underwater to avoid being shot.

It was . . . confronting.

But also, it was the least of her problems.

Cal looked like a dropper in the darkness. He had the bulky physique, the dark clothing, the way of moving that spoke of physicality and competence.

No one would look at him twice.

Walef had a slimmer build, more rangy and thin than bulky, but Ritt was similar in size and shape to Cal. Both might pass muster, especially if no one was looking too hard, except Walef's clothing was wrong. He was wearing a light shirt which would probably earn him a second look.

She, Livia and Demi were going to stand out.

For some reason, all the droppers were men.

It was perplexing, and Anja wondered the reason for it.

She shrugged the question away—it didn't matter why, only that it was so, and that was going to make talking their way out of trouble if they were caught all the more difficult.

The droppers had moved to the roof of the spaceship, and began to disappear. Going inside. Straight to work.

The last of the droppers climbed down the hatch and Cal moved silently after them and stood above it, looking down, waiting for them to move away.

The team reached him, cautious and tense, and Anja peered down herself.

The droppers were gone and Cal turned and put his foot on the first rung.

From above them came the roar of a runner engine, and then another.

Sirco had waited for the droppers to land, and now he was coming in, and he'd brought another runner with him.

They watched as the runners landed on the clifftops and began powering down.

"Get a move on." The bark from below snapped their attention back to the hatch.

Cal looked down at whoever called up to him. "Just watching the runners come in."

"They're here?" The voice sounded sour. "That means the clock's started. So get down this fucking ladder and get to your assignment."

Cal tipped his head, grabbed the poles on either side of the ladder with both hands, and dropped straight down.

The man below made a sound, a half-shout, half-cry, which was cut off suddenly.

Anja crouched by the hatch and looked down.

Cal was calmly using restraints on his unconscious victim.

She turned and went down the same way as he had, aware that she had never gone down a ladder like this before, but choosing to ignore that.

It was quick, and they needed things to be quick. If the past beneficiary of the silver ball had done it this way, who was she to complain?

She got down in time to grab the man's other side and help Cal drag him to a small cupboard, stuff him in it, and gag him before they closed the door.

The others were waiting for them at the bottom of the ladder when they got back.

"Sirco and whoever was in the other runner will be coming down this way soon, so let's go." Cal began to move, and they fell into step, Anja right at the back, turning occasionally to make sure there was no one behind them.

A string of temporary lights had been set up since they had last been here, running along one wall, making it easier to move around. She could always use her fingertip to plunge everything back into darkness, though. She smiled at the thought.

That wasn't a bad idea.

She realized her right hand was clenched close to her hip, her left extended, palm up, fingers slightly curled, as if she was holding something long, and forced her arms to drop to her sides.

We are not your former protected beloveds. I'm not carrying a . . . she didn't know what it was the person before her had in his or her muscle memory.

Weapon, the silver ball inside her whispered.

She had the sudden image of something black and sleek. A long barrel and a trigger under her right finger.

Well, I'm not carrying one. Keep up with your new reality.

14

THE PASSAGEWAY THEY WERE TRAVELING DOWN WAS AS WET, DANK and slimy as the passages she remembered on the floor below. She could hear people moving about, the thump and ring of boots on metallic floors, the shriek and grinding of rusted doors being forced open, the clatter of things being thrown.

Cal stopped, pressing himself up against the wall as they came to a turn in the passageway.

Anja listened. Her hearing was better than it had been, along with her night vision.

Everyone had gone silent—listening like her, Anja realized.

Cal caught her eye, just for a moment. Then he moved, taking the corner and everyone followed, moving in that formation again, seamless and quiet.

It was a thing of beauty, she grudgingly admitted.

A crash up ahead made them all come to a silent halt. Someone had thrown something out of a door farther down the corridor.

Anja moved slightly, so she had a clear view, and saw it was a large piece of machinery.

Then she realized the room the machine had been in was the command center.

Just as Livia had guessed, they were marking things to be stolen, and they had found one of the more interesting rooms in the ship.

"We could lock them in there." It felt as if she spoke before she'd even fully formed the thought.

"Could we?" Cal turned to her.

She nodded, and he smiled.

"Let's do it then."

They reached the heavy, reinforced door, and Ritt and Cal lifted the piece of machinery that had been moved out onto the top of the landing out of the way.

The door opened inward, so Demi and Walef grabbed the circular handle and pulled it toward them. It closed with a high shriek of metal grinding on metal, and slammed into place.

Anja stepped up to the scan plate to the door's right and pressed her hand against it.

"That's how you got in here the first time?" Demi asked her.

She nodded, and then heard the grind of gears as the door locked.

No sound was audible from within any longer.

"They can get out through the hole in the roof," Walef said after a beat.

"But it'll take them extra effort, and I don't know if they can get any of the equipment they want to steal out that way." Cal gave a nod of satisfaction.

Voices echoed, four men talking loudly as they strode down the passage toward them.

"Sirco," Cal murmured.

As soon as he said it, Anja recognized his voice.

"Good time to double back, if he's busy here, take out the weapons on those runners." Ritt cocked his head.

They all nodded in agreement, the movement that freaky, too-coordinated thing again.

But there was no place to hide back the way they had come.

They would have to go down the stairs and then bypass Sirco somehow.

Cal balanced on the hand rail and pushed himself off, sliding down the banister silently, and they followed him, one by one.

The bottom level was still in darkness.

Either Sirco's crew hadn't had time to set up temporary lights here yet, or they didn't have enough for both floors, and needed to set them up level by level.

Anja hoped that was the case. It meant there shouldn't be anyone down here with them.

And if the worst came to the worst, they had an escape route down here.

It wouldn't be pleasant, but they could go out the same way Devinia and Kada had come in.

They crouched behind the steps, completely engulfed in darkness, and listened as Sirco and his three companions reached the command center.

"They must have put this equipment out for us to take, but how do we get in to look at what else is there?" The person who spoke was female and she sounded surprised.

"It was open when we first found it. Maybe it swung closed?" Sirco didn't sound too worried.

Someone thumped on the door.

"What if they're stuck in there?" The man who posed the question sounded annoyed.

"They aren't, there's a huge hole in the ceiling. We can access the room from the top of the ship." Anja could almost see Sirco's grimace. "But it might be more difficult to get whatever's in there out if we can't open this. The hole has made that part of the roof unstable. I don't think we can winch anything heavy out without collapsing it some more."

"They were told to be careful." The fourth member of the group spoke at last. He was in charge, Anja decided, and he was unhappy.

"This is an ancient spaceship that's been submerged for thousands of years in a freezing ocean, Jake. Nothing in their background would have prepared your people for all the eventualities here." Sirco's voice was clipped.

There was a beat of silence, as if Jake didn't like Sirco's pushback and in the quiet, she heard someone running down the passage toward them.

"The crew in the command center shouted up to those of us on the roof to say the door swung shut on them and they can't get it open. It's rusted fast." The messenger was out of breath.

"We worked that out." Jake's voice was clipped. "Can you lift the equipment out?"

"Maybe." The messenger sounded uncertain, but unwilling to voice any doubts. "We'd need to set up a winch."

"Then get to it."

With a murmur, the order was obeyed, and Jake waited until the man's footsteps had faded before speaking again. "What's down these stairs?"

"Haven't looked yet." Sirco sounded defensive. "We haven't got enough lights and we're going through things methodically."

"I'll have a look around. Seb, you come with me. Liia, you make sure that winch system is being set up."

"And me?" Sirco sounded distinctly annoyed.

"You just do your job." Jake's voice was low. "Make sure the crew is making good choices on what they're marking for removal."

"They're your crew." Sirco's voice carried the unspoken tone that this wasn't his problem.

"You've got an issue with doing your job?" Jake asked, and Anja thought one of the other two, maybe Seb, drew in a quick breath.

"My job was to find the signal, see what was there. I've delivered that with fucking bells on. If I don't get back to Rinc soon, with an extremely convincing story about what's happened to the search and rescue team who were with me, then people are going to come looking."

There was a startled silence. "You brought people with you?"

"I had no choice. A wave rider went missing and the only way I could stop anyone else coming this way with a team was to volunteer to bring a team myself."

"Fuck. What did you do with them?" Jake sounded less happy by the second.

"Threw them into the sea."

There was a beat of utter silence, and then Jake laughed.

"Seriously?"

"Seriously."

Down below the stairs, Anja shared a look with Demi. She did not like Jake.

Judging by the expressions around her, none of them were too keen on him.

But interestingly, Sirco didn't mention they'd survived and he'd gone after them a few more times.

"So when you don't return, they'll think . . . what? That you ran into trouble?" Jake's voice had less of an edge, now.

"Probably." Sirco sounded off-hand, which was strange after his defiance a moment ago.

"We need you here. If someone comes, let them come. It'll be another search and rescue team, right, unarmed?"

"Yes." Sirco sighed.

"Then it's decided. Go check on the crew. Make sure they're making wise choices. We can only take so much up with us, and we have to assume there'll be no coming back. As soon as the VSC get wind of this, they'll be all over this island and the Jero system will be crawling with military ships."

Jake's voice was more conciliatory now, as if he realized he would get more out of Sirco with that tone than snapping arrogant orders.

Sirco didn't respond in words, but Anja heard his footsteps as he left.

"You, too, Liia. Go make sure those idiots don't bring down the ceiling on us."

"Will do." The woman's lighter steps faded.

"Got a light?" Jake asked the final man, and Anja remembered he'd called him Seb earlier.

"Yes." Seb must have taken it out and turned it on, because the beam played down the steps above their heads.

Anja watched it calmly.

They could take Seb and Jake. Especially after that strange, absolutely cold laugh from Jake when he'd been told they'd been thrown into the sea.

She realized the sudden tightening in her chest was impatience. She wanted the two men to hurry up, to come down into her clutches.

On either side of her the team had shifted position, getting ready to take the two men just as she was.

Like a hunting pack.

Something bloodthirsty and eager woke up inside her and opened both its eyes.

When she glanced across at Livia, she saw the same eagerness reflected on her face.

Walef took a step forward and tilted his head left and right, as if warming up.

Cal lifted a hand to tell them to hold.

"Let's go." Jake started down the stairs, but he hadn't got more than two steps down before a massive crash shook the ship.

The whole structure groaned, and Anja felt the vibration through her boots.

"I guess Liia didn't get up to the roof in time to keep an eye on the winch system," Demi whispered over Jake and Seb's shouts.

Of course. The droppers had obviously tried to lift something out of the control room and it had collapsed the roof further.

"What do we do?" Ritt's voice was just an exhalation of breath, not that it was necessary. Anja could hear Jake and Seb running for the hatch.

"We need to get up to the runners. Destroy their weapons systems." Cal's words were almost obscured by another crash, and Anja felt the stairs above them shudder.

She moved out from under the stairs into the open, looking at the landing above.

The roof above looked buckled in.

"I'll go check it's clear." Cal ran up the steps and Anja followed after him, the eagerness of the hunt still riding her.

Besides, they should move in teams.

The thought soothed her. That sounded right.

They had just reached the top when there was a strange rippling sound, as if someone was scraping a metal pipe across the roof.

Cal reached back and grabbed her jacket, hauled her toward him in the moment between a sudden shriek of metal and the roof collapsing.

Walef was already on the stairs, a quarter of the way up, and she just caught sight of him jumping back as the ceiling caved in.

Rust floated in the air around them, but at least there was fresh air coming in from above.

Cal had his arms around her, and he tightened them even more as she looked up at him.

"You all right?"

She nodded. "You?"

"I'm fine." He glanced toward the railings, or where the railings had been, but now there was no way to look over the side down to the passage below. It was blocked by rusted metal.

The top of the stairs had disappeared as if they had never been.

"The others will have to go out through the hole in the atrium." Cal crouched down and knocked out a pattern on the metal floor.

From below, someone knocked back.

"They're all right." The stranglehold on Anja's chest lifted, and she looked down the passage at their only way out. "Do you think Sirco and the others will grab what they can and go?"

"Jake seems to be in charge and as he said, this is his one and only chance to strip the ship. He doesn't seem very concerned with the welfare of his crew, so he'll force the others to keep going until they have enough to satisfy him."

"So we still need to get up there and disable the weapons on the runners."

Cal nodded. "It'll take the others a while to swim out the cave. We'll have to do it ourselves."

She nodded. She'd guessed as much. She looked down at her finger. Felt a strange tingle in the tip. She'd shorted the lights in the spaceship. She could short the laz cannon.

"Ready?" Cal brushed a thumb over her cheek, as if he couldn't not touch her, and she turned her head and kissed his hand.

The sound of footsteps coming toward them had them both turning to face their new threat.

She hugged the desire and connection between them close. Smiled, despite the circumstances.

She didn't feel frightened or concerned.

In fact, she was looking forward to meeting whoever was coming toward them. It felt like he was invading their space. Encroaching on their territory.

The lighting had been damaged near the control room where the roof had collapsed, but it was still working farther down the passage, throwing off a harsh light that hurt the eyes and threw shadows everywhere.

For a moment, though, it seemed as if she was looking at the world through a dim, wavering light under the sea.

A ballooning need to feel flesh under her teeth swamped her and she realized both she and Cal had sped up. She stumbled to a stop, reached out to grip Cal's arm.

"You're as eager to meet whoever is walking toward us as I am." She made it a statement, her voice thick.

He paused. Gave a cool nod.

"That's not like me. I've never fought before."

Cal put a hand over where hers held on to him and squeezed. "We can take him."

"I *know*." She hissed the words. "That's what's concerning me. I'm looking *forward* to taking him."

He blinked. "Now that you mention it . . ." He took a deep breath, shook out his shoulders. "The silver balls spent a long time in Devinia."

"She's a top predator." And she did not tolerate others in her waters. Anja pushed hard against the eagerness for blood, and it slowly diminished.

"I think I've got myself back, more or less." Cal squeezed her hand again and stepped away.

She felt more herself as well. "Let's go."

The footsteps that had been coming toward them had slowed and then become muffled, which probably meant the dropper had gone into a room.

Cal took the lead and Anja let him because he looked like a dropper; broad, muscular, in dark clothing. It would give them an advantage if whoever met them in the corridor thought they were part of Sirco's crew.

The footsteps became louder again.

A man appeared in silhouette from behind a bright light, and then stopped.

"You." His voice seemed unsteady.

"How many times have you tried to kill me, now?" Cal asked, conversationally. "Five? Six times?"

As Cal lunged forward, Anja caught her first glimpse of the man, recognized the glider pilot who she'd shot at with the flare.

She moved carefully as the men clashed, looking for an opening to assist Cal, but he didn't need her help.

He carefully laid the unconscious pilot down onto the floor.

The ceiling creaked again, like a giant yawning, and they started jogging toward the hatch.

Anja had a brief moment of uncertainty about the pilot. If the whole roof collapsed, he would be trapped or killed. But he had, as Cal said, tried to kill them numerous times. They had given him a better chance than any he had ever given them.

There was someone going up the ladder when they reached the hatch, a dropper, and without speaking, they both began to run at full speed.

They jumped together, grabbing him and pulling him down, and Anja thought the primal part of the ball within her, with its deep connection to Devinia, was satisfied immeasurably by the action.

The dropper landed hard on his back, winded. Before he could react, she and Cal lifted him up and tossed him into the room closest to the hatch.

Cal pressed a hand to the door and it closed and locked.

They stood for a moment facing each other, not even breathing hard, and Cal opened his mouth to say something, then shook his head and turned back to the ladder.

They ran up it fast and light, to find chaos above.

Men were shouting, and poles with lights attached illuminated the collapsed roof.

They ran over the roof and jumped up onto the rock above the spaceship, skirting the panicked activity and making for the runners.

But they had barely taken a few steps before both runners' engines started up.

It looked like they were too late.

15

———————

Cal kept running forward, even as the runners fired up their engines.

Beside him, Anja kept pace.

The way they had worked together to bring down the dropper had shaken him with the seamlessness of it, and now she was with him all the way again, easily matching him step for step.

Perhaps at some time in the future he would mourn the loss of his old self, the before-the-silver-ball self, but right now, he welcomed the edge it gave him, and the way he, Anja and the others had formed a team.

The runners were parked on the clifftops, and Cal's gaze went out to the ocean, but there was no sign of a search and rescue team, no sign the runners were getting ready to take off to attack anyone.

The relief lifted a heavy weight off him and he slowed as the hot air of the engines blew grit and sand in his eyes.

He put out a hand to stop Anja, but she had slowed with him.

"If they aren't off to attack, what do you think they're doing?"

She turned her head away from the runners as she spoke, her eyes closed against the flying debris.

Before he could answer, Jake's runner lifted off and flew to hover over the collapsed ceiling.

A metal cable lowered from underneath it.

"We should have guessed." Cal pulled Anja down behind a large boulder as Sirco's runner lifted up and joined the first one.

"That's their main priority. They need what's in that control room." Anja's head turned sharply, and she put her finger to her lips.

The sound of a conversation was only just audible over the runners' engines, and Cal turned, so he and Anja were back to back.

A dropper walked along the clifftop, a view enhancer in his hand. He stopped often, looking out to sea.

A second watcher appeared out of the darkness near them, and moved in the opposite direction to his partner.

When they were further away, and their attention was on the sea, Cal tapped Anja's shoulder and they slipped away.

"We can wait for the others at the boat," Cal whispered to her, and she nodded, but touched his arm when they had been going for a few minutes, and veered left.

He realized she was making for the droppers' stash.

He should have thought of it himself.

They could take dry clothes for the others, who would be freezing by the time they'd swum from the cave to the boat, and some food and water, as well, if they could find it.

They could.

They emptied a number of packs and repacked two with dry clothes, and as much food and water as would fit inside.

They stacked the packs again, so the pile looked undisturbed, and slipped away into the darkness with their spoils.

When they got to the tiny cove where they'd left the boat, Cal looked around for a place to start a fire that wouldn't attract attention, and began stacking wood under a deep overhang.

"The others will need a fire and something hot."

Anja brought him sticks and damp driftwood, and eventually they got a smoky fire going.

They ate together, sitting on a rock a little away from the fire, which had become too smokey to endure.

At least the wind was blowing out to sea, so no one at the spaceship site should see or smell it.

Cal set up a tiny water heater, and they made jah.

Anja leaned against him and tilted her head up to look at the stars as she sipped from her cup.

"Do you think we'll live to regret this?" he asked her.

She took a slow sip, and then turned to look at him. "The silver balls?" she asked.

He nodded.

"I've already regretted it a few times. But regret is a wasted emotion when I don't think they'll be leaving us anytime soon."

"No. I suppose we might get rid of them if we hand ourselves over to the gentle ministrations of scientists of the VSC."

She gave a low chuckle. "*I'm* a scientist of the VSC."

He had forgotten that. He grinned at her. "Maybe it isn't such a bad idea after all."

"I'm hopelessly compromised where you're concerned." She went silent, and when she turned to him again, the teasing tone had disappeared. "What is this between us, Cal? We haven't spoken about it at all—haven't had time to. But the kiss in the control room . . ."

"In the control room, I stopped trying to keep my distance. I've thought about you since we met at The Ice Breaker in Rinc." Cal ran a finger down her cheekbone. "I looked out for you since then, hoping you'd come back to visit."

She lowered her eyelids, then looked back up at him. "I wanted to come sit with you by the fire that night. Just sit quietly and sip my drink." She looked down at the cup in her hand, gave him a slow smile, and took a sip.

"Why didn't you?" His voice was a little rough.

"You seemed so self-contained. So content in your own company."

"I usually am. But you are always welcome to come sit with me." He took her cup of jah, set it on the rock, and slid his hands into her hair.

He kissed her slowly at first, soft, gentle touches of the lips, but then she shifted, aligning their bodies closer, and the kiss took on a life of its own. Cal lifted her up, impatient that she wasn't closer still, and she straddled his lap.

At the back of his mind, he knew the explosiveness of his desire, the sheer pleasure from every brush of her fingers and lips, was unusual. He was feeling more than he ever had.

Anja gasped as he fixed his mouth on her throat, and arched under his hands.

"I feel—" She slid a hand down the front of his pants, opened the front fastening, and squeezed him. He was harder than he could remember.

"It's the balls." He spoke against her skin.

She let out a laugh. "I know." She stood, kicking off her pants and then her humor cut off as he cupped her, rubbed her with his finger.

She was wet, clutching his shoulders with hard, urgent hands, and then she was guiding him into her, lowering herself down, her muscles fluttering and stretching to accommodate him.

Her skin was hot, and their bodies burned where they touched, every sensation heightened.

He used the strength of his arms to lift her up and down, to establish a rhythm, and she let her head fall back, eyes closed.

Starlight and Jero illuminated the slopes of her breasts, the shadow of her lashes against her cheeks.

It was the most erotic sight he'd ever seen.

When they were both damp and boneless, leaning against each other, she kissed the side of his neck and he could feel the curve of her lips against his skin.

"You're still amused about the balls?" He let his own amusement warm his voice.

"It was pretty funny." She stood slowly, balancing against him with one hand on his shoulder as she wriggled back into her pants, and then straddled him again, still wearing a grin. "But aside from the word play, it *was* the balls. I've never felt anything like that."

"Cal?" Livia heaved herself out of the surf and staggered toward them, and Cal could see his sister's eyebrows rise up as she noted how they were sitting.

He stood, lifting Anja up and setting her down beside him. She swore softly as she accidentally kicked her now-cold cup of jah onto the sand.

They dropped down onto the beach, and he bent and retrieved the cup before putting his arm around Anja's shoulders.

"Any trouble?" he asked.

Livia shook her head and then walked straight toward the fire. The smoke had mostly cleared and she stood as close to it as she could, shivering.

"We stole some clothes from the droppers. They'll be big for you, but they're dry." Anja crouched beside a pack and pulled out shirts and pants as the others staggered up from the beach after Liv.

They were too cold to talk until they were all changed and crouched around the flames, shoveling food into their mouths while Cal and Anja made more jah.

"So, did you two kill the laz cannons?" Walef asked.

Cal shook his head. "The runners had taken off and were hovering over the control room, trying to stop the roof collapsing. We decided to get more supplies and meet you here, then make plans on what to do."

"Good idea." Demi hunched closer to the fire, turning her head so her hair could dry easier. "I could have wept when you handed me some dry clothes."

"It was cold," Ritt agreed. "But even so . . ." He glanced at the others.

Livia lifted a shoulder in reluctant agreement. "Even so, the swimming was . . . exhilarating. I felt like I was home."

"Echoes of the silver balls' time inside Devinia?" Demi didn't sound as if she disagreed, though. "The way we cut through the water . . ."

"It felt good. Until I started running out of energy, toward the end." Walef took the cup of jah Anja handed him gratefully, took a big gulp even though it was too hot.

"Yes. The end did leave something to be desired. But when we're rested and fed . . ." Ritt took his jah and smiled up at Cal with dreamy eyes. "It will be glorious."

16

Anja brought up the rear again.

It seemed to be her default position in the group.

She didn't mind. It felt right. She and Cal were bookends, keeping the group together and safe.

They had eaten and rested for a few hours, then decided to make their way back to the spaceship, to watch and wait for another chance to disable the weapons on the runners.

As they got closer, the noise and chaos seemed to be less now than it had been earlier.

Either Sirco and Jake had found a solution to their collapsing ceiling problem, or they'd given up for the night.

The runner engines were quiet, and that's all she cared about.

Cal led them along the far side of the island, so they came toward the runners from the opposite direction. It meant there was less chance of bumping into one of the crew.

There were still watchers on the clifftops, though.

Anja could see them silhouetted against the lightening dawn, using their enhanced viewers to look for anyone coming from Rinc.

The rising sun meant they needed to hurry. Darkness was their friend in this situation.

But as they crouched behind a cluster of rocks close to the runners, one of the watchers signaled using a high-pitched whistle.

Someone opened the runner door and stuck their head out, voice clogged with sleep and irritable. "What?"

It was Jake.

"Runner coming in low across the water," the watcher called back.

"Shit." Jake disappeared and his runner's engine started up.

Then Sirco, face strangely illuminated by the light he'd tucked under his chin, staggered into view, hopping into his boots one by one as he hurried toward the runners.

She met Cal's gaze and they rose up and started to run toward the runners as well.

Demi cursed softly behind them and then followed. She veered off toward Sirco's runner when Anja and Cal chose Jake's.

Anja looked over at her and gave a nod of approval, saw the other three were coming too, split into two groups—Livia following her and Cal, Ritt and Walef following Demi.

Jake was too fast, though.

His runner lifted off and shot off the cliff, and Anja changed trajectory, angling toward Sirco's runner.

He had climbed in and started the engines, but it was still firmly on the ground when she reached it.

"How do we disable the cannons?" Demi called, running to the front of the runner where the weapons were mounted.

Anja pressed her fingers against the side. Nothing.

Not there. She didn't know how she knew, but she understood she needed to go to the rear of the runner.

She ran to the back as the engines revved louder.

There would only be seconds before Sirco lifted off.

She put her hands on the cold metal again, and felt it. A cluster of electronics just beneath the thin metal skin.

She held her fingers lightly above them, felt a spark, like touching something charged with static electricity, and the runner's engines cut off.

The ship died.

And they were exposed.

The sun had cracked the horizon, and with a jolt of shock she saw Cal was already fighting someone.

Somehow, she thought she should have known the moment he engaged.

She ran toward him to help, but Walef beat her to it, reaching Cal's side and so she slowed, taking in who they were up against, how many.

Sirco had jumped out of the runner, and he was shouting for help toward what she could see in the growing light was a small group of tents.

"What did you do?" He spun to face Cal.

Cal turned, two droppers at his feet, as Walef tossed a third dropper off to one side.

Ritt had begun to move toward them, but he'd paused, looking in her direction as if for instructions, and Livia and Dem waited at the back of the runner.

Sirco was at its nose, but droppers had responded to his shout and were coming from the right, some still sleep-creased, with hair mussed.

She and the others were horribly outnumbered, but she didn't feel that worried about it.

She caught Ritt's eye and tipped her head toward Walef, and with a nod he ran forward.

Demi had already begun to move toward Sirco, and Anja left her to it, trusting her to get it right with Livia's help.

Cal ignored Sirco. Now he'd dealt with the immediate attack, he looked out toward the ocean and Jake's runner, headed straight for their rescuers.

Anja saw Walef and Ritt had waded into the droppers who'd come at Sirco's call and ran to back them up. She had just reached them, just engaged with her first enemy, when Demi gave a cry behind her.

She put the man in front of her down hard, so he wouldn't get back up, and spun.

Demi lay with a hand to her shoulder, while Sirco stood over her with a laz. Livia was crouched beside her.

She should have remembered he had a laz. He had shot her and the others with it before, after all, when he'd pretended to come to their rescue.

Across the water, the purple light of a laz cannon bloomed, and with a boom, the search and rescue runner hit the sea's surface.

"I'll shoot them both," Sirco shouted, to get through to Walef and Ritt, and they both danced back to see what was going on as Cal turned from the ocean to take in Sirco holding a laz to Demi's head.

A feeling rose up inside Anja, a deep-seated feeling of rage and a need for vengeance.

Sirco would be sorry he had done that.

Very sorry.

She glanced at Livia, and saw an expression on her face that mirrored how Anja was feeling, and when their eyes met, Anja felt a little jump in her chest.

She turned to look at Ritt and Walef, and they were staring at Sirco, their faces grim.

Cal's gaze swiveled from Sirco to the downed runner. "You'll regret this."

Sirco gave a snort. "No." He waved at them, now surrounded by droppers, and then at the runner bobbing uselessly in the water as

Jake circled it. "I don't think I'm the one with any regrets." He banged a fist against his runner. "What did you do to it?"

"What could we have done?" Anja asked. "We don't even have any tools on us. We escaped with nothing but the clothes on our backs, remember?"

Sirco angled toward her. "I remember. What I can't understand is why you came back here. You should have stayed on that other island and waited until we left."

No one said anything to that.

Jake had turned his runner around and was flying back.

He landed on the cliff in a spray of dried vegetation and sand and jumped out before the engine had shut down.

"What have we here?" He took in Demi lying, gray-skinned with pain, with Sirco's laz pointed at her head. At Livia crouched beside her, and then the rest of them, standing loosely surrounded by droppers.

"These are the original search and rescue team and the scientist from the southern peninsula."

Jake turned his head. "I thought you dropped them in the ocean."

"It seems they can swim really well."

Jake gave a choked laugh at that. "I wondered why you didn't come join me in your runner."

"My runner won't start."

Jake suddenly didn't look amused anymore. "What did they do?" He turned to look at each of them in turn. "What did you do?"

"They say nothing. It's true they don't have any equipment with them that could have caused any harm." Sirco sounded nervous. "And they were outside the runner, not inside it."

"So what, it just died?" Jake shook his head in disbelief.

"It looks like it." Sirco lifted his shoulders. "We'll have to have the engineers look at it."

"The engineers are busy enough." Jake's words exploded out of his mouth. "We don't have a lot of time, and we need both runners."

"I know that. *I* didn't break it." Sirco stuck out his jaw belligerently.

Jake swung around to look at each of them in turn. "What did you do?" He turned to the droppers. "Look around on the ground by the runner, see what they used."

A few of the droppers did as he ordered, and Anja turned her head a fraction, caught Cal's gaze.

A picture formed in her mind.

Yes, she thought at him. *Yes, that is what we should do.*

She looked over at Livia, still crouched right next to Demi.

Livia blinked at her, very deliberately, and then changed her stance a little, scooping her arms under Demi as if to hold her close.

Anja glanced over at Walef and Ritt and they started to move a little, loosening their arms and shoulders, distracting the droppers still watching them.

"There's nothing," one of the droppers looking around the runner called.

Jake's lips formed a tight, straight line. "Kill them." He looked over at Sirco.

"What?" Sirco lowered his laz.

"I said, kill them. You can stop when one of those who are left tells you what they did to the runner."

Sirco shook his head. "No."

Jake tilted his head in an exaggerated move. "You were going to get rid of the scientist here a few days ago, and when this lot came looking for her, you threw them in the sea, but now you won't kill them?"

"I never told Halito and Drummon to kill her, just keep her from reaching Rinc. They might have decided to take things into their own hands, but that wasn't on my say-so. And yes, I threw the search and rescue team into the water, but I didn't have the capacity to keep them prisoner. I didn't know what we were going to find when we reached the signal. Right now, we can easily lock them up somewhere, or dump them on another island and leave them. I won't kill them just because you're in a bad mood, Jake."

Sirco had been happy to try to kill them when *he'd* been in a bad mood, chasing them down in his runner and shooting so close to the pod, but Anja didn't mind his change of heart.

"I'll do it, then." Jake moved toward Sirco, hand out for the laz, and everyone's attention focused on the two men.

With a battle cry she didn't know she knew, Anja ran toward the two men, arms out wide to make herself bigger.

Cal did the same, racing toward them.

Livia scooped Demi up and ran as well, straight for the edge of the cliff.

Anja caught a glimpse of her, leaping into the air, back arched, legs bent back, Demi in her outstretched arms, before she slammed into Jake.

She bounced off him, but he took the impact, too, and he stumbled and fell to one knee.

Good enough.

Cal had grabbed Sirco and thrown him to the side, and the laz flew out of his hand, bouncing on the hard, rocky ground near the edge of the cliff.

She ran around Jake before the droppers could close in, heading for the edge with Cal.

He reached out a hand and she took it, and as they jumped off together, she saw him kick the laz over with them.

Ritt and Walef had jumped a few seconds before they had, taking advantage of the droppers' distraction as she and Cal attacked the two leaders.

She thought for a moment she should be concerned, that they

didn't know how deep the waters below the cliffs were, and then she laughed out loud, the wind whipping the laughter away as they plunged down.

These were Devinia's waters, and now they were hers, too.

She knew them well enough.

They hit the icy sea. It felt like a homecoming.

When they surfaced, she swam to Livia.

"I'll take Demi. You and Cal get to the search and rescue runner." She knew they both thought their mother was onboard, and Cal's attention kept going to the downed vessel.

Livia loosened her hold on Demi and let Anja take her. "Thank you."

"You sure?" Cal was suddenly beside her, the water turning his lashes into spiky points around his clear gray eyes.

She nodded. "Go. I'll be right behind you."

He pressed a kiss to his fingers and touched her cheek, then turned, so sleek and sure in the water.

He swam away, with Livia, Ritt and Walef in a diamond formation behind him.

It surprised even her how quickly they disappeared.

She turned on her back, pulling Demi up her chest so her head rested on her shoulder, and followed.

17

Cal looked back every few strokes until Anja and Demi disappeared behind the choppy waves.

He forced himself to focus on the search and rescue runner floundering up ahead. The worry that had sat like a lead weight in his stomach since the moment Jake had shot it out of the sky got heavier still as it slowly listed to one side.

He hoped his mother hadn't been inside, but he knew her.

With both himself and Livia missing, she would have come looking herself, despite all the reasons her staff would have given her for letting someone else do it.

As a former wave rider and current volunteer with the search and rescue department, no one could say she wasn't qualified to come.

He and the others were making good time in the water, and he remembered Ritt telling him that under the right conditions, swimming together would be glorious.

The circumstances detracted from the pleasure of being in the water, but he understood what his fellow wave rider meant.

They were slicing through the waves like a hunting pod, and it felt . . . like he was in his element.

He didn't push hard against the feeling—he needed the speed and the focus—but he worried they were still too caught up in Devinia's old reality. The silver balls would take time to shake Devinia's nature and environment off and embrace a new one.

The runner was close enough now for him to see a few figures clinging to the sides, and he felt a fizz of relief in his blood.

At least some had made it out alive.

"Mom," he shouted as he got within earshot.

"Cal!"

He slowed, treading water to see where the cry had come from, and then finally saw his mother holding on to a hoop of metal from the side of the runner, Yavish and Donnella on either side of her.

"Is that Livia, too?" His mother's voice was thick with emotion as they reached the side. "Oh, thank the stars."

"Is everyone all right?" Cal pulled himself up next to her, and she threw an arm around him, pulling him close.

"Evan was with us. We're hoping he's on the other side," Yavish said.

"I'll go look." Walef swam off, calling Evan's name as he rounded the back.

Cal assessed the survivors.

Donnella was his mother's friend, and Demi's mother. Cal guessed she'd used the fact that she was a doctor to justify her inclusion on the rescue mission to find her daughter.

Yavish was close to his own age. He worked in the Fynian government's administration department, but he was also a search and rescue volunteer. He looked fit enough, but he wasn't wave rider fit, and even if he had been, there was no way any of them could swim to any of the islands before hypothermia set in.

Livia had reached their mother and also received a close hug.

"Are there inflatables inside?" Cal asked when she released Liv.

"Yes, but I don't think there's a way to get them safely," his mother said.

"We need them." There was no choice in the matter.

Livia seemed about to push herself off the side and go under, when their mother grabbed at her.

"It's too dangerous, Liv."

"Ritt and I will go." Cal shared a look with his sister and she gave a reluctant nod.

Someone needed to stay and keep everyone calm.

"Where's Demi?" Donnella had been quiet until then. Cal hesitated, then pointed behind them.

"Coming," he said, then tapped Ritt's shoulder and went under, leaving Livia to explain.

The runner had tipped completely on its side, but the open door was easy to find below the surface, and he and Ritt swam into the storage bay without any problems.

The three inflatables were stored where they should have been stored.

They swam them out one by one, inflating each one before going back under.

By the time they came out with the last one, his mother, Livia and Donella were in one of the inflatables, Walef and Yavish were in the other. There was no sign of Evan.

He would have been piloting the runner. Cal knew him well enough to know that.

His throat tightened. "Evan?" he called out to Walef.

His friend shook his head.

"We'll circle the runner, just in case."

Walef nodded, but from the bleak look in his eyes, Cal didn't think there was much hope.

He turned to look back at the island behind them, at the

activity on the top of the cliff. At least two droppers were watching them, vision enhancers pressed to their faces.

Jake had shot the search and rescue runner down with an absolute callous disregard for the people within. Had demanded Sirco kill him, Anja and the others in the same casual way.

Someone needed to stop him.

Cal was happy to be that someone.

INFLATABLES WITH TINY, almost silent motors appeared out of the thickening morning mist.

Anja had been able to keep afloat, to keep Demi's head above water, but the cold had gotten to her and she wasn't making nearly the progress she had in the beginning. She was relieved to see Cal leaning over the side of one of the boats, hand extended.

They were hauled in, shivering, and handed towels, and Cal helped strip her clothes off, while another woman did the same to Demi, crooning to her as she did as if Demi were her daughter or someone precious to her.

She probably was.

When she was naked and covered in a warm blanket, hot jah was thrust into her hand and then dry clothes.

They were a little big, but they were the warm, smart-fabric outfit of the wave riders, and she put them on with grateful, shaking fingers.

Cal helped her pull the shirt over her head, and did up the buttons on the pants when her fingers refused to cooperate.

His motions were no-nonsense, practical, but his fingers brushed her waist, her neck, her ear, light and intimate.

When she was finally dressed and had the blanket back around her, and another hot cup of jah in her hands, the woman who had helped Demi change and then found her a comfortable place to lie down with a blanket over her, came to sit beside her.

"Thank you for helping my Demi. Livia said you offered to swim with her so Liv and Cal could go ahead and help us. I'm Donnella. Demi's mother."

"I'm very pleased to meet you." Anja put out a hand to her, and then looked down at it, confused.

What greeting was that?

The woman looked flustered. "I'm not familiar with Aponi greetings." She held out her hand, nevertheless, and going purely on instinct, Anja grasped hers and gave it a squeeze.

"Well." Donnella looked bemused. "I'm very pleased to meet you, too."

"Are you all unharmed?" Anja looked over at the other two inflatables, taking in the huddled survivors and wondering if Cal's mother was among them.

Donnella's mouth formed a hard line.

"No. Evan, our pilot, drowned. The rest of us are all right, though, aside from a few scratches and scrapes."

"I'm sorry." Her gaze went up to the cliff, which was slowly disappearing as they made for the island where Devinia and the pod were still calling and hooting.

Jake had done this to them.

She glanced over at Cal, and saw he was staring at the cliffs, too, until the thick mist swallowed them up.

As they came into the bay, Kada moved suddenly, explosively toward them, and though her instinctive reaction was to rear back in fear, she forced herself to lean forward and project a clear message. Telling him it was them. Reminding him of her friendship with his grandmother.

With a huff, he sank back into the water and emerged beside Devinia again.

"What was that about?" Donnella asked, a hand over her heart, as if to stop it leaping out of her chest.

"He's protective, that's all," Anja said. Devinia was still lying on her side, her eyes open but no longer with the snapping, laser focus of before.

They were fading to a pale lavender.

"She's in her final hours." Cal put a hand on her shoulder as they passed the pod and headed for the beach.

She absorbed the comfort, lifting her own hand to grip his.

Someone coughed to the left of them, and she turned to look, saw an older woman staring at her with a sharp gaze.

Cal's mother, if she were to guess.

She smiled and gave the woman a friendly nod, then moved lightly to the front of the inflatable to jump off and haul it up onto the sand.

Livia did the same, and then she and Livia worked together to help Ritt with his inflatable. They worked silently, coordinating without a word.

When they were done, they stepped back in unison, and the three newcomers stared at them before slowly climbing out.

"You practiced that before?" Cal's mother asked, her gaze going between Anja and her daughter. "I didn't realize you knew each other so well."

"Mom, this is Anja." Livia must have heard something in her mother's voice that made her step forward hurriedly. "Anja, this is my mother, Leonie."

"Pleased to meet you." Anja stared at her, thinking there was something so familiar about her. It could just be that she reminded Anja of Livia and Cal—she was their mother, after all—but it was more than that.

It took a moment to sink in.

"The head-of-planet." She turned, looking for Cal, her eyes narrowing, but he had his back to her, pulling supplies from the inflatables, so she turned back. "Apologies, it took a moment to recognize you."

"You didn't know my mother was the head-of-planet?" Livia frowned. "Didn't Cal tell—?" She trailed off, her mouth forming an oh.

Anja recalled Dunc leaning in after he'd introduced Cal months ago, his manner suggesting he was about to share some interesting information, but then they'd been interrupted and he had never finished what he was going to say.

He had been about to tell her the wave rider she'd just met was the son of Fynian's head-of-planet, no doubt about it.

"We should get a fire going." Cal was weighed down by two boxes from the inflatables. He stepped between them, making his way toward the fire pit they had dug the last time they were here.

"Liv was just introducing me to Anja." His mother's voice held a hint of amusement, and Anja began to relax a little.

Cal stopped, turned, and gifted his mother with a smile. "Sorry, I should have done it." He set the boxes down, took Anja's hand.

She caught his gaze and he faltered.

"You never mentioned your mother was the head-of-planet." She kept her voice light.

He blinked, then squeezed her hand. "I meant to, but we've been busy. It doesn't matter, does it?"

She thought about it, realized it didn't actually make any difference, other than add another layer to their interactions with Jake.

The head-of-planet was theoretically no more important than anyone else in an egalitarian society like the Verdant String, but practically, more people would be looking for Leonie Mordova, and her disappearance would cause a bigger reaction than the disappearance of any of the citizens in her charge.

She squeezed back. "I suppose not."

"Then let's get a fire going." He looked back at the inflatable, where Donnella and Walef were helping Demi out onto the sand. He picked up the boxes and moved away, and for a moment, Leonie and Anja stared straight at each other.

Leonie suddenly smiled, and the way her lips curved up was exactly the same as Cal's. "I'm not sure what's going on here, but despite the circumstances, it really is good to meet you, Anja."

18

"An ancestral spaceship." Leonie Mordova turned to look in the direction of spaceship island, even though the mist still hung thick over the water and blocked it from view. She sat back on her heels at her place beside the fire, and shared a look with Yavish.

"That would explain the information we got last night," Yavish said with a nod.

"What information?" Cal slowly crumpled up the container his meal had come in and threw it into the fire.

"When the solar flare died down, the satellites we use for outward communication with the VSC started transmitting information back to us on who was in the Jero system." Yavish shrugged. "There was a ship in our nearspace that had not requested permission to be there, and there were no comms from VSC headquarters or the Arkhoran authorities that they had a ship so close."

"The ship that Jake arrived on," Anja said.

Cal nodded. "No doubt about it."

"We took the rare opportunity of being able to send comms direct to the satellite, rather than send up a runner to transmit, and asked Arkhor if it was theirs, and if so, why they hadn't asked our permission to be here." Leonie tapped a finger to her lips.

"That will give the Arkhorans an incentive to come take a look." Walef's tone was a little dry.

"Knowing them, they'll break every record to get here as fast as possible." Livia gave a lopsided grin.

"That's a good thing, surely?" Anja asked.

"Yes, but we're mostly second-generation Arkhorans on Fynian, given the Arkhorans found Fynian originally. Even though we're an independent VSC territory now, they still like to interfere with us as often as they can. It causes a little resentment down here."

"Not this time," Ritt said. "They can interfere as much as they like on this issue."

"Yes." Leonie looked up at the swirling clouds above them, which were slowly dissolving in the strengthening morning sun. "I'll grin and bear a bit of Arkhoran interference when it comes to this. We'll pay for it—Arkhor will be all over this discovery afterward—but we don't have the expertise or the equipment to deal with a find like this anyway, so it doesn't matter that much."

"When you say they'll break records to get here, how long are we talking?" The thought of an Arkhoran military ship pinching to the black to reach them, armed and ready, was very appealing.

"Could be as early as tonight," Leonie said.

A lot could happen in that time.

The clouds were lifting faster and faster, and the top of space-ship island appeared out of the mist. They could only see the back of it from here, but they all heard the roar of a runner engine starting up.

The sound traveled clearly across the water, strangely distorted by what was left of the mist.

"Where's he going now?" Walef wondered.

"Back up to get another runner, since Anja destroyed the other one?" Livia asked.

"You destroyed their runner?" Donnella asked.

"We tried to destroy both of them, to stop them shooting you down." Cal glanced at Livia, and she lowered her eyes, realizing her mistake.

"How did you do it?" Yavish asked.

Anja cleared her throat. "I didn't destroy the runner, really. I blew its main circuit. It'll take time to replace, but the runner itself isn't damaged."

"I thought you were a marine biologist," Leonie said in surprise.

Anja lifted a shoulder. "I am, but some of my postings have been in very isolated spots, just like the southern peninsula, so I've trained in electronics in case any of my equipment malfunctions. If I had to go back to civilization every time I had a circuit blow out, I'd be away half the time."

It made sense, and it was true, as far as it went, but her ability to tinker with her recording equipment was not what had helped her kill Sirco's runner.

"The runner sounds like it's coming closer." Ritt pushed up to his feet, turning toward the sound.

He was right.

Anja stood as well, just in time to see Jake's runner burst through the final wisps of mist.

"What's he doing?" She didn't expect a response. Everyone was as mystified as her.

They were no danger to Jake anymore. They couldn't have been more at a disadvantage.

He had no reason to come at them, other than spite.

Something in her brain clicked.

Spite. And loss of face.

The runner's laz cannons opened up, strafing the leviathan pod lying in the bay, and then firing at the beach.

The shock at his attack on the pod froze every single one of them.

They didn't move until the first laz beam struck the beach, taking out one of the inflatables, and then hitting the wall of cliffs behind them.

Rocks tumbled down and the runner was forced to turn, banking sharply over the water.

From her position lying on the sand, where she had finally dived for cover, Anja saw Jake had been forced to turn the runner low and slow, and suddenly the water exploded beneath him.

Kada and another leviathan came out of the water like the wrath of a vengeful god.

They slammed into the runner from below, flipping it on its side.

The narrow wing caught the water and the runner somersaulted like a stone skipping over a lake, bouncing once, twice, three times, and then finally getting enough speed to keep in the air.

It sputtered, the engines dealing with sea water as it coughed and shuddered back toward spaceship island's clifftop.

Kada reared up again, roaring in rage and pain, and Anja found herself racing toward the surf, pulling off her clothes as she went.

She had just reached the lapping waves when she realized the others were with her, even Demi, who had been groggy and quiet since they'd been pulled out of the water.

Someone was screaming at them from behind, but Anja didn't have time for that as she half-turned to kick her pants back onto the sand—she just needed to get into the water, make sure the pod were safe.

She dived, and knew Cal was beside her.

They came up for air, and she felt a satisfaction, a sense of rightness, that all six of them were there, in their formation.

They went back under, and the food and rest they'd had since earlier that morning meant her body sang as she powered through the water.

They emerged beside Devinia.

The matriarch had been hit a second time in two days; a long, ugly burn visible on her side crossing over the other score mark. Two others in the pod had been hit as well, she could see the damage across a back and a neck.

The way Kada was behaving, he had taken a hit, too.

The juvenile was roaring and hitting the water with his neck, leaping fully out of the water as he circled the place where he had struck the runner.

The leviathan who'd helped him had slowly made her way back to Devinia, but Kada continued to be outraged.

Anja came up close to Devinia's head, and the old Anja, the scientist, wondered what she was doing here, what good she could possibly do, but she reached out to the matriarch anyway, and ran a hand down her cheek.

If felt as if her fingers sparked, and then Cal joined her, and then the others, soothing Devinia together, and she sighed, and settled in the water, as if they had taken some of her pain.

Maybe they had.

Maybe the silver balls had a way to help her.

Whatever the reason for the compulsion to come out to her, it had been worth it. The rest of the pod calmed, and even Kada stopped leaping from the water. He continued to circle the spot where he'd hit the runner, but he no longer seemed so angry.

Anja felt as if she was coming back to herself, as well. She glanced at Cal, suddenly aware of how focused she'd been on getting into the water.

They had left Leonie, Yavish and Donnella on the beach, and she had no idea if any of them had been hit by the laz cannons.

She had no idea if Cal had been hit.

"Are you hurt?" She leaned toward him, and he blinked, shook his head as if he were also just coming to himself. His eyes, dark gray rimmed around silver, held hers.

"You?" He ran a hand from her shoulder down her arm as she shook her head.

His gaze fixed on the top of her breasts, and his eyes widened.

"You just realized now we're all naked?" She sent him a grin. It didn't worry her, but from earlier reactions, she guessed the Fynians would be mortified.

Cal gave a snort at her words, and then grew serious. "Anyone injured?"

The others murmured they were fine, but Anja didn't think she was the only one feeling a little embarrassed at their headlong, unthinking race to the pod.

"And the others?" Ritt asked. "Your mothers?"

Demi spoke almost for the first time since she'd been shot. "I didn't even check." She put a hand over her face.

"Me, neither," Livia said, voice quiet. "That's bullshit." She smacked her head with an open palm. "Bullshit, you hear?"

"You think the silver balls are listening?" Walef asked, voice sarcastic.

"They *are* listening." Livia bared her teeth at him in a way that was pure leviathan.

At the move, everyone froze.

Then Livia gave a laugh, a quick exhale that exploded from her. "I'm turning into a matriarch."

Anja didn't know why her words broke the tension, but they did. Maybe naming it helped them come to grips with what was going on.

"I think it was the final goodbye. Before she fades away." Cal's voice was quiet. "I think we need to leave her to her family now."

The other leviathans had come in closer, and with a nod, everyone slipped down below the surface and swam away.

They formed a group a little way from where the pod began to press in against Devinia, and Anja found herself in the middle of it.

"There'll be questions when we get back." Demi spoke as if it was not a question. "Not least of which will be why we're naked."

"It's easier to swim naked, and we don't have that many dry clothes." Ritt pointed out the obvious, but the others glanced at him and he closed his mouth again.

Those seemed very reasonable answers to Anja, but obviously she wasn't Fynian.

"We won't have to face them right away. We can get ourselves together first." Cal didn't give a reason for his pronouncement, but no one challenged him.

"I actually feel hot in the cheeks just thinking about how we just dived in and swam." Walef moved uncomfortably. "I don't like not being in charge of my thoughts and my body."

"No." Anja agreed. "But I think Cal's right. This was the last farewell. I don't think she has long, and we were able to take away her pain, so her final hours will be peaceful."

She could forgive the silver balls taking over for a short while to accomplish that.

The others seemed to feel the same, because she felt as though they were calmer as they swam the last stretch to the shore.

As they came closer, Anja noticed the destruction of one of the inflatables, the damage to another. The third seemed untouched, but it was too small to fit them all.

Maybe that had been Jake's plan. He might have been aiming for the boats, to make sure they were stuck here. Seeing them leaving the downed runner on the inflatables earlier might have made him nervous that they would return and have another try at his own runner.

Why he shot at the leviathans, she had no idea.

It had certainly backfired on him.

She hoped the damage would prevent the runner making it back to nearspace, and she wondered how he would explain what happened to his masters higher up the chain.

A leviathan had never attacked a runner in all the years since Arkhor had discovered Fynian. They were known as gentle giants, and Jake had provoked the first attack.

He didn't need to know Kada was probably slightly different to the other leviathans around him, carrying the evolution of Devinia's silver balls in his veins.

Kada had managed to get another leviathan to attack with him, as well. It was actually fascinating.

Maybe that second leviathan was one of Devinia's grand-daughters.

Anja looked back at Kada. He had left his circling and gone back to join the others crowded around his grandmother.

It would be interesting to see how his own offspring behaved in the years to come.

Her feet touched the bottom and, water streaming down her body, she waded in with the others.

Cal was right about having a little time to gather their thoughts, because at the sight of their nakedness, Leonie, Yavish and Donnella, who all seemed unhurt, turned away in embarrassment.

Because they had been wearing the spare clothes from Cal's boat, while they waited for their own clothing to dry by the fire, none of them had been wearing underwear.

Anja glanced over at Cal and found he was looking at her, eyes hot.

She had never seen him fully naked. They had made love in

the dark, only half-dressed. She hadn't had a chance to explore his body as she would have liked.

And what a body it was.

Wave riders were beautifully muscled, the women and the men, and Cal was magnificent. She couldn't look away as they gathered up their clothes and shimmied into them.

Soon, Cal's eyes promised as he slid his pants up over narrow hips, and she knew exactly what that promise meant.

She felt heat bloom low in her belly at the thought.

When they were dressed, Leonie and the others turned to face them. Anja read bafflement, hurt, and suspicion on their faces.

She wondered what their headlong run into the ocean had looked like from Leonie's perspective.

From the look of her, not good. Not good at all.

19

———

"I don't understand." Donnella tucked a blanket around Demi's shoulders.

They had moved to the fire and found their clothes had dried, allowing them to change out of the ill-fitting spares. The flames still crackled away merrily, as if the attack and its aftermath had never happened.

Unfortunately, Cal could see his mother and the others were not equally inclined to forget it.

"We were worried about Devinia," Demi told her mother, clutching the corners of her blanket close.

"You were more worried about Devinia than you were for yourself! You were shot with a laz this morning." Donnella lifted her hands in confusion. "The others ran and you just joined them."

"How did you help her?" Leonie asked the question softly.

There was a beat of silence.

His mother put her hands on her hips. "I was a wave rider long enough to know there was nothing you could have done to help a leviathan who was badly injured like that. Especially not one who was already fading. But you did. Somehow, when you got there, she calmed, and that calmed the rest of the pod."

"It was instinctive." Cal rubbed a hand through his short, wet hair. He looked around at the team, silently asking for permission to reveal their secret, and one by one they each gave a nod of agreement, until he reached Anja.

She hesitated.

The others were either family or close friends with Leonie, Donnella and Yavish. But she was neither.

And it was a big secret to reveal.

He knew that once these things were let loose in the world, they were hard to contain.

And she would know, as a scientist herself, there would be queues lining up to study them if the information ended up in the upper leadership of the VSC.

The silence stretched so thin, it was at breaking point.

Cal reached out a hand and gently rubbed her shoulder, leaving her to make up her own mind.

"Please, Anja." Livia spoke first. "They can be trusted. I know you don't know them, but remember, anything they do that will hurt you will also hurt us, and my mother will never let that happen."

"Hurt you?" Leonie's focus sharpened, and her bruised feelings turned to curiosity.

Slowly, Anja dipped her chin down then up, and Demi heaved out a sigh of relief.

Cal widened his stance, as if about to do battle. "We didn't get to the spaceship first. The pods did. They moved the ship under the island."

Yavish shook his head. "How could they have done that? Why would they have done that? It doesn't make any sense."

"They definitely did." Ritt lifted a log and set it closer to the fire and sat down on it, shivering slightly. "When you see the inside of it, you'll see it was at the bottom of the ocean for a long time before it was moved, pulled up from the seabed and dragged under the arch."

"But why?" Leonie shook her head.

"They did it because Devinia told them to. Years ago. Maybe as many as fifty years ago. She coordinated it." Cal spoke up, and his mother, Yavish and Donnella stared at him.

His mother looked like she wanted to laugh at the absurdity of it, but Cal knew she knew he wouldn't say something like that lightly and she controlled herself.

"Explain." She kept her voice even.

"There was something in the spaceship. Some kind of artificial intelligence in the form of nanotech. Six silver balls' worth." Cal rubbed his hair again.

"I think they were once part of six people," Anja said quietly. "And when those people died in the crash into the ocean, the nanotech reconvened back in its original form, six silver balls."

"What do you mean, part of six people?" Yavish didn't have the same wait-and-see approach that his mother did. Cal knew he worked as an administrator in Fynian's government, and he obviously had a very low tolerance for nonsense.

Except this wasn't nonsense.

"She means the ancestors had super soldiers, or a team of enhanced crew who were probably there to help with the dangers and challenges of finding a new world to inhabit." Cal kept his voice even, but even he heard the warning in it, to let Yavish know he better watch his tone.

His mother narrowed her eyes. "What happened to these silver balls?"

"When Devinia found the spaceship at the bottom of the sea, they chose to inhabit her." Demi cleared her throat. "She wasn't their intended . . . receptacle . . . but she was alive and intelligent enough. Through her, they managed to get the spaceship off the seabed so it wouldn't deteriorate as fast, hid it away, and waited for a chance to find—"

"Find what?" Donnella asked, and there was a tremble in her voice.

"They waited until Devinia was tired of the extra life their presence afforded her, and then they left her." Livia hunched over and glanced at their mother.

"Left her?" The way his mother said it, Cal could hear she had a good idea who the silver balls had left Devinia for.

"We aren't the same as we were," Walef said, which Cal realized from the reaction around them was the exact wrong thing to say.

"But we're getting there." Demi spoke quickly over Walef. "I swear, Mom, we're still ourselves."

"Are you?" Donnella asked.

Demi stared at her, tears in her eyes. "Yes."

"What do you mean you aren't the same?" Yavish was the only one without children among them, and Cal guessed he was more able to step back and look at things objectively.

"We heal faster. Move faster. We're stronger. And we seem to know what the others are going to do before they do it. We're a very good team." Cal kept the facts about their strange dips into leviathan reality to himself.

"You're more than a team." Donnella was shaking her head. "You were like a single entity. Or like a hunting pod."

"A hunting pod." Yavish repeated her words slowly. "Because the balls were in Devinia for a long time?"

Ritt cleared his throat. "Maybe. But I think the team was always meant to be a team."

"Do the people stealing the spaceship tech know about this?" his mother asked.

Already, she'd moved past the craziness of it, to the practical.

Cal smiled.

Anja gave a laugh and shook her head. "No. We'd be part of their salvage if they did."

"Why did they shoot at us, then?" Donnella sounded calmer.

Cal wondered that himself. It didn't make sense. "He was aiming for the inflatables. Maybe he thought to trap us here."

He'd been watching Anja as he spoke and she suddenly shivered, and stepped closer to the fire, as if her body had run out of reserves.

Cal came up behind her, put his arms around her so his body heat warmed her from behind.

She sighed back into him, closing her eyes and angling her head to rest on his shoulder.

He bent his head and his lips brushed her ear.

Everyone went quiet, and he lifted his head to find every head turned their way.

"What?" he asked, annoyed.

"You're not usually quite so openly affectionate," Livia said.

Cal ignored them and kissed her temple, then rested his chin on her head.

"Kada seriously damaged that runner." His mother obviously decided to ignore his behavior. "What do you think they'll do next?"

"Now they have no working runner, and no way to contact the ship waiting in Fynian's nearspace, unless the solar activity is still subdued." Ritt's gaze was focused on spaceship island.

"If that's the case, it won't last," Walef glanced upward. "But let's say Jake's runner does have standard comms and the solar flare is low enough they can get a message through. They'll have to abandon the salvage operation and grab their guys, or they'll have to send down another runner to grab the equipment Sirco and his droppers stripped from the ship. But how many runners of the size Jake brought down can a spaceship reasonably carry?"

"I'd say they won't bother to grab their guys." Cal only had to think of the hard look in Jake's eyes when he ordered them killed to know it. "Jake will look after himself and the tech from the spaceship. His bosses also won't want him in VSC hands with the kind of information he must have in his head."

"So at least one runner will come down, even if it's just to fetch Jake." His mother sounded as if she agreed.

"More likely they'll risk loading up the most interesting looking equipment," Anja said. "If this is the same group who tried a similar operation on Faldine, then they won't like their plans being blown up a second time."

"Third time, if they're also the people behind the Cepi disaster," Cal reminded her.

"Does anyone know who they are?" Donnella asked.

"VSC information on the matter says it's whoever was left from the Core Companies after the VSC took back Garmen and Lassa. Some of the top people managed to escape in the confusion." Leonie shrugged. "They had some Caruson ships and enough credits to disappear, but I'm guessing wandering around space playing hide and seek with the VSC military fleet is getting old. If they turn themselves in, they'll be imprisoned. So they're probably looking for tech to help them find a planet and set up operations again."

"They're interested in seeing what tech the ancestors used to colonize the Verdant String." Cal felt like finally he was starting to see the picture.

His mother nodded. "No one wants another breakaway planet like Garmen or Lassa, though. And that tech isn't theirs. It belongs to the whole Verdant String Coalition."

"That may be true," Cal told her, "but with only one inflatable still intact, there's nothing we can do to stop them."

20

———————

They didn't have any intact inflatables.

On closer inspection, all three had taken hits. One was absolutely destroyed, but the other two might as well have been, given the massive rips in their sides.

"Well, they aren't going anywhere, either." Yavish tried to be cheerful.

"We could swim over, in case another runner does come down before the Arkhorans arrive," Anja said. "So we're in a position to stop them if possible."

She agreed with Leonie, she didn't want Jake to get away with this.

"Maybe." Cal spoke slowly as he looked across at spaceship island, now clearly visible in the midday sun.

"The water's too cold. There's no way you'd make it." Yavish shook his head.

"It would be hard, but doable." Cal turned back. "The problem is we'd need to take supplies, to refuel at the other end, and I don't think we have enough."

"Demi can't go anyway." Donnella's tone brooked no argument.

"If the others go, I'll go, Mom." Demi's voice was quiet. She hadn't said much since they'd confessed they were no longer quite themselves.

Demi had been hurt by her mother's horror at their new reality, and Anja felt protective of her, ready to step in front of her as a shield.

"As much as I don't want them to get away with any part of the ancestral spaceship, I don't want any of you in danger even more." Leonie rubbed her eyes. "Nothing is worth your safety."

While she'd been talking, Anja thought she heard the faintest throb of an engine, not from a runner, a much quieter engine.

She turned at the same time as Cal, and the others turned too, in one of those movements that were a little too similar for comfort.

Cal's boat was coming toward them across the tiny bay. Kada gave a snort at the sight of it, but he didn't move from his place beside his grandmother.

When Anja saw Sirco was piloting it, she decided he was lucky Kada thought of the boat as Cal's.

"He must have found it on the beach at the back of the island." Walef put his hands on his hips as they watched Sirco steer toward them and then land on the beach.

Walef and Ritt hauled the boat up and then stood back.

Sirco hesitated, looking at them ranged in front of him, and then with a shrug and a wince, jumped onto the sand.

He looked behind him at the pod and shuddered. "That was the most frightening ride of my life, going past those creatures. I was just waiting for one to lunge out and smash the boat up after what they did to Jake's runner."

"What are you doing here, Sirco?" Cal didn't hide the steel in his voice.

"I refused to kill you, if you remember." Sirco had both hands up in front of him. His face was battered, and he moved carefully, as if he had other injuries, too.

"We remember." Cal didn't give an inch.

"As you can see, I'm not very popular with Jake." He waved a hand at his face. "I managed to disappear when he turned his attention to other things. I found your boat round the back and decided it would be best if I was no longer in Jake's sight." He blew out a breath. "I didn't think the boat would make it back to the peninsula, and I didn't know where else to go."

"I think you saw Jake's runner take a knock, and worked out there were only two options available to his bosses. Either they swoop down and grab him, because they don't want him talking to the VSC, or they swoop down, grab him, and mitigate their losses by loading up with the best of the tech you've salvaged. Either way, you must have worked out your name isn't on the passenger list, and your quick escape off Fynian has disappeared. So you decided to switch sides." Anja did not hide her contempt.

Sirco stared at her, a great deal of animosity in his expression. "Maybe so. But it's not like I don't have anything to trade. I know a lot about Jake's operation. More than he realizes. I'm looking for a deal."

"Why'd Jake turn on you like he did?" Livia had trusted Sirco, had gone in his runner to rescue Cal without any reservations, and the bitterness of betrayal in her voice came through.

"He wanted me to kill you. I didn't. Then he decided to make sure you couldn't get off this island, and I told him to leave you alone. You had people who were wounded, you weren't going anywhere. He didn't like my telling him what to do. And when his little side trip turned into a disaster, he had some pent-up anger to deal with." Sirco gave a humorless laugh, and then put a hand to his ribs with a groan. "I didn't realize the leviathans would attack, and neither did Jake."

No one corrected him that they never had before.

"So he got back and beat you up because he was angry?" Demi shook her head in disbelief.

"The man's under pressure. With my runner absolutely dead, and now his runner too damaged to fly farther than an island hop at best, he's failed to deliver. Like Anja said, I could see he'd probably be taken off planet, but *I* certainly wasn't going to make the cut anymore. He's visibly nervous about his boss's reaction."

"And who is his boss?" Cal asked.

"Ricardo Ven." Siro lifted his shoulders. "Some ex-Core Company executive from Garmen. Has the means and the muscle to pull something like this off."

Leonie looked like that was ringing some bells for her. "You were a plant in the Fynian solar flares office, my son tells me. Waiting for your chance to rob my planet." She crossed her arms as she spoke.

Sirco nodded.

"What's happened to Duncan?" Anja realized that at last she could have an answer to that question.

"We needed him out of the way, because as the solar flare activity lessened and our chances of picking up the signal got better, we didn't want him noticing anything strange about my movements. He was sent to a conference in Arkhor." Sirco lifted a shoulder. "I don't know how Jake managed to make it look like it was official VSC Scientific Research Institute business, but he did. He was only able to get it organized at the last minute, though. I told Duncan I'd check in with you every day, but I missed your first call. Your message said you wanted a runner to search for your missing pod, and I panicked. We couldn't have a search team wandering around in exactly the place we thought the signal would be found. I had your line rerouted to a wave rider safety hut and got the two men Jake had sent me to listen in on your comms, told them to make sure you stayed put."

"How did you have a general location for the signal?" Walef wanted to know.

"Someone in the solar flare office wrote a report where she said she was sure it was coming from the southern peninsula last time it was detected. It was filed away and forgotten, until Jake's boss heard about the signal and started to take an interest."

They were silent as they considered the information.

"Do we have a deal? Because there's more. I kept my eyes peeled while I was part of the operation." Sirco kept his gaze on Leonie, the one person whose word would mean he was safe.

"What do you want out of this deal?" Leonie asked.

"I want to go home to Kalastoni and fade into the background, no imprisonment. In return I'll give you everything I know about this operation, Jake and his boss. Don't forget, I refused to shoot your children and got beaten up for it."

Leonie opened her mouth, and Anja was sure she was going to agree.

"Not killing us is a pretty low bar." Cal's voice had not softened one iota. "He also threw us into the ocean from his runner. If Kada and Devinia hadn't saved us, we'd be dead."

"I don't think you told me that part." Leonie shifted her stance, looked over at her son.

"I panicked. I didn't want to kill you." Sirco hunched. He looked past them to the fire, as if expecting there to be more of them. "Who are Kada and Devinia?"

No one answered that question, and Leonie addressed Sirco with a glint in her eye. "I'm not the one you need to negotiate your deal with. The Arkhorans will be swooping in any moment now, and they'll be the ones making the deals. But my guess is they'll be interested in what you know."

"The Arkhorans?" Sirco looked up at the empty blue sky, face set.

"They're on their way to check out the ship that brought Jake here. The one hovering in Fynian nearspace. Looks like your decision to switch sides was an even better one than you knew." Anja realized she was annoyed that he had gotten himself out of trouble. Leonie was right. The Arkhorans probably would like to hear what Sirco had to say.

He wouldn't face the full force of VSC law. Unfortunately.

In the distance, the damaged runner's engine started up. It spluttered and coughed, and then the runner rose up into the sky, clearly visible from the beach.

"Looks like they worked out you aren't on the island anymore." Cal shielded his eyes from the midday sun as they watched it lift and then sink down out of sight, although Anja could still hear the engine in the distance.

"I agree, that's Jake trying to see where I've gone."

Anja had a bad feeling Jake knew Sirco was not someone he could let go without consequences.

Sirco had said Jake didn't know how much he knew about the operation, but from what she'd seen of Jake, he didn't strike her as someone who'd let something like that slip past him.

He'd want to have Sirco where he could see him.

It struck her that Sirco had lied. He hadn't come to them because he didn't known where else to go, he'd worked out he'd have a better chance with the wave riders than out on his own on the ocean in a small boat.

"They'll be looking for you," Cal said, his gaze resting on Sirco. "And they won't care who they hurt to get to you." He glanced at Anja. "We need to get over there and fry those circuits so they can't hunt down Sirco when the engine dries out."

She had come to the same conclusion. She didn't care what happened to Sirco, but even if they sent him to another island, Jake wouldn't bother checking to make sure he was among them. He'd shoot everyone on the off-chance Sirco was there, and check afterward.

"At least you brought my boat back. It means some of us have a way to get over to the island."

"Some of us?" Demi asked.

Cal turned to her. "At least a few of us need to keep an eye on Sirco. Between you and Ritt, you should be able to keep him in line."

Demi's nostril's flared, and her chin lifted. She opened her mouth to protest.

"Please, sweetheart." Donnella put a hand on her shoulder. "You're not completely—"

"That's the thing, Mom. I *am* completely healed." Demi stared at Cal with narrowed eyes. "Why me?"

Cal held her gaze, and eventually she gave a huff and looked over at Ritt. "What do you think about it?"

They were the two who'd taken the most damage. Ritt to his ribs, and Demi had definitely received a higher level hit with the laz than they'd all gotten in the first encounter with Sirco.

"It makes sense." Ritt rubbed a hand over his ribs. He didn't quite wince, but it was a close thing.

It would have taken precious resources away from the healing process to swim in the freezing water, and Ritt had had to go in more than a few times since this started. So he might truly not be fully healed.

But Anja had picked up that Ritt and Demi were close friends since she'd met them, and she had the feeling Ritt might pretend to be a little more stiff than he was, just to keep Demi from overextending herself too early.

"I've already told you, it's not worth the risk." Leonie was shaking her head. "I don't want them stripping the ancestral spaceship or getting away without answering for their crimes, but you're more precious to me than whatever's in that ship." She turned to Sirco. "How many of them are up there? Twenty? More? Against four of you."

"Twenty three," Sirco said.

"Twenty three! Please don't go, Cal."

"We aren't going to take them all on." Cal's lips thinned. "We're going to sneak up and disable that runner. Jake won't want to let Sirco go. I don't think our boy here is as sneaky as he thinks he is. Jake has to be aware that Sirco knows a lot about their operation, and he will not like him talking to us, or the Arkhorans. He's going to come over as soon as he has that runner going again, and I don't think he's going to politely ask us to hand Sirco over. He'll be happy to kill us all."

Yavish was shaking his head. "And if they catch you?"

"Jake will kill you," Sirco said, and Anja knew he was doing it more to stir the pot between Leonie and Cal than out of any concern for their safety. He almost looked as if he was enjoying himself.

"We're hard to kill." Cal glanced at Sirco. "Ask him, he's tried often enough."

"I don't want there to be any chance at all that someone will kill you." Leonie drew herself up. She wanted to assert her role as head-of-planet, Anja could see, but at the same time, didn't want things to devolve to that level.

"Mom, Cal's right. They'll come for Sirco as soon as they can." Livia spoke up. "We'll be careful."

Her words were calm, sensible, but beneath the surface, Anja could sense the same thread of excitement, of straining at a leash to go do what they did best, that was building in her own chest.

She suppressed a shiver.

"At least wait until it's dark. They'll see you coming." Yavish's words earned him a grateful look from Leonie.

"They may manage to dry out the runner's engines by then," Cal said.

The engines were still going, she could hear them. Jake must have decided to run them until they were dry.

Anja decided to keep out of this fight. She felt the same urgency to be off as the others, but she wasn't going to get between Cal and Livia and their mother. Not if she wanted any long term relationship with Cal in the future.

And she did. She really did.

Walef, Ritt and Demi were as quiet as she was.

Leonie sighed. "I agree what you've laid out is a likely scenario, but it is only a scenario. The thought of this Jake character getting his hands on you . . ." The head-of-planet swallowed. "It frightens me."

"It frightens me to think of you being shot with a laz cannon on this beach." Cal looked up at the cliffs, but the only way up was to climb the sheer face of them, there were no convenient paths up a gentle slope, like there were on the mainland.

Even if they did manage to climb up, Anja didn't know if the island had anywhere better to hide than this beach. It seemed all bare rock and rough grasses from where she stood.

"This is one of the few islands in the archipelago with a proper beach like this. Most of the others have cliffs straight into the ocean." Cal's voice was gentle but implacable. "This is the only place you can wait, and this is the first place Jake will come looking."

The tone of the engines in the distance changed, and the effect on the pod was immediate.

Kada lifted out of the water, head turned in the direction of spaceship island, and the other members of the pod began to hoot and call.

Anja spun toward them, and the others did, too.

"Something's stirred them up," Yavish said.

"The runner. Can you hear the engine noise is different?" Livia asked.

"Do you think they've fixed it, and Kada is remembering it

from before, when Jake shot him?" Anja turned to look at Cal as she asked the question, and froze.

While their focus had turned to the pod, Sirco had obviously moved.

He was no longer standing in front of them, he was beside Leonie.

And he held a laz to her head with one hand, and a flare gun in the other.

21

—————

Cal felt the deep, sinking feeling of failure.

He didn't like it at all.

They should have checked Sirco for weapons when he landed, but Cal had never even seen a laz before Sirco's men started shooting at Anja with them—could it really only have been a few days ago? It was not something he'd ever had to check before.

Besides, he'd kicked Sirco's laz off the cliff when they'd escaped earlier.

He had thought them all gone.

His horror at the depth of his mistake seemed to be almost all-consuming, and he realized not all of it was from him. The silver ball was mortified not to have seen this possibility. Too long in Devinia, he managed to discern from the rapid-fire images they were sending him. Too long in something other than a person. Their ability to read a face was rusty.

He shook off the feeling forcefully. It was done. They had to move on and solve it, not wallow in regret.

The others were staring at Sirco in horror, and he thought he could see the same feelings of failure and distress on the rest of the team's faces as must surely be on his own.

Sirco dragged Leonie back a little, to give himself room, and he looked wild-eyed.

"You've decided to go back on the deal? Or the whole deal was a ruse?" Cal forced his voice to come out evenly.

"A ruse." Sirco adjusted his grip around Leonie's neck. "Although I seriously considered making it a reality when you told me the Arkhorans were on the way. I have to admit that's a glitch in the plan not even Jake can fix."

"But you didn't." Anja's voice was flat.

"I didn't because they've clearly got the runner working again, and they're a lot closer than the Arkhorans. As you say, no matter what happens, Jake won't let me simply go. I either go with him, alive and well, or go against him and die." He lifted a shoulder in a shrug.

"And what do you want?" Cal was sure there was something. All the inflatables had been damaged. Jake could have left them here, and they wouldn't have been any threat to him at all.

"The thing is, this whole enterprise has been a two for one deal." Sirco's mouth quirked. "I was originally sent here to steal druk. Jake's boss needs it, and can't buy it, because he's no longer able to show his face in the Verdant String, and every third-party deal he's tried to arrange has fallen through. The VSC vet everyone they don't know who's interested in druk too thoroughly."

"That's why you spent so much time with the wave riders." Cal knew Sirco had spent a lot of time in the restaurants and bars the wave riders frequented, chatting and making friends. "You were gathering information."

"I started out with you, Cal." Sirco gave a wry smile. "You're the head of trade, which in this place means the head of druk trade. But you were not the chatty, friendly type." He gave a shrug.

"So you decided to see what you could get out of me." Livia's words were bitter.

Sirco tipped his head at her. "You were almost as much work as your brother. And ultimately about as useful." He sighed. "So I became every wave rider's friend in order to work out where to find good places to dredge the sea floor."

He waved a hand at Cal. "When I first came, we thought it might be possible to rob the warehouse." He gave a laugh. "Oh, we were so naive. When we realized that was impossible, given your security, we decided to harvest it ourselves." He pointed to Anja. "And her little pod's waters seemed like the best place. The wave riders were too active near Rinc, so I did a few reconnaissance trips to see how isolated things were down here, and realized we could do what we liked, as long as we killed the comms to Anja's cottage, just in case she saw us and got it into her head to warn anyone."

"But we aren't in the southern pod's waters here. Or only the outer edges of them," Anja said.

"The spaceship changed things a bit. I've had to be very flexible the last month or so." Sirco shrugged. "I managed to find out from the wave riders I spoke with that these islands are where the pods come during mating season."

"There's a lot of sea floor around these islands." Cal infused as much contempt into his voice as he could. "Good luck finding tiny pieces of druk."

"True, but these bays are where they mate, aren't they? Nice, calm water. A little shallower. And as the pod homed right in on this bay, I'm guessing it's a regular hangout. So chances are there's druk here. And as an extra bonus, it won't be too deep." Sirco tipped his head toward the pod. "That's why Jake shot at them. He hoped it would make them leave so we could get on with it without them in the way."

"Dredging the seabed will disturb the pod." Leonie spoke for the first time. "It's not just illegal, it'll be dangerous for whoever does it."

Sirco laughed. "I'm aware. That's why I'm not going to be the one to do it."

Cal had a bad feeling about who *was* going to be doing it.

"And the ancestral spaceship?" Livia sounded tired. Cal glanced at his sister, worried about her, but her face was almost impossible to read.

"The researchers Jake's boss hired to look through data on where the most druk was likely to be found on the ocean floor, found mention of the signal. Got them all very excited, apparently."

"So this turned into a double theft. The druk, and the tech from the spaceship." Ritt moved a little, and Sirco's elbow shot up, the laz pressing even harder against the side of Leonie's head.

"Oh, no you don't." He lifted the hand holding the flare gun, pointing it straight into the air, and shot it off.

The flare sizzled as it flew upward, bright pink and cheerful against the blue sky.

"Calling your friends?" Cal asked, although the answer was obvious.

"Jake brought special equipment down with him that sucks up sediment from the ocean floor. But after the leviathans attacked him like they did, he decided it would be better if you got the druk for us."

Cal knew he wouldn't like who was expected to do the dredging.

A faint hiss seemed to emanate from Sirco's chest, and he pulled down his jacket to reveal a small device clipped to his shirt beneath.

"You in control there, Sirco?" The voice was disembodied and sibilant.

"Yes. They'll be coming toward you in the boat in a few minutes. Do you have contact with Jake?" Sirco glanced up at the sky again.

He was sweating about the Arkhorans, Cal realized. He wanted to pass the information about their imminent arrival on to Jake. But whatever comms devices they were using only had a short range.

"The cliffs are blocking us. We'd have to go back out into the open sea to make contact. Is it important?"

"This lot say the Arkhorans are on their way." Sirco made it sound as if he didn't know whether to believe them or not, but Cal knew he did believe them.

He was hedging his bets. Just in case the Arkhorans didn't come and he was blamed for making Jake rush and maybe not get as much tech out as he wanted to.

Cal watched him closely. He was nervous more than hyped up. He was going along with this because he knew with his runner out of commission, he either made himself useful enough to be taken off planet at the end of this, or he'd be left behind to face the consequences.

And as he'd said, the Arkhorans weren't here now, and Jake and his runner with its laz cannons were.

He was a pragmatist.

"Do you want us to tell him?" The voice on the other end wavered in and out.

"Wait until the wave riders get to you. One of you can take their boat out and contact Jake while they're diving."

What came through Sirco's device in response was nothing more than a crackling sound, as if the person on the other end had said something, but had cut off comms before it could be transmitted.

Sirco did not try to get him back to clarify.

Good to know.

Sirco caught Cal watching him and narrowed his eyes. "You take your boat out to meet them. They'll let me know when you get there. After that, I'll get a report from Fida every fifteen minutes that all is well. If I don't, I shoot your mother." He pointed the flare gun at Cal to make his point clear. "I won't kill her. Not right away. I'll shoot her on medium strength with the laz. And if in fifteen minutes I still don't hear from Fida, I'll shoot her again. And again." His lips turned up in a parody of a smile. "You understand?"

His mother might live through one, or maybe two such hits, but not three.

Cal nodded. "I understand."

He wondered if his overwhelming urge to kill Sirco showed on his face.

He could feel it coming from Liv as well, and also from every other person in the team. Even Anja, who didn't know his mother at all.

Some of the feeling was fueled by residual echoes from the silver ball's time with Devinia. He knew because his first image of dealing with Sirco had involved ripping him up with his teeth.

He managed to fight that urge back.

"Do what you have to do to be safe," his mother said. She had kept still and calm throughout, but there was a steely edge to her now, and Cal knew she would take whatever opportunity she could.

Yavish was grim-faced and Donnella looked in shock.

He caught Yavish's eye and the administrator gave a tiny nod.

He would take whatever opening Sirco gave him. But Cal knew Yavish would do nothing to endanger his mother.

That was fine with him.

A throb of an engine sounded near the entrance to the tiny bay but came no closer.

Kada and a few of the other members of the pod turned toward it. Kada let out a warning boom, but none of them moved.

Devinia must be very near the end.

"Get in your boat and go out there to meet them." Sirco eyed the pod warily. "I've stripped it of everything useful, so there's nothing that'll help you in there. They'll tell you what to do."

"Why aren't they coming in closer?" Walef asked, and Cal knew he did it to force Sirco to admit his and Jake's weakness.

"You know why." Sirco understood that Walef was needling him, too.

"Scared?" Anja asked, voice soft and derisive. "Afraid of the big, bad leviathans?"

"They leaped out of the water and fucking knocked Jake's runner out of the sky. We're not insane, so yes, we're afraid of the leviathans." Sirco's words came out between clenched teeth. "Now get in the fucking boat, and go out and meet my colleagues."

Demi and Ritt didn't move. There was no discussion about it, they just stood still as Cal, Anja, Walef and Livia obeyed Sirco's order.

"All of you, I said." Sirco waved the hand with the spent flare gun in agitation, and pointed it at Demi and Ritt.

"They aren't fit enough," Cal said as he got a grip on the side of the boat. "Ritt damaged his ribs when you threw him out of the runner into the ocean, and you shot Demi yourself. You know she isn't up for it."

Sirco hesitated, then waved the gun again. "They can do less strenuous tasks. But I'm not having any of you on this beach with me. Go."

Reluctantly now, when before Demi had fought him every step of the way when it came to staying behind, Demi and Ritt joined them.

"Sorry," Demi mouthed to him.

He shrugged. It wasn't her fault. But it would have been good to leave her and Ritt behind. They'd have found a way to get the laz from Sirco and neutralize the threat he posed, he was sure of it.

Sirco had been afraid of exactly that happening.

They gave the boat a push together and jumped in. It glided backward through the water and then spun just as the engine engaged, turning smoothly as Cal accelerated away.

They sped past the pod, who were still agitated.

Anja leaned over the side as they passed Kada, and he guessed she was trying to communicate with him.

The inflatable that was waiting for them at the mouth of the bay was much larger than the three small ones from the runner; at least a twelve seater.

There were large, flexible pipes piled on one end of it.

Three droppers stood inside, all armed with weapons.

Jake must have brought the weapons down with him. Cal didn't know how anyone would legitimately have access to so many laz.

The droppers watched closely as Cal steered his boat up beside them, and then they spread out, training their weapons on the team as they clambered from one vessel to the other.

As soon as they were in the inflatable, one of the droppers tied Cal's boat to the side.

So they weren't going straight out to let Jake know about the Arkhorans.

That surprised Cal.

One of the men tapped a device similar to the one Sirco had clipped to his shirt, and confirmed they had arrived.

His mother was safe for the next fifteen minutes.

From the corner of his eye he saw Anja edging close to the equipment.

"Stay back, where I can see you." One of the men pointed his laz at her chest and she lifted her hands innocently and backed away.

Something rose up in Cal's chest, an almost overwhelming desire to leap across and knock the laz from the man's hand. Snap his neck.

He had been careless earlier with Sirco and now his mother was in danger, but he would not let anyone touch Anja.

If they did . . .

Anja shot him a quick look, as if she had somehow picked up the feeling roiling inside him.

"Same here," she said to him, and he thought there was a tremble of emotion in her voice.

For a moment, her words made no sense, and then he understood.

Their gazes locked, and Walef cleared his throat behind them.

"Your timing sucks, people."

"No, it's perfect." Anja shot Walef a grin over her shoulder, lightening the mood, and lifting Cal's spirits.

Hard, choppy waves suddenly rocked the inflatable, and Anja seemed to lose her balance for a moment. She put out a hand to brace herself, reaching for the machinery, but she just wasn't close enough.

"What now?" Cal asked the droppers, stepping forward, arms crossed over his chest, to distract attention from her.

Unfortunately, the guard's aim on her didn't waver.

"Now we send you down to hold the pipes," the one who seemed to be in charge said. Cal recalled Sirco mentioning a Fida.

This was probably he.

"How does it work?" Anja asked.

Cal wondered if they were suspicious about how sweetly she asked the question, because there was no doubt in his mind she was going to try to make sure it didn't work at all as soon as possible.

He really loved this woman.

"I'm going to attach the pipes to these valves. You're going to swim down with them. When you're down, you tug to let us know you're on the seabed and then we start up the pump. It'll suck the sand up. You move the pipes around to get as much of the seabed as possible. When you have to come up to breathe, tug and we'll switch off and wait for you to come up."

"You don't have any breathing apparatus?" Livia asked.

"They're using it in the spaceship, in that big underwater atrium. So, no."

"You don't want the pump running when we're in the water, only when we're on the sea floor?" Walef asked.

"It can handle the water, but it's a waste of energy, and we only have so much." Fida clipped in the first pipe, and Cal realized the pump was in the middle of the inflatable, and the valves were spaced evenly around it.

They would be three to a side, like a strange insect floating on the surface with pipe legs extended down.

"How does the pump deal with the sand?" Demi asked. She studied the machine.

"Don't worry about that." Fida clipped in another pipe. "You just swim."

"The moment you start the pump, the pod will react." Ritt had said almost nothing until now. His dark hair was a ruffled halo of curls around his face, and he looked peaceful and calm, but Cal could feel the fury roiling just below the surface.

The three men looked uneasily at each other. The pod had quietened down since the big inflatable's engine had stopped, but they were still alert, looking toward the mouth of the bay.

"Fida?" One of the men asked the leader. He looked very uncertain.

Fida looked back at spaceship island and then toward the pod. He was caught between Jake and the leviathans.

Cal worked out that Fida was more afraid of Jake than the pod when he lifted the last pipe and clipped it in.

So be it.

He would play along with this for a while, see how things worked. And when he found a weakness in their plans, he wouldn't hesitate to pounce.

22

———————

ANJA SHRUGGED OFF HER JACKET AND THEN HER SHIRT, AND FOUND all eyes on her, enemy and friend alike.

"What? You want me to swim in my clothes? That I just got dry in front of the fire?" she asked, seriously astonished. These people were so afraid of the naked form. It was so foreign to an Aponi like herself.

"No." Fida shook his head, but he seemed flummoxed. "Obviously that would slow you down. But we don't have anything . . ." His gaze darted around the boat, as if there might be some swimming gear he had somehow overlooked.

"Well then." Anja folded her jacket and shirt, and sat to pull off her boots.

Reluctantly, very reluctantly, the others did the same.

When she had her pants off and stood in her underwear, she saw Cal relax a little, as if he had been afraid she was going to strip completely naked. She wouldn't have minded, but she knew the Fynians would.

At least this time she actually had underwear on under her

clothes, unlike their headlong dive into the bay to comfort Devinia.

She didn't understand why Cal was so invested in her state of undress, but she looked forward to teasing him about it when there weren't three laz pointed at her.

"Grab a pipe," Fida said. He seemed to have gotten over the discomfort he felt at their lack of clothes, but the other two droppers didn't seem to know where to look.

Anja took the one beside Cal. The pod was not going to like the pump, she guessed. Maybe she wouldn't need to fry it.

Kada could just smash it.

And hopefully not smash them at the same time.

She jumped into the water.

Its icy embrace gripped her, and while she knew she should be in shock at the sudden cold, she only felt delight.

The water wasn't deep. When she touched the sandy bottom, the boat was clearly visible above.

She looked across at the others, saw Cal had been waiting for them to reach the bottom, and he tugged the pipe as soon as they were all down.

A deep throb started up, audible even on the sea floor.

Anja felt the pipe jerk in her hands and almost lost it in surprise, but she managed to hold on and had to fight with it to point the open end down into the sand at her feet.

The suction began, churning up sediment around her. In moments she could barely see her hand in front of her face, let alone Cal and the others.

She tugged at the pipe.

She could hold her breath longer, she could feel it, but the droppers didn't know that, and she wasn't going to make it easier for them.

The others would do the same, she was sure.

The throbbing sound cut off and she pushed off the seabed, still blinded by the sediment in the water.

As she surfaced, pushing hair out of her eyes, she caught a glimpse of a leviathan, high out of the water, neck flung back to smack it down on the boat.

The inflatable reversed, leaving the team in the water, the pipes trailing behind it, as the leviathan's neck slapped the water.

Kada.

She felt no fear, she simply let the waves caused by his attack carry her out of immediate range.

He lifted up again, not quite leaping from the water but definitely getting some height to see where the boat had gone.

The engine cut off, and the inflatable, with Cal's boat attached, drifted silently.

With a grunt, Kada sank beneath the waves and didn't re-emerge, and she turned toward the pod.

Sure enough, his head popped up close to Devinia after a few minutes.

She glanced over at Cal.

Smiled.

Demi was beside her on her right. "Better try to keep a straight face," she told Anja. "Pretend to be just as terrified as they are."

"Will that fly?" Walef swum closer. He, Ritt and Livia had been on the other side, and they joined together in their familiar grouping. "We are wave riders."

"Let's be serious and concerned," Cal said. "See what it gets us."

Livia half-hid a snort. "I don't think they're going to run that pump again."

"I agree." Anja nodded at her. "Let's make a song and dance about being freezing, needing time to warm up between dives, and also offer to dive and scoop druk off the floor by hand."

"Why would we do that?" Walef asked.

"Because we want Leonie and the others to stay alive. This way, they're still getting druk as best they can, so they can tell themselves Jake won't kill them. And we draw it out. Resting often, warming up. Diving for short periods."

"Giving the Arkhorans time to get to us." Cal nodded slowly. "And they haven't passed that message on to Jake, did you notice?"

"They're frightened of us," Ritt said. "They didn't want one to leave. They think they need all three with weapons to manage us."

"Which they do," Demi said. "Anja almost got her hands on that pump."

They had moved through the water as they spoke, and now they were close enough to the inflatable to hear the three droppers talking to each other. One was close to shouting, so it wasn't difficult, but just in case, they went quiet, concentrating on swimming faster to reach the side of the boat.

Cal got there first and pulled himself up, hauling them all in after him one by one.

"Cold." Anja let her whole body shiver and her teeth chatter.

She was actually feeling cold now, but these idiots should have been wondering why they didn't have hypothermia.

She would like to see how they managed even five minutes in the icy water.

"Towels or blankets," Cal demanded of Fida.

But all three men looked like helping the team was the last thing on their minds.

They were arguing with each other about going back to spaceship island, and with a narrow-eyed look, Cal pushed past them to find something himself.

It galvanized the rest of them, and they started looking for supplies. Food, jah, towels.

As she moved past it, Anja let her fingertip trail across the pump and felt a little buzz under her skin.

Now they would have to take the offer of free-diving for druk over sucking up the sand, no matter who won the argument currently underway.

Fida seemed to wake up to the fact that the team were all around him, and that he and his two colleagues were distracted.

"Get away from the equipment," he barked at Anja.

She lifted her arms out at her sides, to emphasize she was nearly naked. "What do you think I can do to it?"

He grimaced, and flinched when Cal tossed Anja a towel and she caught it mid-air.

A chirp came from the comms device clipped to his neckline.

"Were you attacked?" Sirco asked. "I saw a leviathan breaching."

"What do you think?" Fida's voice shook. "Yes, we were attacked. That thing nearly killed us."

"Any damage?"

Fida looked around the inflatable, and Anja had the feeling it was for the first time since they'd reversed and then cut the engine.

"I don't think so." He moved to the pump, checked it, and then swore. "Something might have happened to the pump." His hand hovered over the on button and he hesitated.

One of the droppers grabbed his forearm and shook his head vigorously.

"It's damaged," Fida said, and the two droppers with him almost let out a breath of relief.

"Shit. What are you going to do?"

"It's not my fault a fucking monster tried to land on us." Fida sounded close to hysterical.

"We know whose fault it is," Sirco said. "I wasn't blaming you. Are you going to go back?"

"You know the reception we'll get."

"We can free-dive for druk," Anja said. "But we need to warm up now and eat something before we can go back down."

"The druk is visible?" Fida sounded skeptical.

"I saw some before the pump stirred up so much sediment I couldn't even see the end of my own nose," Ritt told him.

"Did you get that?" Fida asked Sirco.

"Yes. They're being very helpful."

Anja could read skepticism in Sirco's tone, but he had no choice but to accept it, she supposed.

She would do whatever she could to narrow his choices more and more. Until there was only one possible outcome for both Jake and Sirco.

Defeat.

23

"THE SEDIMENT IS CLEARING. I CAN SEE THE BOTTOM." ROALD, ONE of Fida's fellow droppers, looked over his shoulder. "You can go down again."

The old Anja would have dreaded going back into the freezing water.

The new Anja actually looked forward to it, but she pretended reluctance. It wasn't difficult to be convincing.

"Have you felt the water?" she asked him. She hunched over in her seat, shoulders raised.

He curled a lip at her, but refused to look her in the eyes.

He, Fida, and Gyntree, the other dropper, were nervous they were even doing this. Proceeding without the pump.

But the pump would bring the leviathans, and right now, they feared that more than Jake.

Not that the pump would work, but they hadn't tried it again, and they didn't know that.

This was the only way to get druk. And they needed druk. Badly.

"Get in and swim," Fida said, his hand curled around the comms device attached to his shirt.

The threat was clear.

Get in, or he'd contact Sirco and Sirco would harm Leonie.

"What do you want us to put the druk in?" Cal asked. He had risen to his feet as the threat was made, and Fida looked a little wide eyed at the sudden movement.

He was right to be.

It had been purely predatory.

Anja could feel Cal's rage chained just beneath the surface.

It affected her. It affected the others.

Livia's feelings seemed off, but Anja understood that, too.

She had been betrayed and manipulated, and she was as angry with herself as she was with Sirco.

Cal's question had thrown Fida. He looked around the inflatable blankly. "A box, or something?"

"Something. If we have to use our hands, we won't get much." Cal's response was dry.

They had all just eaten a ready-meal and Fida pointed to the empty containers. "Use those. You each have one."

"Will they be big enough?" Roald asked.

"How much druk did you get from the pipes before you switched off the pump?" Walef asked.

All three of the droppers' heads turned to the pump. They had forgotten about the first haul, Anja realized.

Fida moved to the pump and crouched beside it. "I'll have to turn it on to see."

"Then we'll have to see when we get back to Jake," Gyntree said firmly.

Fida nodded. "Take the containers this time round, and we'll look for something better while you're down there."

They still hadn't gone out in Cal's boat to use the short-range comms to tell Jake about the Arkhorans.

They'd either forgotten, or they were reluctant to give him any bad news.

She wasn't going to complain about it.

None of them had put their clothes back on when they'd swum back up. They'd swaddled themselves in the towels and blankets they'd found under the inflatable's seats and now she shrugged off the blanket she'd been using and set it on the bench behind her.

Cal had his back to her as he did the same. His shoulders and back were sleekly muscled and she couldn't help but stare.

He went still and then glanced at her over his shoulder.

He'd sensed her looking. Maybe even sensed her thoughts.

She didn't look away.

Ritt cleared his throat, and she looked over at him.

"Ritt and Demi shouldn't be diving," she said.

Fida straightened up from beside the pump. "Why not?"

"Ask Sirco. Ritt damaged his ribs, and Sirco himself shot Demi with a laz. She's still recovering."

Fida looked over at them. "They went down before."

"That was when we were just holding pipes. This is going to be harder. At least send them down every second time, to give them time to recover."

"We need you all down there." Fida moved his hand dismissively.

"Again, I'll ask, have you felt the water?" She tilted her head back, and looked at him with utter contempt. "You wouldn't last more than a minute in that water, and you know it, yet you want us in there for a lot more than that."

Fida stepped in front of her and grabbed her arm. "You will go down."

Cal's hand was on his shoulder in the next moment, and the dropper visibly flinched.

"Hands off." He spun, laz lifted.

"Just need a container." Cal's expression said that was a lie.

He was pushing Fida, Anja could see it on his face, but he also really didn't like the dropper putting his hands on her.

Fida could see it, too. He moved back, keeping the laz steady on Cal.

"She didn't say she wouldn't go down. Just that you should let Ritt and Demi rest longer." Cal picked up a container from the bench and handed it to Anja.

She let her fingers linger on his as she took it from him.

"I'll allow your friends to rest. But you better make up for it in druk. Now get. In. The water." Fida's words were spoken through gritted teeth.

Anja glanced at Ritt and Demi. Ritt was careful not to meet her gaze, but the way he held himself told her he'd be watching for any opportunity.

Anja stepped onto the side of the inflatable and jumped in.

Around her, the sound of the other three jumping in filled her ears.

She angled down, eyes on the sandy floor of the bay, and saw her first piece of druk.

It wasn't big, around the size of her thumbnail. She picked it up, and realized there was druk all around them.

Whatever Sirco was, he was certainly no fool. And he and Jake had picked an excellent place to harvest druk.

She filled the container, choosing the smallest pieces she could, and slowly rose up to the surface.

The container was grabbed from her before she could pull herself up, and she saw that was because Walef seemed to have tipped his into the boat when he'd surfaced, and Gyntree was scrabbling on the bottom of the inflatable, picking up small pieces.

She shared a quick look with Walef, and forced herself not to smile.

Cal came up behind her, giving her a boost over the side of the inflatable, and she landed lightly and turned, hand out to help him.

As they grabbed towels and dried off, Cal glanced over at his sister, his expression worried.

Livia had come up last, and she was still too quiet.

Anja touched Cal's hand, stood up and found a seat beside Livia as Fida gave them each a cup of jah.

He was pleased with their haul, she could see. He ran his fingers through the druk and there was calculation on his face.

He was thinking about hiding a few pieces, she could tell. He was thinking Jake would never know.

"You all right?"

Livia glanced at her. "No."

"Sirco fooled you, and you feel betrayed."

Livia opened her mouth, closed it, and then looked across at Anja and held her gaze. "Sirco got information out of me that helped him attack you and my brother, hold my mother hostage, and rob my planet." Her mouth was set in a grim line.

"Information he could have gotten from someone else, and they wouldn't have hesitated to give it to him, because he was a friendly scientist from the VSC Research Institute."

Livia thought about it. "Probably. But he focused on me because Cal is trade emissary."

"And got so little out of you, he decided he'd have to drag the seabed for druk instead."

Livia considered her words. Gave a slow nod.

"So . . ?" Anja decided too much talk and Livia would feel like she was being managed.

"So it isn't my fault. But I still feel betrayed."

Anja nodded, clinked cups with Liv. The jah felt amazing as it went down.

She caught Cal's gaze. He was sitting beside Ritt, checking his ribs. He flicked his gaze over to Demi and she gave a slight nod and moved across.

Demi was lying curled on her side on a bench, looking miserable.

"You all right?" she murmured as she felt Demi's forehead for a fever. "What can you tell me?"

"They're petrified of Kada. Like, panic-stricken." Demi's whisper held a hint of amusement. "And they think Ritt is way more dangerous than I am. And if I lie down, they don't look at me at all. Well, once or twice, because I think they were annoyed I wasn't diving."

"Did they contact Sirco?"

Demi nodded. "Fida has a timer to remind him. They spoke for a bit, including about Ritt and me. Then Sirco reminded them about the Arkhorans coming. They'd actually forgotten." She gave a tiny smile. "I think Kada took all their mental energy."

"Are they going to warn Jake?"

Demi gave a shrug. "Don't know. Walef was coming up, so Fida cut the conversation short, but I think they're afraid the sound of the engine will attract Kada's attention."

Anja could see the possibilities with that scenario. She gave a slow smile. "Fida might force you down with us next time, but if we can persuade him to let you rest for the dive after that, look for a chance to do something." She kept her tone crooning, as if she were talking to a sick child.

"Will do." Demi flashed her a quick grin, and then closed her eyes.

Anja left her, moving carefully across to Ritt and Cal as waves hit the boat with short, choppy smacks.

Roald, one of the droppers, flinched with each shudder of the inflatable.

Demi was right. He was terrified.

Anja crouched beside Ritt and Cal, helping Cal strap Ritt's ribs with bandages from a small medkit. She put her head close to his and whispered what Demi had told her.

"They're afraid the sound of the motor will bring Kada back?" He looked thoughtful. "We can use that."

They definitely could.

24

———

Clouds had been building in the blue sky above. Cal could feel the air getting colder.

Beside him, even with the blanket wrapped around her, Anja shivered.

He was tired of this.

He didn't mind going into the water, he liked it, but his body used up precious resources to keep him warm every time he did.

He could see they looked thinner than they had.

"We need food." He swallowed the last of his jah and looked over at Fida. "We're using too much energy trying to keep our core temperature up in the freezing water."

Fida looked like he wanted to argue on principle, but he wanted druk more.

He handed out meals, and they sat in silence and ate.

Close by—closer than he had been—Kada let out a bellow.

Roald made a noise, a half-squeak, half-cry. "He's coming back."

Fida stood, shielding his eyes against the glare on the water. His face looked grim and frightened.

"We have to call Jake." Gyntree glanced at Kada, then at Fida, and swallowed nervously.

"Will the engine noise attract the leviathans?" Fida asked Cal.

Cal nodded. "Usually that's not a problem, we want them to come closer, but this is a wild pod, not one of the groups we harvest druk from off the Rinc coast, so they're not used to coming close. And since Jake shot them, they're angry. I don't think they'll be too happy to hear a motor after what just happened to them."

"Shit," Gyntree whispered. "What do we do?"

"You've dealt with lots of leviathans, right?" Fida asked.

"I'm a wave rider. But as I said, this is a wild pod." Cal made a movement with his hands, conveying that anything could happen.

"Still." Fida looked over at Gyntree. "You go out with him. He steers, you make sure you keep your laz on him, and take the comms device. Keep trying until you get Jake, and then get back here."

Gyntree hesitated, looked over at Kada, and then at the boat.

He was the one insisting on getting hold of Jake, and Cal could see that now he would have to put himself in danger to do it, he was reconsidering.

Cal was tempted to say something to tip the scales, but he kept his mouth shut. Anything he said would be treated with suspicion.

"Well?" Fida asked.

"Don't give me any trouble." Gyntree turned to Cal, laz in hand.

Fida unhooked the comms unit from his jacket, but he activated it before he handed it over to Gyntree. "Sirco, we're going to let Jake know about the Arkhorans. I won't have the comm device until Gyntree gets back."

"Don't hesitate to shoot them if they look like they're going to try something." Sirco's voice was fuzzy and distorted, but his words were clear enough.

"No need to tell me. I'll let you know as soon as Gyntree's back." Fida clicked off, and Gyntree hooked the device to his shirt.

He waved his laz at Cal, and Cal took that to mean he should get into his boat.

He hopped over easily, moving to the motor at the back.

Gyntree clambered more awkwardly into the smaller vessel and then sat on the bench that was fitted into the prow. He faced Cal, the laz steady on Cal's chest.

"Untie the boat." Fida motioned to Anja, and she moved over and untied the knot holding the two vessels together.

Cal caught her gaze and she gave a tiny nod of understanding.

Then he slowly opened the motor and the boat began to move out to the mouth of the bay.

Kada gave a snort behind them as soon as the motor started and ducked under the water, and Gyntree shot to his feet, his whole body tense as his gaze focused on the sea around them.

"Is he coming?" His question was a whisper.

"Sounds like it," Cal said.

Gyntree was clutching his laz tightly, but he was no longer pointing it at Cal.

They were too close to the inflatable for him to make a move, though. Cal needed them to be out of the bay before he took control, out of Fida and Roald's sight.

The water got rougher as they headed out, and then Kada suddenly lifted up beside them, his huge eye peering at them before he sank back down.

Gyntree gave a cry of alarm and discharged his laz, the beam bouncing off the water with a sizzle.

"Stop." Cal turned on him, fury burning in his blood. "You hit him, you'll just enrage him."

"All right, all right." Gyntree lowered the laz, pointing it down. "I didn't mean to do that, I just reacted."

He moved to the side of the boat, ignoring Cal completely.

Kada followed them, coming up on one side, then the other.

Cal didn't know how much of Kada's behavior was due to his direction, but he was certainly sending Kada mental images of playful interaction.

When he came up and exhaled right beside them, sending a spray of water over the boat, Gyntree's knuckles were white where he gripped the side of the boat.

"Do you think he's toying with us?" His voice was not steady.

"Yes." Cal rounded the curve of land that sheltered the bay from the open sea, and as he did, Kada breached, the large flippers on his right side almost brushing the boat as he launched himself out of the water.

It was a magnificent sight, and as Gyntree stumbled back in terror, Cal moved.

He grabbed the laz out of Gyntree's hand, and then pushed Gyntree over the side as the boat lifted up in the massive wake of Kada's landing.

The dropper tried to scream when he hit the water, but the cold seemed to suck the air from his lungs.

He gasped, flailing, and turned desperately to see where Kada had gone.

The ripples were still radiating outward from where Kada had landed, and Cal used the lift of one to haul Gyntree back in the boat.

The dropper tried to scramble away from Cal, struggling to move in his wet clothes, and then, when Kada boomed a call almost right next to them, he curled into a ball.

"Don't put me back in the water with him. Don't."

"Sure," Cal said easily. "What's going to happen is you're going to sit quietly as we go back to Fida and the others, and you're going to pretend everything is fine." He looked around his boat for something to tie Gyntree up with, but Sirco had been telling the truth when he'd said he'd stripped it.

He had the idea to pat Gyntree down, and found two pairs of flexible restraints in an inside pocket of his jacket. He put one pair over Gyntree's wrists and then hauled him onto the bench where he'd been sitting before.

He unclipped the comms device and wondered if it was waterproof. He put it in a pocket, in case it did still work.

"Kada doesn't like people who shoot at him. And Jake hit him with a laz cannon earlier, so he's still carrying a grudge. You do anything to call attention to the fact that I'm in control now, and I will toss you in and leave you there. If Kada doesn't get you, the cold will."

Gyntree nodded, his whole body hunched over and shivering. "How . . . how do you do it? I can't think after being in that water. How do you dive down and get druk when it's that cold?"

"Training and practice." It wouldn't do for Gyntree to think there was something unnatural about their abilities.

He turned the boat, knowing Fida was more likely to be happy to see them returning than suspicious they'd gotten hold of Jake so quickly.

He angled back into the bay and headed toward the inflatable, which seemed empty. As he steered closer, Cal realized Fida had sent the whole team, including Demi and Ritt, down to dive.

He slowed the boat, giving everyone time to come back up before he reached them. The moment Fida realized Gyntree was a prisoner, he would start shooting.

Fida's full focus was on watching him and Gyntree approach, or watching Kada follow them, perhaps.

Cal saw Livia's head pop up at the side of the inflatable, behind Fida. The dropper didn't react or turn. She suddenly lifted right out of the water, as if levitating, stood on the inflatable's side, grabbed Fida, and spun as she threw him overboard.

Walef pulled himself into the inflatable after her.

He must have given her a boost up to take Fida out, Cal thought, impressed.

Roald had turned when Fida cried out, but Anja levitated out of the water as well, lifting so high she was almost level with him.

She grabbed his jacket and as she fell back in, she took him with her.

Ritt and Demi's heads popped up, and they got in the boat, then hauled Anja up as soon as she surfaced.

Ritt bent down and scooped a laz off the bottom of the boat. Roald must have dropped it before he was dragged into the sea.

"That was quite a breach move," Cal called as he brought the boat up alongside the inflatable.

Anja looked over at him, saw Gyntree sitting hunched and restrained at the other end of the boat, and grinned. "Might have had a little help from Ritt and Demi."

Ritt had obviously been tracking the two droppers they'd thrown into the bay, and he joined Cal in the boat as Anja and Livia tied it back onto the inflatable.

He helped Cal haul Roald up, and Cal used the second set of restraints on him and shoved him onto the bench next to Gyntree.

"Fida?" Cal asked.

"Here." Walef pointed off the side of the inflatable.

"Come this side, or we won't pull you up," Cal called to him.

He couldn't see Fida's face, but after a moment he could hear the splash of someone moving in the water, and Fida's head popped up near the prow of his boat.

Cal searched Roald, digging into the inner pockets of his jacket, and pulled out more restraints.

He and Ritt pulled Fida up, secured him, and added him to the bench.

"Good job." Cal jumped back into the inflatable, Ritt right behind him. He pulled the comms device out of his pocket and waved it. "Now let's see if this still works after a dunking in the sea."

25

———

THEY WERE RIDING HIGH.

Anja let the feeling boost her as she dried herself off and handed a damp towel to Cal.

At least their clothes, still neatly folded on a bench, were dry, but she opted to stay out of them a little longer while her smart fabric underwear dried.

Demi and Walef made jah and handed it out, and dug out another meal.

There was enough left over for the three droppers and Anja took the food over to them, already opened so they didn't have to struggle to open the containers with their hands restrained.

They gulped down the hot jah first and then ate, looking miserable.

"The water's cold, isn't it?" she said, conversationally.

Fida lifted his gaze and glared at her. "Let us dry off or we'll freeze to death."

They might actually be in danger of that, Anja decided. Roald's lips were pale blue and he'd stopped shivering altogether.

She got a few towels and gave them to Gyntree and Fida,

tipping her head at Roald. "You'll have to help him, he's in worse shape than you."

It seemed as if they hadn't realized that before. Gyntree dried his hair and face, and then did the same to Roald, but Fida ignored them both, seeing to himself first.

Anja left them to it, and hopped back into the inflatable.

Cal and Ritt were hunched over the comms device. They'd dried it off, but water could have got inside it.

"Let's buzz Sirco like that time before we left the beach, a sort of crackle but no words." Ritt lifted the device up to catch the light, turning it in his hands.

"Wait until it's dark, or almost dark. We can't approach the beach like we are now, he'll know straightaway the droppers are our prisoners." Anja looked up at the sky.

It was no longer clear blue. Clouds had begun to build for another storm and it lent an urgency to their plans they hadn't had before.

It was already mid-afternoon and the sky was beginning to darken. They wouldn't have long to wait.

Ritt lowered his hand, nodded. "It'll give it longer to dry out, as well."

"And if it doesn't work?" Demi asked. She'd dried off completely and dressed, and her short corkscrew curls danced in the breeze.

"If it doesn't work, we have no choice but to go in, keep up a pretense until we land," Cal said. He had come to stand beside Anja, and he drew her close.

She tucked in under his arm, and relaxed for the first time since he'd gone off in his boat with Gyntree.

"Sirco will be suspicious." Walef stated the obvious.

"Sure, but we don't have another option." Cal didn't need to say that one way or another, Sirco was going to be a danger to Leonie, Donnella and Yavish.

"I hate waiting." Livia was still drying her long, dark hair, and she twisted it in her hands to wring out the last of the sea water. "Let's go as soon as the light fades."

"That should be in about an hour." Walef shrugged on his jacket. "Gyntree didn't get hold of Jake, did he?"

Cal shook his head. "He didn't do much once we rounded the mouth of the bay. Thanks to Kada, he was too busy imagining his doom to do more than grip the side of the boat and get off a few panicked potshots."

"Did he hit Kada?" Ritt turned to look at Gyntree. There was something more than a little predatory in the movement.

"No. And I persuaded him he'd be a lot more sorry if he hit Kada than the other way around."

Ritt gave a slow nod, but he watched Gyntree for a few more moments before he turned back to the group.

Anja picked up one of the containers of druk. "Over the side?" she asked.

Everyone had to think about it, first. It probably went against everything in them to throw druk back, but no one wanted Jake getting it.

Eventually everyone nodded. Anja tossed the druk over the side, and then did it for the other containers, as well.

The wave riders looked pained.

"Let's rest a bit," Walef suggested, when the last piece of druk disappeared into the sea. "We've got some time before it gets dark enough to head in, and we need it."

They settled on the benches, and Anja pulled on her clothes, the last one to do so, she saw with amusement.

The Fynians had been in a lot more of a hurry to get dressed than she had.

Cal waited until she'd fastened her jacket and made space for her beside him, so they sat together, leaning back against the air-filled side of the inflatable.

She was almost comfortable, Anja realized. She closed her eyes, warm under the blanket he'd pulled over them, happy to let the boat rock her into a doze.

She could feel the hard outline of the laz in Cal's jacket and shifted it out of the way. "Did that go into the water, too?"

His lips curved against her temple. "No. I took it off him before I threw him in."

"Did anyone check Fida for his?"

He nodded. "It's gone. Probably at the bottom of the sea."

She forced her eyes open and turned to him. "Shouldn't someone in Rinc have come looking for your mother by now?"

He lifted a shoulder. "Maybe tomorrow. They'd assume she'd keep looking for us, as long as she had the light, and return in the darkness tonight. When she doesn't come back, they'll wait until first light tomorrow, and then I'm guessing more than one runner will come this way, given two runners have disappeared already."

"Damn." That was too bad.

"We're a small population, and that's just how we have to live, especially without wireless comms." Cal shrugged again.

"So between now and tomorrow morning, the only hope we have are the Arkhorans."

"Realistically, yes," Cal said. "I'd like to make sure Jake and his droppers can't leave while we wait to be rescued, though. And can't shoot at any other leviathans or runners."

"Agreed." She snuggled in closer, drowsy with warmth.

Nearby, Kada exhaled, and she realized he'd been circling them since Cal returned.

She looked over at him, and sent thoughts of good wishes for Devinia his way.

He sank down under the surface, and when he reemerged, he was lying beside his grandmother again.

Devinia was very still.

If she was still alive, Anja thought she was hanging on by a thread.

"What are the droppers doing?" She yawned into Cal's chest. She noticed he hadn't taken his eyes off them, even though he seemed completely relaxed.

"Trying to dry off. Fida's a little apart from the others, and keeps rubbing something in his pocket."

"Druk." She closed her eyes again and felt an almost weeping relief at being able to rest her body completely for a change. "I thought he wouldn't be able to resist taking some."

"Even though we weren't really trying, we managed to bring up a fair amount." Cal extended his leg a little and poked at one of the now empty containers of druk on the floor of the boat.

"There's a lot down there. Maybe we can free dive for it when this is over. In thermal diving gear."

He brushed a hand over her hair. "What're your plans when this is over? Will you go back to your research?"

She shook her head. "I think I told you before how much I hated the isolation. I decided I was done with my project before Sirco's droppers attacked me."

"But will you stay?" His voice was neutral, but she thought he tensed beneath her. "I know I have no right to ask you, but still, I really want you to stay." His grip on her jacket tightened. "It almost frightens me how much."

She lifted her head, looked into his eyes. "And I was wondering if there's a job for a marine biologist in Rinc."

His body relaxed, and he pressed a kiss to her hair. "Well, if there isn't, you could always be a wave rider."

"Or a druk free-diver. I have a feeling I'll be very good at finding where the most druk is on the seabed. Did you sense it, too? A sort of feeling for where to find it when you get down there?"

"Echoes of Devinia, again," Cal said. "That might be a plan. It would certainly bring in a lot of druk."

And it would keep her on Fynian. It was one of the few places in the VSC where you had to work at an actual job. No one who wasn't born here could take the citizen's dividend and not work, like VSC citizens could do on the seven remaining mother planets if they chose to.

Fynian was too small, had too few resources. Tourists were only allowed to come for a limited time; no extended holidays. You were either born here, here to work, or you left after a month.

Anja let herself doze, feeling happy despite their circumstances.

The silver ball inside her had not liked the idea of her leaving Fynian. Partly because it was invested in Fynian, partly because she got the clear sense the team was paramount.

Not to be broken up.

Would she be able to leave, if she had to?

She didn't know.

It was a good thing she didn't want to.

"It's almost dark, we should contact Sirco." Ritt stirred from his bench, and everyone slowly sat up straight and leaned forward.

Ritt glanced at Cal, and he gave a nod.

Ritt depressed the small button, held it for a moment and then lifted his finger off it.

They waited.

"Didn't get that." Sirco's voice came through scratchy and almost inaudible.

That was good. Because none of them sounded like Fida.

"Coming in," Ritt said. "Jake." He paused. "Use them as hostages." He paused again.

"Still didn't get much." Sirco's response was so distorted, Anja was sure it was only because she had a silver ball helping her hear better that she caught it at all.

"Coming in." Ritt switched the comms device off.

They all shared a look.

Sirco would be expecting them. It was the best they were going to do.

"Ritt and I should slip into the water before you get to the beach and sneak up behind the rocks on the left side. They aren't much cover, but his attention should be on the boats." Demi clasped her hands in front of her. "Of all of us, he'll expect to see Ritt and me up and about the least."

Cal gave a nod. Looked around the group. "Agreed?"

Everyone nodded.

"And if he puts Mom, Donnella and Yavish between the inflatable and himself, what do we do then?" Livia asked.

Walef looked over at the three droppers, and lowered his voice as he tapped the side of his head. "I heard Cal. Just before he took Gyntree out of the bay. He sent a suggestion to Anja that we push the droppers into the water."

Anja nodded. She hadn't had to whisper Cal's suggestion to Walef. He'd already known.

"I didn't get it," Livia said. "Walef had to tell me."

"Me, neither," said Demi. "But I was farther away from him. And if Cal was directing it at Anja, maybe it just leaked out to Walef."

"And maybe I'm just really good at picking up mental messages." Walef cleared his throat. "Like Anja seems to be good at killing machines." The look he sent Cal had Anja fighting a blush. He had perhaps caught a bit more from her and Cal's exchanges than he wanted to.

"How about this?" Cal's gaze swept around, including all of them, and Anja got the picture of everyone rushing Sirco at once.

"That's not a clever idea but I got it," Ritt said.

"Me, too." Livia nodded.

Everyone seemed to have gotten it.

"But that's not the plan?" Demi clarified.

"No. That was a test run. We take it as it comes." Cal fired up the motor of the inflatable and started toward the beach.

They passed the pod, and Anja strained to see Devinia, but there were too many leviathans around her.

Demi and Ritt had pulled off their clothes again and slid into the water.

Walef jumped into Cal's boat and fastened gags on the three droppers.

No sense in taking the chance one of them would try to warn Sirco.

Cal slowed the boat, giving Demi and Ritt time to reach the beach before the inflatable did.

Darkness had fallen swiftly, the last of the sun blocked by the cliffs, and Anja hoped it would be nearly impossible for Sirco to see who was in control of the inflatable.

They'd have only moments before he'd work it out, though.

They'd have to move quickly.

Cal's mother's life depended on it.

26

———

The fire was going strong, Cal saw as he pointed the inflatable at the beach.

The flames leaped high, and he imagined that Sirco had gotten Yavish to scour the shoreline for driftwood.

The flickering light it threw out would hopefully also make it more difficult for Sirco to clearly see who was piloting the boat. He and Walef were similar enough in size and profile to the droppers that they could be mistaken for them at a distance.

Sirco gave a shout of greeting as the inflatable hit the sand and shuddered to a stop.

Cal and Walef jumped out, hauling it out of reach of the frothing waves.

Cal had expected Sirco to approach them, perhaps with his mother still at his side, but he stayed where he was, sitting on a big log by the fire.

His mother knelt in front of him, and Donnella was sitting to the side.

Yavish was nowhere to be seen.

He glanced casually to his left and caught a glimpse of the tops of Demi and Ritt's heads as they used the pitiful cover of the low rocks to work their way toward the fire pit. Then they stopped.

Slowly stood.

Cal frowned as he moved forward, not sure what to expect, when Demi threw back her head and laughed.

Yavish slowly rose from behind Sirco, a laz in his hand.

It looked as if his mother hadn't needed saving after all.

"It's a relief to see you." His mother stood and dusted sand from her behind. "We weren't quite sure how we were going to handle things with three armed droppers."

She looked extremely pleased with herself, and Cal grinned as he pulled her into a hug.

"This was your doing, was it?"

"Well," his mother gave Yavish a sidelong look. "Yavish definitely helped. And Donnella."

Liv was just behind him, and he stepped aside so she could embrace their mother as well.

"We were so worried."

Cal turned back to look at the inflatable. Anja and Walef were getting the three droppers out of the boat, and Ritt had run back to help them move their prisoners to the fire.

"Us, too." His mother followed his gaze. "What are we going to do with them?"

Cal shrugged. "What can we do? Hold them until more help arrives."

"I am not happy with any of this."

Cal gave a chuckle. "I'm sure you're not."

He took a step to go help the others, and his mother's hand closed over his forearm.

"Anja."

He looked over at her. "Yes."

He answered as if she'd asked a question.

She sighed. "Are you sure this thing that's in you now, this nanotech, isn't influencing you somehow? Because I've never seen you so unreserved with a woman before."

He held her gaze. "The nanotech has nothing to do with it."

She looked like she wanted to say more, but then she gave a nod and released him.

"Did you get any druk?" Yavish asked as Cal moved closer to the fire. The laz in his hand was still pressed against Sirco's head.

Cal lifted his hands. "Not sure. Whatever there is, is in the pump, but it's broken." No need to elaborate in front of Sirco. And it might be a good idea for them all to keep quiet about exactly how much druk they'd found down on the bay's floor.

He sent the thought out to everyone, and got tiny nods of agreement back.

They settled down by the fire. The three droppers were put together with Sirco, and given jah and food.

They were running low there, though. Cal had a look at their little pile of supplies. Maybe two more meals, and they'd be out.

"What now?" Ritt handed Demi a cup of jah and sat down by the fire with his own.

"Tomorrow, someone's going to come looking for my mother and Sirco. And given two runners have disappeared, my guess is they'll send at least two runners this time." Cal kept his voice low. They were sitting apart from their prisoners, who were still restrained. There was nowhere for them to run, and Cal didn't think any of them were brave enough to try to escape by stealing a boat and motoring past the pod.

As long as they didn't have access to their weapons, they were no longer a threat. That didn't mean Sirco needed to hear their plans, though.

"Jake still has his runner and its laz cannons." Walef leaned forward, face grim. "And we know he'll use them."

"We were going to try to kill the engines before Sirco arrived. I don't think things have changed since then." Cal looked over at his mother, waiting for her to protest.

She rubbed her face. "These people are so ruthless. It's not something I'm used to, and I'm frightened they'll hurt you."

"We're ruthless, too, Mom." Livia was sitting beside their mother, and she patted her knee. "We are matriarch ruthless."

Cal could see his mother didn't know what to make of that.

"Those search and rescue runners will be flying straight into a danger they won't suspect or even see coming," Ritt said. "We owe it to them to try and make sure Jake can't hurt them."

His mother sighed. "I know."

"We protect each other," Anja said, her voice gentle. "We'll watch each other's backs. And we'll be careful."

That was right.

Cal felt the rightness hit him in the chest, and the others nodded.

"We're a team." Demi's hand formed a fist and she touched it to her chest and then extended it.

For a moment, everyone stared at it, and then Anja leaned forward and put her hand over the fist.

Livia went onto her knees to reach, and placed her hand on top of Anja's and then Ritt and Walef followed.

Cal put his hand on top last and then Demi dipped her hand down and threw it upward.

As they all lifted their hands off, Cal had the sense of a ritual, done many times. A team-building event that was accompanied by a battle cry of some kind.

"What was that?" Donnella asked, voice hushed.

"That was what our ancestors did before they went into battle." Ritt spoke as if he had been knocked off his feet.

Cal felt the same.

"What did they call out?" Walef asked. "They called out something."

"We'll have to come up with something of our own," Anja said. "It doesn't feel complete."

Yavish, Donnella and his mother were looking at them with varying degrees of horror.

"You're shocked." Cal didn't make it a question.

"It's just that you looked . . . different," Donnella finally said. "Harder."

"We are different." Demi hooked her hands over her knees. "Maybe I should feel more worried about it, but I'm not. Without the silver balls, we'd already be dead. Many times over."

There was silence for a while, the sound of the fire and the waves the only noise.

"If the only way I have you here now is because of the silver balls, I'll accept what comes with it." His mother sounded as if she was forcing the words out. "But I worry. And I beg you to be careful." She clasped her hands in front of her.

"I don't understand what's happening to you, and it frightens me." Donnella touched Demi's hand. The one that had formed into a fist.

"All I can say is that it wants to protect us, and it wants to protect Fynian." Cal knew this in his bones. "It was created to help our ancestors settle in new worlds. It means us no harm. If we have a few strange moments, it's because we're adapting to it, and it to us. It's been inside our ancestors—its original recipients, then Devinia, and now us. Give it time."

His mother lifted her head and held his gaze. "Time?"

"Time," he repeated.

He looked over at Yavish and Donnella, then back to his mother.

One by one, they nodded.

Across the water, the sound of Jake's runner starting up broke through the silence, and the droppers and Sirco all turned to look in that direction.

Time had just run out.

27

They approached the tiny beach on spaceship island, where they'd hidden Cal's boat last time. They came in absolute silence, thanks to Kada towing them.

It hadn't taken much to persuade him to do it.

He loved towing Cal's boat. Anja knew that, but she'd thought it would be difficult to get him away from Devinia's side.

Perhaps he needed to move for a bit. Or perhaps Devinia was already gone.

The other members of the pod still surrounded her, but they were quiet, and she didn't know what was usual in these circumstances.

Kada let go of the rope and gave them a nudge with his nose before he sank beneath the waves that slapped at the cliff face.

The beach they'd used earlier was gone, the water coming up the side of the sheer rock face.

"High tide." Walef sounded undaunted.

"There's the path." Demi pointed, and Anja couldn't see where she meant until they got in a little closer.

"Good eyes."

They all seemed to have something that was a little better than the others. Maybe that's how it worked. Each member of the team had a specialty.

It made sense.

She wondered how the silver balls decided who got what, and then let the thought go as Cal used the motor at last, needing it to maneuver them close enough to the rocks so Ritt could jump out onto a narrow ledge of rock.

Anja jumped out beside him and the two of them held the boat as best they could while the others got out, then they lifted the boat up and propped it against the cliff face.

They couldn't tie it to the rocks, it would be bashed to pieces by the waves against the sharp, spiky limestone.

"Let's hope the tide doesn't get any higher, or bye bye boat." Livia moved back as the water lapped over the top of the ledge and around the soles of their boots.

"It's going out." Demi pointed to the water line at knee height on the rock behind them. She sounded sure about it, and Anja was happy to trust her.

They found the path they'd taken up from the beach before easily enough, and moved silently upward.

When they reached the top, they turned to look back at the island they'd just come from.

"Do you think they'll be all right, alone with those droppers?" Livia asked.

"They've got a laz," Walef said. "Don't forget, they got the drop on Sirco all by themselves."

Livia nodded, and they turned to face the direction of the spaceship.

Since he'd started up the engine to his runner earlier, Jake had lifted up, turned the runner in a full rotation and then landed again.

Anja guessed he was still having problems with it.

It had barely made it back after Kada had knocked it into the sea.

The cannons probably still worked, though. So it was still dangerous to whoever might head out to look for them tomorrow.

The engine was silent now, and as they got closer to the spaceship and the two runners parked on the cliff, she heard raised voices.

Not arguments, more the shouts of people moving heavy things.

It was early evening, and lights had been rigged above the spaceship, pointing down into the collapsed roof. An automated arm lifted slowly, swinging a massive, heavy-looking console out from the control room.

They shouldn't have that. It wasn't theirs.

Anja stood still in the darkness and watched as the console was carefully maneuvered onto the rocky ground beside the runners.

Droppers rushed to unclip it from the arm, which swung back out and dipped down into the control room again.

They hadn't set the console down on the rock, she saw now that she focused on it, they'd placed it on poles laid beside each other. They began to roll them forward, someone pulling away the pole that was freed up behind, and running to add it back to the front as they progressed.

Basic, but very effective.

They were moving the console to Jake's runner.

Perhaps the irregular lift-offs and set-downs were to see how much weight the runner could take. Because the console was heavy enough to make ten droppers sweat, and that was with the help of the poles they were using to move it.

"They're having to decide what to take," Cal murmured beside her, and she nodded.

"With Sirco's runner out of commission, they're having to

calculate the amount and importance of the equipment they plan to steal."

It wouldn't matter how heavy the console was when they broke through to nearspace, but they'd have to generate enough thrust to get free of Fynian's atmosphere first.

"Looks like they've stripped the spaceship bare," Walef murmured.

He was right.

A pile of equipment sat to one side, way more than could be fitted into the runner.

Some of it had been sorted. Prioritized, Anja guessed.

That must stick a little in Jake's throat.

He wouldn't want to leave anything behind.

She hoped she could ensure he took nothing.

"There're a lot of people around the runner." Demi leaned in, keeping her voice whisper quiet, although the darkness and distance meant it would be impossible for them to be seen or heard where they were.

"Too risky to approach now," Cal agreed. "Let's see if there's a pattern. Or a lull."

They settled in, finding a small stand of bushes they could hide behind.

Anja lay on her stomach, looking through the branches, and after less than half an hour, Jake strode up from the spaceship, looking over the pile of equipment and then walking over, hands on hips, to look up at the console, which had been rolled into the runner.

A dropper came to stand beside him, one of the two men who'd originally tried to kill her and who'd shot Kada, Anja saw.

They had an animated conversation, with the man gesticulating at the console and then out toward the island where the pod, Leonie, and the others were waiting.

"They're wondering where Sirco and the other droppers have got to," she murmured.

"That was inevitable." Cal was beside her, and she had to admit this particular problem hadn't crossed her mind until now. But it had crossed Cal's.

"That's why you were so insistent on coming here." She glanced at him. "Because they would come looking for Sirco, no matter what happened. Jake needs the druk."

The search and rescue runners they were expecting aside, Jake would come in guns blazing if he thought his plan to steal druk had been ruined. And it could well be much sooner than tomorrow morning.

Cal's face was grim. "Yes."

No wonder Sirco had been nervous. Not because he'd had the tables turned on him, but because when Jake came looking for him and the others, chances were, he wouldn't be gentle.

"We need to get closer. Hear what they're saying." Cal rose up a little from his position, but just then, the runner's engine roared to life and the back closed up.

Jake shook his head and motioned to the dropper to follow him, and they walked back toward the spaceship.

The runner rose up, and after a short time aloft, settled back down again.

"They're close to the cliff's edge." Anja lifted up a little, calculated the distance. "If we come up the cliff face, I could get to it."

Cal pressed up against her side and studied the runner.

He nodded. "Let's try it."

They backed away, moving carefully and slowly, leaving Ritt and Demi behind to watch from the other side.

As soon as the rest of them were out of sight of the runner, they cut left, reaching the cliff at the point where it curved right, back the way they'd come.

Anja crouched on the edge and peered down. "It looks possible."

They'd decided two would go down, Anja and Cal, and Livia and Walef would shadow them above, at a distance.

Anja lowered herself over the side, found a thin ledge that ran some of the way in the direction she needed to go and waited for Cal to join her.

His big boots barely fit on the narrow ledge, but they moved along, crouching to keep their heads below the clifftop, and then the ledge ended and they didn't have to crouch, because the only foot and handholds were lower down.

It felt good, Anja realized. Stretching her body, using her arms to hold her whole bodyweight.

It was almost as if the silver ball was getting to know her strengths and flexibility as she moved, adjusting here and there to help her.

She could already hear the sound of voices up ahead but they were suddenly overwhelmed by the sound of an engine coming from above.

She looked up and sure enough, winking in and out as it dropped, came a small runner.

She pressed herself against the rock, although hopefully neither she nor Cal were visible.

She glanced at him, found him looking up as well.

"From the ship waiting for Jake in nearspace?" she guessed.

He nodded, but he didn't look happy.

Now they had two runners to disable.

She started moving again.

The runner landed, the heat of its engines wafting over her for a moment before they were shut down.

She had to go down the cliff a little way before she could go up again, and Cal cut in front of her, his longer reach giving him access to handholds she couldn't quite get to.

He waited for her a body's length below the clifftop, reaching down a hand to help her up, so they were crouched together just below the edge.

The small runner had set down a little away from Sirco's dead runner and Jake's working one, closer to where Demi and Ritt were hiding than the clifftop, but very much in an open area with no cover.

The runner's engines had been shut down, but the motors were still in cooling mode, and hearing anything over the noise was difficult.

Jake stood talking to a man and woman, neither of whom looked like droppers. They wore the correct clothing for the icy weather, but it looked tailored to fit them perfectly.

They did not look happy.

Neither did Jake.

He was waving a hand toward the island where Leonie and the others waited.

The woman turned away sharply and walked toward the pile of equipment stripped from the spaceship, leaving the two men to continue what was clearly an argument.

Jake seemed aggrieved. He pointed to the collapsed roof of the spaceship, and then gesticulated toward his own runner and then smacked a fist into his palm.

Anja was sure he was describing being attacked by Kada.

The woman called over to both men, her face animated as she held something from the pile, and her companion started toward her, then turned back to Jake, pointed to the small runner, and then turned back to the woman again, his attitude dismissive.

Oh, Jake didn't like that.

Not at all.

He stared after the man with narrowed eyes, and then spun to face the open door of the small runner and climbed into it.

"He was told to check on Sirco and the druk." Cal had seen it, too.

"He doesn't want to go." Anja could see it in every jerk of his body as he climbed into the runner.

"Who would, after meeting Kada in such a way?" Cal rose up a little more for a better view. "Is there a cannon on that thing?"

Of course, when Jake found out he had no druk, he might start shooting.

"Not a cannon, but I think there's a weapon of some kind. Smaller than a cannon, but . . ." All he'd need to harm Leonie and the others. Devinia and her pod, too.

The moment Jake shone the spotlight she could see mounted on the front of the runner on the beach, and saw the droppers sitting together, restrained, he'd work out what had happened.

Anja wouldn't put it past him to open fire.

"That runner can't take off." Cal gripped the top of the cliff with both hands, poised to haul himself over the top.

He was right. They couldn't let it lift off, but between the top of the cliff and the runner were plenty of droppers.

Neither she nor Cal would get there in time, and they'd be killed or captured, which would be a waste for no possible gain.

So if they couldn't go to the runner, they'd have to get the runner to come to them.

Jake closed the door and the engines fired up.

Cal rose, muscles in his arms bunching as he prepared to vault over the top.

He was going to risk it, because he couldn't let Jake reach his mother.

She put a hand on his shoulder and pushed him down. His quick look was sharp; surprised and impatient.

"Wait."

The runner lifted off the ground, hovering instead of taking off, the engines churning up debris that made everyone turn away, eyes shielded from the flying sand.

"What would cause Jake to come this way, nice and low?" she asked Cal.

He frowned at her.

"You look too much like a dropper, he wouldn't look twice at you. I'm thinking, a glimpse of me." She hauled herself up the side and stood on the edge of the cliff facing the runner, and gave a wave.

No one else had seen her yet, they were trying to avoid the whirlwind of sand that Jake was causing, and he had paused to enjoy seeing the objects of his ire bent away from him, arms covering their eyes.

"Anja."

She didn't know for a moment if Cal had spoken to her in her head, or out loud.

She glanced down at him. "Trust me. And get ready to throw me."

She turned back to Jake. She could see him through the clear screen of the runner's front window. Saw his eyes widen, and then narrow in fury as he noticed her. Recognized her.

He sent the runner straight for her, as if intending to hit her.

Which he clearly did intend to do.

"That's right. Come to me."

She dropped lightly back onto the small ledge beside Cal as the runner roared closer and then stepped into Cal's cupped hands.

He was crouched down, and he stood as he tossed her high, giving her as much lift as possible.

She flew upward, then twisted and stretched her body, reaching out as the runner passed overhead.

Her hand caught the step built into the side of it, and she

dangled in the air as it dipped toward the water. Jake banked, and she was able to use the momentum to flip onto the roof.

If Jake didn't realize she had hitched a ride before, the sound of her boots above him would have made it clear.

She had moments before he flipped upside down or went high enough into nearspace to kill her.

She ran the few steps to the back, put her hands flat on the surface, and let the silver ball do its thing.

The engine cut off abruptly, and the runner dropped, a dead weight falling out of the sky.

With seconds to spare before impact, Anja dived off.

She landed in the sea, not far from the cliff.

She looked up, and saw Cal was already halfway down the side, coming to her.

There was water in her eyes and she blinked as she thought he might be free falling a short way, grabbing a rock, free falling again.

She shook her head and started swimming.

She looked behind her a few times. The runner was bobbing in the water.

It didn't sink, but it didn't go anywhere, either.

That was good enough for her.

Droppers lined the cliff's edge above. Someone had brought one of the large lights, pointing it in the runner's direction. No one seemed to notice her.

Hopefully in the dark, it would be almost impossible to see her.

She was fast in the water. It gave her joy, and she had to admit that this was one part of her new self that she could not regret, even though she knew her body was paying a price in resources to keep her warm.

By the time she reached the bottom of the cliffs, Cal was waiting for her.

He had managed to climb down the sheer rock face faster than she would have believed possible.

She grabbed his hand and he pulled her bodily from the water, making it seem easy.

For a moment she leaned against the rock face, water pouring off her clothes, and closed her eyes, catching her breath.

Cal moved beside her, and she turned her head and opened her eyes. Found him close, his forehead almost touching hers.

"Anja." There was an exasperated warmth in his voice as he pressed his lips against her temple.

"It just came to me. The silver ball knew it was possible."

He sighed. "Mine did, too. It kept me from jumping after you. Although I wanted to."

She thought about it. "It wouldn't have let me do it if it hadn't known there was a high chance of success."

He gave a slow nod, his face thoughtful.

The exertion of the swim had warmed her, but now she was still, she began to feel the bite of the cold, and she shivered suddenly.

"Let's get back to the boat, get you a spare set of clothes."

She was lucky they had thought to bring them, but they had agreed before they set off, anything could happen.

Even she hadn't imagined leaping off a cliff onto a runner, though.

"At least Jake won't be shooting anyone in that runner. Although the other one is still working." She let Cal help her up and then waited for him to lead the way.

"Whoever came down on that small runner will need to go back up, and Jake's runner is all they have. They can take even less equipment with them now." Cal swung across a deep crack in the rock and waited for her on the other side.

What he didn't say is they still hadn't managed to neutralize the remaining runner. Its laz cannons were still just as much a threat as they'd been before.

As Anja stretched her arm to grab a handhold, a strong beam of light seemed to blossom around her.

She squinted, angling her head to look upward.

The big light was pointing down at her and Cal now, and when she looked out across the water to the runner she'd brought down, still floating in the waves, she saw Jake standing on the roof, pointing to her.

Damn. He'd managed to get out and alert his friends.

Someone shot a laz in their direction, but the angle was too difficult and it passed harmlessly overhead.

"They're going to follow us if we take the cliff." Cal was looking up as well.

It would be all too easy for the droppers to keep pace from above.

There was only one solution.

Anja shivered, but she couldn't pretend she was sorry she had to go back in the water.

With a nod, she dived in, and heard the splash as Cal joined her.

They sank beneath the water, and turned toward the back of the island and their boat.

Hopefully the rest of the team had seen what was happening and had gone back themselves.

Even better would be if they had launched the boat back out and could pick her and Cal up as they rounded the cliffs, because she was very sure droppers would be headed for their little landing spot right now.

It would be a race to see who got there first.

28

———————

Cal heard the motor of his boat long before he saw it.

It was a huge relief to hear it at all, though. He could sense Anja was flagging as much as he was.

They had made excellent progress around the side of the island, but the sea was even colder now than it had been this morning, and they had had almost no rest.

Hands reached down to lift them out of the water, and then someone, Walef, he realized, helped him out of his clothes while Liv did the same for Anja.

They were rubbed down and given an energy bar each, which he ate in slow bites as Walef helped him tug on dry socks, a warm shirt and insulated pants.

They headed for the pod and his mother, Ritt steering.

"We were worried you wouldn't make it to the boat in time." Anja spoke as if her jaw was stiff.

"Nearly didn't, but we got there." Liv was drying Anja's long hair, rubbing it vigorously with a towel.

"How did you make that jump?" Demi had been brewing jah

while they got dry and dressed, and now she handed them each a cup, then poured out more for the others.

Anja tried to chuckle, but her throat must have been too tight. "Cal," was all she said.

Demi turned to him.

"I threw her."

"Shit." Walef sat back, cupping his jah to warm his hands. "That was crazy. I couldn't believe what I was seeing."

"We couldn't let him reach the island. There was a weapon on the front of that runner." Cal swallowed jah and wondered if he'd ever had anything as good.

"I saw it." Demi looked flinty-eyed.

"I had to hold her back from running through about ten droppers to get to it," Ritt commented from the steering lever. "She had the same thought about him opening fire at everyone on the beach."

"Well, it's not going anywhere anymore." Walef looked toward the spaceship.

They were out of range of the lights, but the outline of people running around on the clifftop was clear enough.

The only thing that worried Cal was they still had one runner left, and by the sound of it, it was working well enough.

"We heard a few things when that man and woman arrived," Ritt said. "The Arkhorans arrived in the Jero system an hour ago, but they've sent someone down to Rinc to talk to Leonie. They haven't found the thieves' ship in nearspace yet."

"That's why they came down, to tell everyone to wrap things up?" Cal asked.

Ritt nodded. "They wanted to have a quick look before they pinched to the black. They were not happy about Sirco's dead runner, and that the boat wasn't back with any druk."

"You'd think with the Arkhorans already here, they wouldn't

want to risk getting caught. They must be desperate for that druk." Liv hunched over her cup of jah, looking exhausted.

They all were.

When last had they slept? Cal wondered. He couldn't even remember. "You'd think," he agreed.

The sound of the runner's engine firing up sent a crackle of hope through him. Maybe they were leaving. He'd like to have grounded them completely, but having them gone was the next best thing.

The runner rose up and then hovered.

Cal waited for it to suddenly accelerate upward to nearspace, but instead, it turned in their direction.

"Why?" Anja breathed. "They're really risking everything for druk?"

"It doesn't make sense," Demi agreed.

"To us, it doesn't." Cal glanced at Ritt, and his friend indicated he was already pushing the boat as fast as it would go.

Anja turned on her seat, looking toward the narrow opening into the sheltered bay.

"You're talking to Kada?" Liv asked.

"Trying to." Anja looked back at them. "I don't know how well it works. How well it's ever worked."

But then he heard it, a hoot and bellow from the pod.

The runner was above them now, and it passed them, engines glowing in the darkness.

Cal heard a splash, as if Kada had leapt from the water, but the runner was keeping high.

They were being cautious, he realized. They couldn't afford to lose their final runner and trap themselves on Fynian.

A sudden purple flicker and then another roar from the pod electrified Cal. They were shooting at the leviathans.

"The fuckers." Ritt leaned forward, as if he could make the boat go faster by doing so.

"Why?" Livia's voice was anguished.

"Trying to get them to move so they can land on the beach without worrying about a leviathan attack?" Anja had moved to the bow, almost leaning out of the boat.

Her face was a mask of concentration.

She was trying to get the leviathans to move, so they would no longer be targets, Cal guessed.

When she looked back, her eyes were stark.

"Kada says Devinia is dead. And one of the other leviathans, the one who would have taken Devinia's place as matriarch, is badly injured. They're moving away from the beach."

Which left his mother and the others exposed, but Cal wouldn't have it any other way.

The leviathans were innocent bystanders in this mess. He didn't want any more hurt or killed.

The thought of Devinia being dead opened a yawning black hole inside him. It was the silver ball making him feel this strongly, he knew, but it was real enough.

On the heels of the grief came fury, and a need for revenge.

Enough now, he thought. This needed to end.

"Cut the engine," he said to Ritt.

The others turned to stare at him in disbelief. All but Anja.

She was standing on the prow, and the wind whipped her hair as she glanced at him, eyes gleaming, and gave a nod.

She was with him all the way.

His throat closed at the surge of emotion he felt for her, and he couldn't speak for a moment.

"They'll hear the engine and they may turn the laz cannons on us," he said to the others. "We swim in."

Ritt cut the motor, and the boat drifted forward, getting them through the narrow mouth of the bay, and into the calmer waters beyond.

Up ahead, the runner hovered in front of the beach, over the shallow water, the lights illuminating the beach and everyone on it.

Anja's head turned to the right, and Cal suddenly knew the pod lay in that direction, away from the beach but still within the protective arms of the curving cliffs.

No one moved, letting the momentum of the boat take them as far as it could before they'd have to get back into the cold water.

The runner moved to the left, looking for enough space on the beach to land, flinging up sand as it went.

Anja had jumped down from the prow and was busy taking off her clothes.

She was too thin, he saw. The constant exertion was taking a toll.

His sister folded her clothes next to Anja, and he noticed she was too thin, too, and had what looked like a healing bruise along her side.

He handed everyone an energy bar. It wasn't enough, but it was better than nothing.

They ate in silence as the boat drifted closer to the beach.

The runner had landed close to the cliff, pointing in the direction of the campfire, the bright beams of its lights illuminating most of the beach but leaving the shallows in darkness. The engines were still running.

"I'll kill it," Anja said.

Cal nodded. "The rest of us will deal with the passengers."

The passengers were already disembarking. He didn't see Jake among them.

Cal wondered if he'd been left on the floating runner, abandoned by his masters in their haste to be gone, or killed first, so he couldn't say anything to the Arkhorans when they finally arrived.

"Time to go." Cal crouched on the side of his boat and then lowered himself silently over the side.

The droppers and their masters probably wouldn't hear the

splash over the sound of the waves and the engine, but no sense in taking chances.

Anja came in straight after him and he caught her in his arms in the water, her bare limbs entwining with his, and kissed her.

She pulled him close, her hand on his neck, and kissed him back, her body slick and smooth against his, and then she was gone, disappearing in the darkness.

"I think you just warmed the water a few degrees." Walef looked in the direction she'd gone. "Thanks for that."

He shot Cal a quick grin and then went under himself.

"You do generate heat." Demi was watching the beach, looking for any sign of her mother, Cal guessed.

He didn't respond, and she flicked him a similar smile and headed for the shore.

Cal began after them, his gaze moving to the left every now and then, looking for signs of Anja.

He found none.

The woman he'd seen on the cliff with Jake was nowhere in sight, but the man who'd come down with her had stepped out of the runner, and had brought two droppers with him.

Two droppers were probably all the runner would take, given the weight of the console and whatever else Jake had loaded into it.

Cal wondered if the two men would be allowed up into near-space, or if they'd be left down here on the beach.

His feet touched down on the sandy seafloor. He'd overtaken the others and now he waited for them, waist deep in the swirling water. The lights of the runner reached only so far, and they would be impossible to see in the deep shadow.

He, on the other hand, could see everything clearly.

His mother was on her feet, and was shielding her eyes against the bright light, trying to see who was coming toward her.

"Which one is Sirco?" The man called out, and his mother focused in his direction.

One of the droppers pointed Sirco out.

Of the four prisoners, only Sirco didn't look happy about the runner's arrival.

He knew they weren't being rescued.

Just robbed and abandoned. If they were lucky.

"Where's the druk?" The man strode forward, unconcerned by Yavish, who stepped forward, laz in hand.

"Get back." Yavish adjusted his grip on the laz. He radiated nerves and discomfort with the weapon.

The man stopped and looked at him dismissively. Flicked a finger.

One of the droppers shot him, and Yavish fell like a tree in a hard Fynian storm.

Donnella gave a cry and ran to him, and Cal thought he saw her kick sand over the laz Yavish had dropped, to hide it.

"Where's his weapon?" The other dropper had come up beside her, and she shook her head, playing dumb as she felt for a pulse and turned Yavish on his side.

"Don't know."

The way the light was angled, every movement threw wild shadows, and the dropper looked on the ground, frowned, and then stood over her, gaze watchful.

"Who are you?" His mother narrowed her eyes at the newcomer. She'd started moving toward Yavish, but had stopped when Donnella had reached him first. "What do you want on Fynian?"

The man ignored her, his focus on Sirco. "I said, where is the druk?"

"In the pump." Fida was the one who spoke first. He waved at the inflatable that they'd pulled up the beach.

"You haven't removed it?" The man looked at Fida a beat too long to be friendly.

"The sound of the motor caused those monsters to attack. We couldn't remove it *and* get more druk. It was one or the other." Fida's tone was defiant.

The man hesitated, as if in surprise at the reasonableness of his logic. "Get it now. They're gone."

Fida shuffled toward him, restrained hands held out in front of him.

The man waved a hand, and the other dropper came forward and released him.

"I'll need at least one other person to help." Fida glanced behind him.

Sirco shuffled out. Not because he was eager to please, Cal thought, but because he thought he might be able to escape if he was in the boat.

He knew he was dead if he didn't.

He was a man with nothing to lose, and that suited Cal just fine.

A flash of laz fire to the left had him turning.

Anja.

For the first time he noticed a third dropper, lying on the roof of the runner, laz in hand.

He'd fired at Anja, but she must have dodged. She didn't look as if she'd been hit, but she had come to a halt, hands raised in surrender.

He'd underestimated them. Again.

His mother, Donnella, and everyone else turned to look at what was happening.

The man in charge made a come here gesture and the dropper on the roof jerked his laz in the direction of the campfire. An order to Anja to head over there.

She did so, moving away from the water's edge, keeping all eyes on her.

Protecting the team from discovery.

When he should have been protecting her.

29

Anja moved slowly.

She hadn't seen the dropper on the roof.

He must have taken up position while she was swimming in.

There was no shame in it.

You couldn't predict everything. What mattered was how you managed when something unexpected did occur.

She'd dodged in time to avoid being shot, and now she was giving the team time to work out a new plan while she kept all eyes on her.

She hadn't realized Yavish had been shot until she saw him lying on the sand, unconscious, with Donnella crouched beside him, being guarded by a suspicious dropper.

Leonie watched her approach, and Anja couldn't read any expression on her face.

Maybe that was just as well.

"Who are you?" The man she'd seen on the clifftop with Jake wasn't trying to hide his feelings. He was coldly furious and impatient.

"Dr. Anja Farucci." She gave her full title. "Who are you?"

The man sneered at the question. "What were you doing trying to sneak up to my runner?"

"I was trying to stop you." She spoke without heat or inflection. "Were you with the Core Companies on Garmen?"

He paused, the action so infinitesimal she would have missed it but for the silver ball. "Where did you come from?"

He wasn't going to give away anything about who he was and where he was from, but that pause told her he probably had been running a Core Company out of Garmen before things had gotten very messy for him and his kind.

"I slipped into the water when we heard your runner coming." She knew Leonie wouldn't contradict her, but Fida, Sirco and the others might. So she kept her voice low.

Gyntree and Roald were still on the other side of the fire, too far away to hear her. Sirco and Fida were standing beside the inflatable, close enough, but only Fida turned when she told her lie.

He said nothing, though, as if he didn't want to bring himself to the man's attention.

"That true?" The Core's man glanced at them.

Fida shrugged. Behind him, Sirco nodded yes.

That surprised her, but maybe it shouldn't. Sirco was bright enough. He'd know there was no way off Fynian for him now. The best way to help himself was to help her and the team. Help Leonie.

The Core's man dismissed her, turning back to the inflatable. "The druk," he said.

Fida hopped into the boat and crouched beside the pump. There was a long moment of silence as he fiddled with it, and Sirco, who'd been leaning against the side, watching, eventually climbed in with him.

"What is it?" The Core's man walked closer, and his dropper came with him.

"It won't switch on." Fida flicked a quick look at the laz in the dropper's hands.

"And why is that?"

Fida swallowed. "We were attacked, as I said. The monster nearly landed on top of us. It must have damaged the pump."

"It doesn't look damaged." The Core's man was leaning over the side of the boat to get a better look.

"Then you try." Sirco stepped away from it, and put one leg over the side of the inflatable to get out.

The man's arm shot out and grabbed Sirco's upper arm. "That's not very respectful."

"I'm not feeling very respectful." Sirco gave a toothy smile. "I've lived in this weird place for months, done most of the groundwork for this project, found a fucking ancestral spaceship into the bargain, and here I am, freezing on a tiny beach on an island in the middle of an icy sea, being ordered to get a broken pump to work."

The Core's man didn't like that answer.

He struck Sirco, an open slap across the face.

Every eye was on the confrontation.

Anja sensed Cal before she saw him. Her gaze went to the beach, and he stepped out of the darkness.

Perfect timing.

As if he'd heard her, he sent her a quick smile, and then shot the dropper next to her with the laz he had in his hand.

The man screamed as he went down, and suddenly laz fire was everywhere.

The laz cannons on the runner.

Anja dropped, shouting at Donnella and Leonie to do the same, and the stream of fire came over the top of them.

The Core's man swore and dropped down beside the inflatable, and his dropper fell back, hit by friendly fire.

When the burst from the cannons stopped, everyone stayed where they were, frozen in place.

From somewhere out in the bay, a leviathan hooted in fury, agitated by the sound.

The Core's man went still, halfway through the act of standing. He stared off into the darkness, then turned to look at the runner.

At the woman inside, Anja decided.

She had changed the tone of things, but she had almost taken out her partner into the bargain, and she had drawn the interest of the pod.

Don't come this way. She sent the thought out to Kada. The woman in the runner would turn the cannons on the pod in a heartbeat if they came close to the beach.

"There are more of you." The Core's man finally turned his gaze to Cal and the team, lips thin and tight.

They were crouched low, frothy waves foaming at their feet, still in perfect formation.

The Core's man was sizing up the situation, Anja realized.

Both his droppers on the ground with him were down and out. He didn't particularly trust Sirco and Fida, and while the laz cannons had the capacity to kill, killing wouldn't get him what he wanted.

And they were more than a little indiscriminate.

Not something he could trust his life to, as the dropper lying at his feet attested.

"You two." He waved at Roald and Gyntree.

They stood slowly, still not fully recovered from their time in the water.

"Now." The Core's man barked the command, and behind him, Anja saw Sirco make a face.

The two men shuffled a little faster, and came to stand in front of him. He cut off their restraints in quick, impatient movements, then handed Gyntree the laz that had been in the dropper's hand before he'd been hit with cannon fire.

"You." He pointed at Anja. "Pick up the laz your friend just used and the one next to you, and bring them over here. Hold them with two fingers," he showed her, "and if you even twitch, you're dead."

"They had two of their own. Yavish had one, she had another." Gyntree pointed at Leonie.

"Now that is useful information." The Core's man gave Gyntree an approving look. "Bring all three."

Anja glanced at Leonie, and the head of planet closed her eyes in frustration, then slowly pulled the laz from the back of her pants.

Anja felt a surge of delight inside her. She kept her eyes down as she took Leonie's weapon from her, then bent and picked up the dropper's one with the other hand.

She felt the tingle as the silver ball destroyed both weapons' inner workings as she walked toward Cal.

He was still crouched low, the laz in his hand, and he held it out in a flat palm to give no cause for suspicion.

Anja turned to look at the Core's man. "I can't hold three with two fingers."

He considered it. "Put two on an open palm, carry the third in two fingers."

She took Cal's from him, and knew they were both suppressing a smile of satisfaction.

She carried them over to the Core's man like precious gifts, rather than useless lumps of metal.

He took one, waved at Roald to take the other and tucked the third in a pocket.

She flicked a longing glance at the laz in Gyntree's hand, but decided she better not risk trying to grab it.

The cannons were much bigger than a normal laz, and she

could see the dropper who'd taken a hit from them was dead, not just unconscious like Yavish and the dropper Cal had hit.

"Go back and stand where you were."

She backed away, and as she stepped closer to Donnella, she felt something under her bare foot.

It was under the sand near Yavish. His laz?

She glanced at Donnella, but the woman was very deliberately not looking at her.

So, it was his laz. And Donnella knew it was there. Probably had hidden it when she came to his aid.

Good for her.

She stopped with it between her feet.

The dropper who had been lying on the roof of the runner and had shot at her earlier scrambled to his feet and stood, laz lifted, watching them all from above.

She hadn't been paying attention to him. That was a mistake.

His gaze kept straying to the dropper lying in the sand by the inflatable.

They would have worked together. Perhaps had been friends.

He was now dead, by his employer's hand.

If he had second thoughts about his life choices, though, it wasn't apparent in the wide-legged stance he took up on the roof, weapon in hand.

Cal and the others slowly straightened up again, now the threat of the cannons was over.

"If they move, kill them," the Core's man said to the dropper on the roof.

Cal's eyes glittered in the light from the runner's spotlights, and Anja could feel the frustration pumping off him in waves.

She fixed her attention on Cal and Walef, and thought about the laz under a thin layer of sand between her feet.

Both of them turned their heads to look at her, and then looked down at the ground.

She gave a tiny nod of confirmation.

"The pump," the Core's man snapped, and she switched her attention back to the inflatable.

Fida and Sirco were standing beside it now, and Gyntree had climbed in.

He shook his head. "It won't turn on." He didn't look particularly sad about it.

"I can get the druk out," Anja said.

The Core's man swung his attention to her immediately. "How?"

"I recognize the pump. I'm a marine biologist. I've worked with them before. We use them to take seabed samples."

The Core's man regarded her for a beat. "Why should I believe you?"

"Ask Sirco. We worked together at the VSC Research Centre."

The Core's man glanced at Sirco and he gave a nod.

"Don't know why she'd help us, though."

She waved at the runner. "The sooner you get your druk, the sooner you'll leave. There is only so long we can stand around in this temperature without clothing and not be affected."

"That's true." The Core's man looked her over, taking in her practical underwear as if noticing her state of undress for the first time. He glanced at the rest of the team, at Cal and the others with icy water dripping off them, and nodded. "Move wrong and you'll regret it."

She just needed to get close to Gyntree and his laz. And if that wasn't possible, have an excuse to walk to the runner itself. That would be the main prize in this game they were playing.

She reached the boat, climbed in and moved to the pump.

She had destroyed the circuits, and there was no bringing them back, but she actually had been on a project that used a similar pump before, and she knew there was another way to get to the material it had collected.

She grabbed the narrow handles on the bottom of the cylinder, where it attached to the main pipe, and twisted.

As soon as it turned in her hands, she lifted the heavy cylinder up, and a mixture of wet sand and druk began oozing out, sluggish and viscous.

With a grunt of surprise, Fida jumped back in with her, taking the cylinder out of her arms.

He nearly dropped it, not anticipating how heavy it was.

He sent her a strange look, as if he couldn't believe she'd had the strength to hold it on her own.

She would need to be careful. The silver ball had obviously helped, and she would need to remember she was enhanced, and make sure she didn't attract suspicion.

Fida shook it, and more sludge dribbled out, pouring sand and druk all over the floor of the inflatable.

"Catch it in something," the Core's man snapped at Sirco.

"Catch it in what, exactly?" Sirco waved at the empty boat.

"Get something from the back of the runner," the Core's man said to Roald and after a moment of hesitation, he started shuffling across the beach to do as he was ordered.

He moved with unsteady legs.

He looked terrible and Anja lifted her gaze to Cal. Hoped she was able to transmit to him that Roald's laz was useless.

Then she blinked.

Ritt and Demi, who had been at the back of the group, had disappeared into the shadows cast by the runner's bright beams.

Only Walef, Livia and Cal were crouched on the beach now.

The dropper on the roof was so focused on the inflatable, he hadn't noticed they'd slipped away.

"Why don't you flip the pump upside-down and take it as is?" Anja lifted her hands in a dramatic gesture. Mainly it was to keep attention on herself to let Ritt and Demi do whatever it was they were doing. But she could also see no way to reach the runner and kill the engine right now, unless she was ordered over to it. Making it easy for them to leave was the next best thing.

Fida struggled to flip it, and the Core's man pushed Anja aside and hopped in to help him.

"There's still a lot on the floor." He sounded both annoyed and pleased.

There *was* a lot of druk embedded in the sludge, Anja noted. Enough to make the Core's man happy.

She glanced back at Roald. He had made it to the runner, and stood by the door, as if waiting for someone to invite him in.

"Scoop it up and put it back in the pump." The Core's man waved at Gyntree and Sirco and took a step back.

"Why should I?" Sirco asked. "You aren't going to take me with you."

"Do it, or I'll kill you." The Core's man turned to look at Sirco, rubbing his thumb over the top of the laz, and then looked over at the runner, with its laz cannons.

He seemed to be surprised to see Roald over there, as if he'd forgotten he'd ordered him to go fetch something to put the druk in. "What's the problem?"

No one said anything for a moment, because the problem was clear. No one could give Roald what he needed without someone abandoning a strategically important position.

The dropper on the roof, or the woman behind the laz cannons.

Unless Roald went inside and got something himself.

But he didn't. Couldn't. He stood, swaying slightly in front of the runner as if he'd forgotten what he was doing there.

It was the perfect moment to move.

30

Cal moved.

He'd been watching for the right moment, and this was it.

Everyone distracted, no one knowing quite what to do.

"Now," he ordered Walef and Liv, and then ran for the spot where Anja had stood earlier. Where she'd communicated to him that Yavish's laz was hidden.

His mother and Donnella were standing close by, but he didn't have time to speak to them.

Not that his mother would need reassurance. She was watching everything carefully, like the strategist that she was.

Walef and Liv had taken off, running left toward the runner. As he scrabbled in the sand for the laz, he saw them take Roald to the ground and then roll underneath the ship with him, where the cannons couldn't reach them.

The dropper on the roof stepped forward to aim at Cal.

If what he'd picked up from Anja was right, aside from the runner's laz cannons, the rooftop dropper and Gyntree held the only working weapons, other than the one Cal had just scooped up from the sand.

Cal flicked a look at Gyntree.

The man had started to lift his laz, and Anja, still standing beside the inflatable, threw herself at him, taking him down to the ground.

The Core's man ran forward a few steps and lifted his laz, but Cal ignored him, using the chance Anja had given him when she tackled Gyntree to turn and aim at the dropper on the roof. Before he could fire, Ritt appeared on the roof behind the man and shoved him off his perch.

He fell with a cry of surprise and landed hard on the sand, wheezing as he tried to get air back in his lungs.

Liv darted out from beneath the runner, grabbed the laz that he dropped as he fell, shot him with it, and then threw it up to Ritt.

She rolled back under the runner, and flashed Cal a grin.

The cannons began to hum.

He'd expected some kind of reaction, had expected the cannons to come into play, but fear shot through him at the possible consequences.

"Get down!"

Anja was down already, and his mother and Donnella, standing a little behind him, threw themselves flat on the sand.

When the cannons fired, spitting crackling purple beams, they were aimed over everyone's heads. Over the head of the Core's man, still standing exposed in the middle of the beach, unable to comprehend that his laz hadn't worked.

The cannon fire was just a warning shot.

A reminder of who had the heavier weaponry.

But the fixed cannon was not quite as useful anymore, now that most of the droppers were down.

As the short cannon burst ended, the Core's man turned, lifted his laz again, and shot at Anja, who'd rolled away from Gyntree and was pulling herself up into a crouch.

When nothing happened again, he threw it away and fished the second one out of his pocket.

Cal shot him.

As soon as he hit the ground, the cannons fired again, lower this time, and Anja dived forward and rolled toward Cal.

He was still lying on his stomach, looking toward the inflatable, and he shot Gyntree, who had chosen to stay on the ground after Anja's tackle, out of cannon range. Yavish had set the laz to slightly higher than the stun setting, which meant he was probably out for an hour.

He'd like to take them all out of consideration, but Sirco and Fida had ducked behind the inflatable as soon as the cannons started up, out of sight.

As soon as it was obvious the cannons were only useful in keeping everyone low, but posed no immediate threat, the woman cut them off.

"Either leave or surrender." Cal lifted into a crouch and raised his voice so she could hear him through the open door of the runner.

There was silence.

The woman would be facing difficult choices.

"Bring him to me and I'll go." Her voice came over the speakers that were set in the nose of the runner.

There was no confusion over who she meant. The Core's man.

"No." And there was nothing she could do to make him, short of taking off and shooting at them.

That would mean she'd have to kill everyone on the beach, land again and then load up her friend.

Cal wondered if she was that desperate.

They'd soon find out.

While she thought through her options, Cal saw Demi creeping toward the door of the runner out of the corner of his eye.

The woman must have seen her, too, because a sudden burst of cannon fire erupted, and then the doors swished closed.

Demi had ducked out of instinct when the laz fire crackled, although she wasn't in danger from it, and now she looked over at Cal and gave a grimace at her defeat.

But they weren't that much worse off.

Demi slipped behind the runner, and then Cal heard a splash.

She was going to bring in the boat, he realized. Give them their clothes back, for a start.

The air had turned colder as the night deepened, every breath a puff of condensation, and he looked forward to getting warm again.

"The dropper we have under the runner needs to go back to the fire," Liv called up to the woman. "We're letting him walk to it."

She was right about Roald looking like he needed the fire.

His skin had a gray tinge, and he seemed barely able to understand when she gently urged him to go warm up by the fire. He staggered out into the cannon's sights, and finally made it to the fire pit.

Cal had wondered if the woman would shoot him out of spite, but she let him go.

No reason to bring down a man who was as unsteady as Roald.

"What's the best option. Let her go, or make her stay?" Anja murmured, crouching close to him. "I could crawl across the sand to the runner—I don't think the cannons can get me if I stay that low—and blow the engine."

"We should trap them here for the VSC, but I just want them off my moon." Leonie spoke from behind them.

Anja turned to look at her. "Then they might come back and try again."

Cal thought the same. They really wanted the druk. The Core's man had risked a lot to come get it before they left. They knew the Arkhorans were already here, trying to get in touch with Leonie in

Rinc and that every extra second they stayed was dangerous for them.

And yet still, they'd risked it.

The sudden sound of engines high above them had Cal looking up.

The Arkhorans, he hoped.

It was possible the thieves had another runner to send down, but then it would surely already be here.

The runner on the beach revved its own engines in response, and Ritt ran to the edge of the roof and slid down the side, just in case it took off while he was still up there.

Liv and Walef ran, bent over, out from underneath it, and it started to lift up.

The cannons had already moved and were shooting upward.

So probably it was the Arkhorans, coming to save the day.

But Cal wouldn't put internal fighting out of the realm of possibility with this group.

Anja sprinted toward the runner as it lifted and turned, but it was just out of her reach when she jumped up to touch it.

It didn't go straight up, as Cal expected. It hopped over the beach to land in the water beside the inflatable.

The woman was trying to grab her partner and the druk.

They really were desperate for the stuff.

"I'll take you with me if you help me load Ven and the druk," she shouted through the speakers to Fida and Sirco.

Cal hadn't forgotten about the two men, but they were out of sight, keeping their heads down, and had been no threat until this moment.

Sirco complied immediately.

He had done everything he could to make sure he'd get off Fynian before the VSC caught up with him, and he wasn't going to stop now.

Fida was a little more circumspect.

He had realized by now he would have been left behind, and it was only desperation giving him a chance now that he'd thought was his right to expect before.

He didn't trust the woman.

Anja started running toward the inflatable and the runner, and Cal sped up to join her. To have her back.

Fida bent and when he straightened, he was holding the laz Gyntree must have dropped when Anja took him down.

She didn't even slow down when he pointed it in their direction, which told Cal she'd managed to neutralize it.

Fida looked down in disgust when it didn't work, and then tossed it aside to jump into the inflatable with Sirco and grab Ven by his arms.

They dragged him across the boat and over the side, and the runner's door opened for them.

Anja reached the runner as they shoved him in, Cal right beside her.

Sirco lunged at her but Cal cut him off, grunting at the impact as Sirco slammed into him.

Above them, the engines of whatever was coming down through the sky toward them grew louder.

"The druk," the woman shouted as Cal shoved Sirco back toward the open door of the runner, and Fida staggered through the foaming waves toward the inflatable to grab the cylinder.

The engine of the runner cut off between one breath and the next, and so did the lights.

The sudden reduction in the noise level felt like bliss.

Anja had gone behind the runner when Sirco had leaped for her, and now she stepped out, water swirling around her knees.

"What did you do?" The woman appeared in the doorway, eyes wild, standing over her partner where he had been dumped by Sirco and Fida.

Anja waded through the shallows to stand beside Cal without responding.

The woman screamed, leaning out toward them, face twisted in rage, and then she stepped back into the runner and the door began to close slowly.

She was using a manual mechanism, Cal guessed, since Anja had shorted the electronics in the ship.

He left her to it.

Getting her and her friend Ven out could be the Arkhorans' job.

He looked up, in time to see a massive runner take a hit from above.

White light, like a lightning strike, hit the runner and encased it.

The bulky carrier began to free fall, sinking backward so the nose pointed straight upward. Cal knew the design. It was an Arkhoran runner.

Their rescuers had been taken out of the game.

"They're going to fall into the bay." Cal felt as if his throat was lined with sandpaper.

"The pod." Anja's hand gripped his shoulder. "The pod is out there."

She ran to the left, along the beach, looking in the direction the pod had gone earlier to avoid the runner's laz strikes.

"Dive." She must be thinking it to Kada, but she shouted it, too.

Cal joined her, his thoughts on the falling craft, the need to get deep below water.

With a boom the Arkhoran runner hit the surface, and moments later the waves hit him at chest height, forcing him back.

He grabbed hold of Anja, anchoring her to his side.

"We going to rescue them?" Demi was suddenly in front of them in the boat, and as Anja dived into the water to swim to her, he spun around to find his mother on the sand behind him.

"Catch," he called as he tossed her the laz. "Shoot whoever's left standing. It's safer."

She caught it one-handed, and the glint in her eye told him she likely would shoot Fida and Sirco. Roald might get lucky.

And if the woman or her partner appeared, they'd be met with laz fire, too.

He turned back and dived in, found Walef, Ritt and Liv were pulling themselves into the boat from the other side.

"Will this day never end?" Ritt flopped down as Demi turned them toward the downed runner, but he didn't sound that unhappy about it.

Cal realized his body felt as if it was humming. Geared up to throw himself into the rescue.

"Why did they engage with the Arkhorans, rather than get away?" Anja craned her neck, looking upward.

It was difficult to see what had shot the Arkhoran runner down, but suddenly white light crackled high above and the outline of a sleek black ship was revealed, and then the bulkier, massive shape of an Arkhoran warship, the mother ship of the downed runner they were headed toward.

A battle in nearspace was not something Cal ever thought he'd see over Fynian.

"They should have run, but they didn't. And now they've caught the attention of the warship." Cal agreed it made no sense, unless . . . "They didn't want to lose those two in the runner. And the druk."

"And maybe the tech from the spaceship." Liv was looking upward as well.

"That smacks of desperation." As Walef spoke, the warship returned fire, the flicker of laz light illuminating the strange black ship a second time.

Even though it was clearly outgunned, the black ship seemed to hesitate.

And then it was gone, and a bang reverberated from above. They had pinched to the black so close to the nearspace limit, they had nearly ripped themselves to shreds.

Cal knew the theory of it. Ships could only pinch to the black with enough space around them and a good distance from planetary atmospheres. Otherwise, they could suck something big, like a satellite or a small runner, in with them and tear themselves apart.

In practice, no ship to his knowledge had ever been reckless, or desperate, enough to try doing otherwise.

"Not our problem," Demi said, dismissing them. "Nothing we can do about it. This, on the other hand . . ."

They were approaching the floating runner.

Anja had been leaning over the side as they got closer, her face set, and Cal crouched beside her.

"Kada?" he asked.

She nodded. "They are unharmed but very unhappy."

A hoot and the boom of a neck hitting the water reached them.

"Very unhappy." Cal grimaced.

"I'm trying to tell him we will deal with it. He is resistant."

"What does he want to do, move the runner?" Walef asked, joking.

Anja twisted in her crouch and looked back at him, and his mouth dropped open.

"That's what he wants to do?" Walef looked stunned.

"They did it before," Cal reasoned, thinking of the spaceship tucked under the island.

"Hold him off, Anja. We can't rescue the Arkhorans if the pod is trying to push the runner out of the bay." Walef was standing now, looking in the direction of the surfaced and angry pod.

"I'm trying. Sending calming thoughts. Telling him this is the end of it now. No more laz fire. No more attacks."

Cal rubbed the icy skin of her bare back and tried to send similar thoughts toward Kada as well.

The boat thumped against the side of the runner and Demi and Liv looped the rope over something to attach them to it.

A latch opened above them.

"Who are you?" an unfriendly voice called.

The tone was somehow, after everything that had happened, the last straw.

"We're Fynians who thought you might need a ride to dry land, but if not, no problem, we'll leave you to it." Cal was quite happy to motor back and let them sort themselves out. He could be somewhere warm. Somewhere warm, with food inside him, and Anja a little more naked than she was now, lying beside him in a comfortable bed.

Anja turned to look at him, a slight frown on her face, and then her expression cleared.

"Let's leave them to it," she agreed.

31

They weren't able to leave them to it.

Anja hadn't thought they would, but it had been a lovely idea.

And they would get there, her and Cal, to that warm, comfortable bed. She would make it her mission.

The first two groups of crew from the runner were already huddled around the fire on the beach, and Demi was coming back from dropping off the third.

Cal stood with Anja on the roof of the runner beside the captain and her two senior officers. The runner was listing a little, but was still floating on the surface.

They were all watching Kada and a leviathan Anja guessed was the new matriarch circling them. She was pleased the new matriarch seemed to be moving well after being hit.

"They're friendly, right?" the captain asked.

"Not right now, they're not," Cal said.

Anja tried to see how Kada was in the light thrown out by the runner.

There was definitely a deep line running along his side, but he, too, seemed to be moving well enough.

"They've been attacked with laz fire a few times over the last few days," Anja said into the surprised silence that greeted Cal's words. "They came here because their matriarch was dying, and instead of the peace she deserved, she was shot repeatedly and her pod was threatened. Then this runner landed in their safe haven, which has made them angry and defensive. They want to push it out into the open sea."

"How do you know that?" one of the lieutenants asked.

"Because I'm a marine biologist who's spent the last four months studying them."

That led to another silence.

She and Cal were still in their underwear, and even an Aponi like her was now uncomfortable enough with the looks to wish she had her clothes back.

"Do I know you?" The captain had been casting glances at Cal, not just because he was almost naked and very nice to look at, Anja guessed, but as if she was trying to remember where she'd seen him before.

"I'm Calder Mordova, the trade liaison for Fynian."

"Mordova?" The captain frowned. "Any relation to the head-of-planet?"

"My mother," Cal said.

The thump of Demi bringing the boat alongside the runner cut off anything the captain planned to say in response, and they climbed down and got in, the last to leave.

Cal went straight to their clothes and handed hers to her, and she shivered in relief as she pulled on her shirt. The smart fabric immediately made a difference to her core temperature.

They both dressed in quick, efficient moves, and then Anja crouched down and touched the water. She didn't need the physical connection to communicate, but it somehow helped her connect better to Kada. She let him know if he absolutely had to push the runner out of the bay, he could do it now.

She had closed her eyes to concentrate better and when she opened them, she found the Arkhorans watching her strangely. Her gaze flicked to Cal, and he stepped beside her, just as Kada lifted out of the water and slammed into the runner.

The new matriarch followed, her big body exploding out of the sea to smack the runner in the same place Kada had.

Anja glanced back at the captain, saw her horrified expression.

"What are they doing?" she whispered.

"Shoving it out to sea," Anja said.

"I thought they were tame," one of the lieutenants said, eyes wide. "Don't you climb into their mouths?"

"We do, but they aren't tame." Cal kept his voice even. "And after the last few days, I don't know if they'll let us harvest druk for a while. They're traumatized."

He wasn't wrong, Anja thought. Although the pods around Rinc hadn't been involved in this, they would have heard something happening, and Kada was part of their pods, and would presumably return.

Good thing she and the team knew where to find a lot of druk without needing to harvest it from a leviathan.

Demi had been sitting quietly at the tiller, steering them to the beach, and the hull scraped onto the sand.

Anja let the Arkhoran crew haul them up the beach—she wasn't going to get her clothes wet again if she didn't have to—and then she accepted Cal's hand to help her down from the prow.

Leonie was sitting by the fire, and Cal took Captain Zirna over to introduce them.

"They'll already have sent a runner down for us," Zirna predicted, and she'd barely said it when they all heard the sound of engines from above.

"Not sure where they'll land," Cal said.

Zirna looked around, and had to agree.

With no comms available, the runner circled, saw the problem, and landed on spaceship island.

"I hope they realize no one there is friendly," Anja said.

Zirna turned sharply. "What do you mean?"

"They're all paid mercenaries over there, employed to help strip the ancestral spaceship."

Laz fire sparked from across the water, and she grimaced.

"I guess they know now," Zirna said, voice low. "Ancestral spaceship, huh?"

"I want to go to bed." Livia leaned against Walef and yawned.

Anja gave a groan of agreement and closed her eyes. She was leaning against Cal's shoulder and they were all sitting in the waiting room off Leonie's offices.

Cal's mother had disappeared inside with the commander of the Arkhoran warship and a few of his senior officers, including Captain Zirna.

"Let's go," Cal said suddenly. "If they want us, they can come get us."

Everyone lifted their heads to look at him, and Anja felt the sensation she was starting to think of as group-sense tighten about her. Everyone was in agreement.

Maybe it was only when they all felt the same way that this feeling rose up inside her.

It would take some getting used to.

The idea of leaving, of finding a bed and resting her tired, aching body, sounded so good, though, she didn't care.

They all stood. Anja felt a little unsteady on her feet.

Ritt was closest to the door, and he'd only taken a step toward it when someone appeared from inside Leonie's office.

"Where are you going?"

They turned to look at the officer frowning at them from the doorway.

From the way his eyes widened, Anja wondered whether the turn had been a little too coordinated.

"To bed." Cal kept moving and the others followed his lead.

"Stop."

It was Leonie, who was now standing beside the officer.

She shook her head with regret. "You should be resting, I know. Just answer a few questions for the commander, and we can debrief him on the less important details when you've had some sleep."

With a sigh they turned back and walked into her office.

The chairs were all occupied by Arkhoran officers.

Unable to face the idea of standing, Anja found a wall to lean against and then slid down to the floor.

Cal joined her, and the others flopped to the ground around them.

There was a moment of shocked silence in the room and then the commander cleared his throat.

"Any information you have on the identities of the insurgents would be vital, but first, can you tell us what you used to burn out the electronics of the runners the thieves were using? The scientist who arrived on Fynian under false pretences as a solar flare scientist, Reg Sirco, claims someone called Anja did it."

"I'm Anja." She lifted a hand heavy with fatigue. She'd guessed questions would be asked about the string of dead runners she'd left in her wake. Had thought about her answers. She forced her eyes open. "I used a device I found in the ancestral spaceship." That was technically true.

"Where is it?" One of the senior officers leaned forward in excitement.

Anja flexed her hand. "The last runner I disabled, on the

beach, was in the water. We were under attack and the tide was coming in. I'm afraid I lost it in the waves."

The officer and her commander shared a look.

"We could scan for it," the commander said.

The officer shook her head. "Not on this place. Not with the current solar storm activity."

They looked back at her, accusingly.

She lifted her shoulders, unconcerned. "Maybe there are more of them inside the ship."

The officer gave a slow nod. "Maybe. We'll look. What does it look like?"

She made the shape of a small rectangle with her hands. "Smooth. Metal."

"How did you know what it was for?" the officer asked.

"I didn't. But when I pressed it against the wall of one of the rooms in the spaceship, it plunged the whole place into darkness and—"

"The lights were working when you got there?" the officer interrupted, tone urgent.

She nodded. "Yes. It was when I was holding the device and leaned against the wall that it all went dark, right?" She looked over at the others. They could take some of the scrutiny for a bit.

"Yes. One minute, low-level emergency lighting, the next, absolute darkness," Ritt agreed.

"I didn't know for sure if that's what had happened, but I suspected, so we tried it on Sirco's runner, and it worked," Anja said.

She closed her eyes again.

"And the druk?"

Anja had forgotten about the pump, full as it was with druk. But it had still been in the inflatable when the Arkhorans had arrived, so they would have found it.

"They sent us out for hours, sucking up the sea floor, to get what's in that pump." Cal spoke for the first time.

And they *had* been out there for hours, but the druk in the pump was the result of the less than two minutes the pump had been operating.

Anja wondered why he was fudging on that, and then she realized. No sense in letting Arkhor know where all the druk was.

Fynian needed a few strategic advantages.

"They were desperate for it," Livia spoke up. "They risked themselves over and over to try and get it. They would have left Fynian an hour before you arrived if they hadn't tried to retrieve it."

"Sirco also admitted they'd tried to buy it through fraudulent deals, then considered stealing it from the warehouse in Rinc, before they decided to suck it off the sea floor," Walef said.

"The Core's man, the one in the runner on the beach, his name is Ricardo Ven." If they were interested in identities, Anja had a feeling this was information they'd be happy to receive.

She was right.

"How did you know he was associated with a Core company?" the commander asked.

"Because that's what the speculation is about what happened on Faldine a few months ago. That Cores execs who escaped from Garmen and Lassa were behind it." Cal kept his body relaxed, his fingers interlaced as his arms rested on his knees.

"The commander says they'll get some people from Garmen and Lassa to confirm, but most of the droppers are likely former security and enforcers for the Core companies on the breakaway planets." Leonie ignored the oppressive look the commander sent her at divulging that information.

"Their ship got away." Demi's voice was hoarse with fatigue.

"Unfortunately." The commander's lips formed a thin line.

"We never expected them to pinch to the black so close to near-space. They almost blew themselves up."

"Desperate," Livia said again.

"I think my people need to rest now." Leonie had been leaning against her desk, and she straightened up. "You can talk to them later, if you have any more questions."

"We'll need a full account of what happened," the senior officer said, also pushing out of her chair to stand.

"That will wait until they've had some sleep." Leonie gave a polite smile, and Anja pushed herself back up the wall to standing.

The officer looked at her in surprise.

Maybe that had been too athletic?

She was too tired to wonder or work it out.

They filed out of the office, and she was gripped by group-sense again. They all felt as if they'd had a lucky escape, like misbehaving students somehow avoiding punishment.

She tried to suppress a giggle, but it came out as a snort anyway.

Cal took a deep breath beside her, and Livia started to cough.

Ritt held the door out into the atrium open for them, and Anja sped up to get through it.

As soon as it closed behind them, they started to laugh.

"I'm putting this down to going through exhaustion and out the other side," Demi said, gasping for breath.

The sound of a door opening behind them forced them to close their mouths and keep walking, heads down.

Livia coughed again, and by the time they made it out to the street, they were snickering.

They stood for a moment in the cold midday air, light, soft flakes of snow falling all around.

People walked past, lights shone from shop windows. It was so normal, so safe. It was heavenly.

Cal put his arm around Anja's shoulder and steered her to the left as the others turned right.

"My place is this way," he murmured into her ear.

She turned and lifted a hand to wave goodbye to the others, and then leaned into him. "At last," she said.

At very long last.

32

———

"Dunc." Anja smiled and stood as her old colleague waved to her from the bar.

She had been sitting beside the fire with Cal and the team in The Ice Breaker, and she gestured to him to pull up a chair.

"Anja." He lifted his hands toward her in greeting, and she covered them with her own before retaking her seat.

"Calder." Duncan nodded at Cal and then the rest of the team, who nodded back politely.

Beside her, Anja sensed Cal tense, and knew he was still not happy with her former boss.

"I gather things went to hell for you while I was away." Duncan sat carefully, and Anja realized he was ill at ease in the company of the wave riders.

She hadn't noticed that last time.

"I was alone and couldn't get hold of headquarters," she said. "And that was before people started trying to kill me."

He lifted the drink to his lips, sipped and then looked down. "I should have told you personally I was going off-planet. It was so last minute—" He shrugged and looked up. "But I had no idea that Sirco wasn't who he said he was."

She already knew Duncan had been cleared by the Arkhorans of any involvement.

Cal had told her.

"I know."

He drew in a deep breath. "They were trying to steal druk? And they decided to steal it from the sea floor near your research station?" He shook his head. "And then they found an ancestral spaceship?"

"Technically," Cal spoke up, "we found it first."

Duncan shook his head again. "And it all ended in a battle in Fynian nearspace. Incredible."

They sat in silence for a moment.

"Are you sure about leaving the research unit?" Duncan leaned forward. "I know you went through a lot—"

"With no support," Cal interrupted.

Dunc faltered. "I thought Sirco was reliable. I would never have left Anja with him as her comms manager if I'd thought otherwise."

"I know." She tried to send him a reassuring smile. "But I was too isolated, Dunc. I realized how isolated I was feeling when I couldn't get hold of anyone for days. How bad it was for me, personally." She lifted her shoulders. "If you want my input for improvements to the job, you need to get the researcher back to Rinc for a weekend at least twice a month."

He nodded. "Not that there's anyone interested at the moment. But when we find someone, I'll implement that." He paused. "So you're becoming a wave rider, now?"

He sounded a little skeptical. As if he couldn't believe it was true.

"Yes." She grinned at him. "I want to stay on Fynian, and working with leviathans is definitely in my skill set."

"And something about a search and rescue team?" He looked around the group, eyebrows lifted.

"We worked well together out there, during this craziness." She gestured to the group. "Leonie has made us an official search and rescue team. The first permanent team on Fynian." And Leonie had other plans for them, too, she knew.

Cal had told her he thought his mother was interested in using them as a first line of defense against any outside attacks on her moon.

It made sense.

While druk was available only to members of the Verdant String, those who wanted it and couldn't get it would be thinking of ways to take it by other means.

She had finished her drink before Duncan had arrived, and now Cal put his empty glass on the table.

"Ready?" he asked. He'd been . . . edgy tonight. As if he had something to do that was making him nervous.

She nodded. "It was good to see you, Duncan. I'm sure I'll see more of you now that I'm based in Rinc than I did when we worked together." She and Cal stood, and Duncan stood with them.

"I'm glad you're staying," he said, and dipped his head in Cal's direction. "Anja says she wouldn't have gotten through things without you, so thank you."

Cal relaxed a little, gave a nod back. "She saved me, too."

They called their goodbyes to the team and then walked out, Cal's arm around her shoulder, hers around his waist.

"Did you see the Arkhorans in there?" Cal murmured in her ear as they stepped out into the hushed, snow-covered street.

"I did." She had noticed them everywhere since their final debrief. Lurking. Watching. "What do you think they suspect us of?"

"I think they're looking for the device you 'lost' in the waves."

She lifted her hand and slid it under his shirt and rested it against his ribs. Gave him a little tickle.

His own hand clamped down on hers through his clothing and gave it a squeeze. "Now, now. That's a dangerous ancestral device you're wielding there."

She grinned. His body threw off wonderful heat and her hand was happy where it was, so she left it there. "So someone did search the house?"

"I think so."

He didn't sound too annoyed about it. After all, there was nothing to find.

"And has your mother told you anything more about why Jake and Ven were so focused on druk?"

"Jake's dead and Sirco's the only one talking. He doesn't know as much as he pretended he did, but the Arkhorans reckon they needed to go somewhere where there's a lot of space debris, and the only way to get safely through is with a spaceship well-coated in druk to repel the shrapnel."

"So to get to the place they've found to re-establish themselves, they may have to go through some kind of asteroid belt?"

Cal hummed at the back of his throat. "It makes sense. But where exactly is anyone's guess."

They had reached his house, the eaves heavy with snow, the warm light they'd left on in the kitchen sending out a welcoming glow.

She turned toward him, forcing him to stop. "I know the silver balls have made this—us—easier." She found it easier to say this in the still night air, standing in the shadows thrown by the light from within.

He opened his mouth and she put a finger against his lips to stop him.

"But I'm not sorry for it. I'm grateful."

"My mother asked me if I was sure I wasn't in love with you

because of the silver balls, and I told her no." He lifted a hand and slid it behind her neck and into her hair. "I knew I wanted you the first time I saw you in The Ice Breaker. And that only strengthened when you came straight at me, riding that hover up the cliff path. Neither of us had a silver ball then."

"True." She relaxed into him, tipped her face up to his. "But the silver balls have smoothed things. I don't second-guess my feelings, and they tell me I can trust yours."

He bent his head and touched his lips to hers. "You can." He pulled back and put his hand in his pocket, and that edgy expression came over his face again. "All this talk of silver balls. I had something made for you."

He extended his palm and she saw he was holding a ring.

She picked it up, curious.

It was fashioned out of polished silver metal, and an almost perfectly round, silver piece of druk was set into it.

He took it back, lifted her hand, and put it on one of her fingers.

"I'm not sure if that's right," he murmured, looking at where he'd placed it. "But it doesn't matter. We're not them."

She looked down at the ring. She understood what he meant. They weren't the original silver ball carriers, but somehow, for some reason, giving rings was a tradition to those people.

Cal must have felt the urge and decided to indulge it.

She held out her hand, examining how the ring looked on her finger. It felt right. Like a tribute. And the silver ball of druk was just playful enough to make her smile. Telling the truth without actually telling it.

"Yes," she said.

"Yes, what?" He smiled even as his forehead wrinkled in confusion.

"I don't know. Yes to all this." She waved her hand.

He lifted her up, swung her into his arms so she laughed out loud as he made his way to the front door.

"Yes works for me."

SIGN up to Michelle Diener's New Release Notification list to find out when to expect the next book in the Verdant String series.

Also, let other readers know what you thought about Wave Rider by leaving a review on Amazon.

ABOUT THE AUTHOR

Michelle Diener is an award winning author of historical fiction, science fiction and fantasy romance.

Michelle was born in London and currently lives in Australia with her husband and children.

Connect with Michelle
www.michellediener.com

ACKNOWLEDGMENTS

Thank you as always to all the people who help make my books the best they can be. This includes Edie and Jo, as always, as well as Diane, Suzie, Cherry, Christine, Sandra, Lynn, Jennifer and the other members of my ARC team.

Thank you to Creative Paramita for the beautiful cover.